"My lord, I am not worthy—"

He drew nearer to her, enticed by the lushness of her mouth. "You are more than worthy, madonna," he whispered. "You have no idea who it is who asks you this favor. Please, call me by my given name."

Her pink tongue darted out and moistened her lips. "Since you and I have concealed our true identities for tonight, I will do as you ask. But on the morrow—"

"Let the devil take tomorrow, sweet Jessica," he murmured.

Desire, fueled by an overwhelming urge to protect her, rushed through him like a wildfire. Gathering her into his arms, he held her snugly in his embrace. "What is my name, Jessica?" he whispered into her black, silken hair.

Softer than a butterfly's wing, her long eyelashes fluttered against his cheek. "Francis," she breathed. Her rosy lips beckoned his kiss.

Sizzling fireworks exploded within him....

Praise for Tory Phillips's previous titles

Lady of the Knight
"Ms. Phillips weaves an adventurous story...
a good, fast-paced read."
—*Romantic Times Magazine*

Three Dog Knight
"Readers will be held in thrall...a gem of a tale."
—*Romantic Times Magazine*

Midsummer's Knight
"...a fast paced plot...fully and funnily
Shakespearean...wonderfully written..."
—*Publishers Weekly* (starred review)

One Knight in Venice
Harlequin Historical #555—April 2001

ONE KNIGHT IN VENICE

Tori Phillips

HARLEQUIN®

TORONTO • NEW YORK • LONDON
AMSTERDAM • PARIS • SYDNEY • HAMBURG
STOCKHOLM • ATHENS • TOKYO • MILAN • MADRID
PRAGUE • WARSAW • BUDAPEST • AUCKLAND

ISBN 0-373-29155-8

ONE KNIGHT IN VENICE

Copyright © 2001 by Mary W. Schaller

This edition published by arrangement with Harlequin Books S.A.

Visit us at www.eHarlequin.com

Printed in U.S.A.

Available from Harlequin Historicals and
TORI PHILLIPS

Please address questions and book requests to:
Harlequin Reader Service
U.S.: 3010 Walden Ave., P.O. Box 1325, Buffalo, NY 14269
Canadian: P.O. Box 609, Fort Erie, Ont. L2A 5X3

Dedicated with much love to our family's favorite aunt,
Katheryn Nink.

"In mine eye she is the sweetest lady
that ever I looked on."
—*Much Ado About Nothing*

"What think you of falling in love?"

—As You Like It

Chapter One

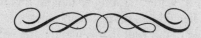

Venice, Italy
February 1550

"*Madonna*, there is a man waiting to see you," said the dwarf.

Blowing a tendril of her black hair out of her eyes, Jessica Leonardo smiled at her diminutive friend and confidante. "Many of my clients are men, Sophia. What is so unusual about this particular one?"

The little woman pursed her lips. "He is tall. His head brushes the ceiling." Sophia shrugged. "Well, almost. And…he is foreign. A Viking, I think." She shuddered.

Jessica suppressed a grin. "You are not sure?"

Sophia fluttered her pudgy fingers. "God in Heaven, how can one tell? The man speaks our language but with an accent and he is dressed in all the fashions of the world. His hose reek of Paris while his doublet could only be from Verona. His overcoat looks like something the English would fancy, and his bonnet? I cannot begin to guess what nationality his hat calls itself.'' She narrowed her eyes. "But this I *do* know. Though his clothing fits him well, he looks to me as if he wears borrowed finery.''

Jessica cocked her head. "How now? You speak in riddles, Sophia.''

"Then let me tell you plainly. Though he is dressed like a wastrel, he learned his manner in a monastery. I swear that he could hear a merry tale, yet never crack a smile.''

Jessica wiped her marble pestle clean of the dried lavender she had ground. Then she rinsed her hands in a nearby basin of water. "I long to behold this wonder,'' she said, drying her fingers on her work apron.

She crossed to the wall that separated her still room from the antechamber. Sliding back a small rectangle of the paneling she squinted through the peephole. *"¡Dio mio!"* she whispered under her breath.

As Sophia had described him, a giant of a man paced around her comfortably appointed waiting room like a mighty lion in a too confining cage. He clutched his ruby-colored feathered bonnet in his right hand while he ran the fingers of his left through hair that was the color and sheen of old gold. Jessica scrutinized him with a practiced gaze that had beheld many men's bodies of all ages and stages.

The stranger's red-and-white-striped hose accentuated the muscles of his unusually long legs. He sported a golden codpiece in the shape of a scallop shell and his tight red-velvet doublet ended just at the waistline instead of below it. A shirt of cream silk billowed through the slashed gold-embroidered sleeves, making his shoulders appear even wider than nature's design. The sleeveless outer coat that dropped almost to his knees was fashioned from gold brocade and lined with red fox fur—very costly. The short scarlet cape that covered his shoulders gave him the appearance of having wings. Cheerful crimson pom-poms crowned the straps of his golden square-toed shoes.

Yet the gentleman's most arresting feature was his face. Finely chiseled, as if he were a saint carved by the great sculptor Sansovino, the stranger's expression belied the gaudy cheer of his apparel. He looked intense, intelligent and extremely dangerous.

"Am I not right?" Sophia whispered behind her. "I told you he is not what he appears to be."

An icy chill clutched Jessica's heart. *Could the stranger be a priest from the Holy Office disguised to test my faith?* She shivered. *Please, dear Lord,* she prayed, *give me strength and courage.*

Then she noticed that the man rubbed his right shoulder and flexed the fingers of his right hand. Though his expression did not change, a whisper of pain flickered in his sky-blue eyes. No matter what he pretended to be, Jessica could tell that her mysterious client suffered true discomfort. After replacing the peephole cover, she turned to Sophia.

The little woman cocked her head to one side. "Will you see him? Shall I tell Gobbo to wear his stiletto?"

Taking a deep breath to quell the spasms in the pit of her stomach, Jessica nodded. As she untied her stained apron, she asked, "Did you tell the gentleman of my conditions?"

"*Sì,*" Sophia snapped, "though he knew about them before I even spoke." She drew closer to Jessica. "Take care, *madonna.* This man has no mirth in his soul."

Jessica swallowed a hard knot in her throat. "Of course not. He is in pain."

Sophia jutted out her double chins. "Ha! He has no laugh lines around his eyes. You shall see."

Jessica lifted her leather mask from its peg by the door.

The white-painted face depicted Columbina, one of the characters from the popular Commedia dell'Arte. Jessica threaded its black ribbons over her ears and tied a tight knot under her thick braid. Her mask must not slip down at the wrong moment.

She turned to Sophia. "Is it on straight? Does it cover the—" She could not bear to say the word "mark"—not when an officer of the dreaded Inquisition might be the man that waited so impatiently for her appearance.

Sophia stroked her cold hand. "He will see nothing he should not."

Sending another quick prayer to heaven, Jessica opened the door to the adjoining chamber and stepped inside. The giant lord instantly stopped his prowling. *He is even taller than I thought. He must be close to seven feet.* Jessica dropped a curtsy. Under her green woolen skirt, her knees trembled.

"Good morning, *messere*. It is an honor to welcome your lordship to my establishment. I am Jessica Leonardo. How may I serve you?"

To her surprise, he sketched a small bow in return. Obviously the man had recently arrived in the city. No proper Venetian gentleman ever gave reverence to a common woman. *Does he mock me or does he hope to put me off my guard?*

"Greetings, Signorina Leonardo," he replied in a deep melodic voice. "I thank you for seeing me on such short notice."

Jessica indicated one of the padded half-moon chairs. "Will it please you to be seated, *messere?*" Her hand shook a little. She tucked it within a fold of her skirt.

To her relief, he eased his long frame onto the seat. Now she could see his face better. How beautiful his eyes were—

yet filled with more than mere physical pain. "Tell me how I may help you?"

He blinked. "I have an old injury—here." He touched his right shoulder. "The damp, chill weather has aggravated it."

"Ah," Jessica remarked, drinking in the music of his voice. "Then you have not lived long in Venice?" she asked in a casual manner. Observing the way he held his body, she noticed that he favored his right side.

His lips parted as if to smile but stopped before they could complete the action. "I was born in England."

Jessica nodded. "A very cold, wet country, I am told."

"Indeed," he replied. His even white teeth flashed in the pale morning's light that glinted off the water of the narrow canal outside Jessica's grilled window. "That is why I have spent my recent years seeking warmer climes."

Jessica had the uneasy feeling that her visitor pursued goals other than the sun's rays. "You speak Italian well— even our own dialect that many visitors to Venice find confusing."

He lifted one of his dark golden eyebrows. "I have a good ear for many languages. It is one of my few talents."

A scholar! Definitely he must be from the Inquisition. Her apprehension mounted. "How…how did you learn of me?" she asked in a faint voice. "I mean, my healing abilities?"

Again a whisper of a smile hovered about his lips, though his eyes remained cold. "A lady of my acquaintance, Donna Cosma di Luna, knew of my…discomfort. She recommended you."

Jessica snorted inwardly. Cosma di Luna was no lady; she was an extremely expensive courtesan. This Englishman must be rich indeed to afford a night of pleasure with her—if he was not a priest. "My thanks to Donna di

Luna," she replied. "She comes here occasionally for a massage."

His mouth finally completed a smile—a small one. "Cosma tells me you have an angel's touch."

She moistened her lips. "Donna di Luna is most kind," she murmured. She touched the mask that hid her shame from the world's prying eyes. "And she told you about this?"

He nodded. "She did, though she did not explain why."

Fear rippled through Jessica. *I must take care. If he sees this devil's mark, I will be taken away and burned at the stake.* She fought to control the level of her voice. "My face is disfigured, *messere,* and has been so since my birth. The sight of it would sicken you. Therefore, I wear a mask in deference to the sensitivities of others."

He gave her a long, searching look before he said, "I am sorry to hear of this misfortune for your lips remind me of the red roses of my homeland and your voice is sweet as a lark."

What does he really want from me? I have done nothing to betray my parents. Jessica cleared her throat. "Did Donna di Luna describe what I do?"

He nodded. Absently he rubbed his shoulder again. "She said that you can massage away the pain. If this is true, Signorina Leonardo, I will be forever in your debt. I have lived with this torment for many years."

Jessica stared directly into his sad azure eyes. Taking a deep breath for courage, she replied, "I can mend the pain that plagues your shoulder, my lord, but I fear my craft cannot heal the wound in your heart."

A muscle twitched on one side of his jaw. "Cosma did not warn me how perceptive you are, *signorina,*" he remarked in a wary tone.

She looked away from him, her heart hammering in her

breast. "It is easier to understand another's pain when one has been wounded as well."

For the first time his face softened a fraction. "I am sorry," he murmured in a gentle voice.

A warmth flooded Jessica's being at the sound of his words. She glanced at him out of the corner of her mask's eyehole. The Englishman was exceedingly handsome. She could well imagine him in a courtly setting instead of sitting in her plain little house. Her fingertips tingled. Behind her back she balled her hands into fists. She turned toward a second door in the room that led into her treatment chamber.

"If you wish me to help you, please follow me." She opened the door.

He stood up. Once again his bulk filled the space. Jessica backed away. He held up his hand to her, palm out. "Pray forgive me, little one, I did not mean to startle you."

She gave him a shaky smile. "In truth, my lord, I have never met anyone quite so...tall."

He arched one brow. "Height runs in the family."

Jessica moistened her dry lips. "Then you must live in a large house to hold all of you at one time." She bit her tongue. *I am chattering like one of those silly little monkeys they sell on the Rialto.*

The Englishman followed her into the treatment room. "Have no fear. The family resides in England," he remarked. His caped silhouette danced along the wall like a winged creature. He smelled of cloves and wood smoke.

Seeing that Sophia had already prepared the chamber, Jessica smiled. In the far corner, a brazier of pierced brass stood on a tripod of slim iron legs. Hot coals glowed within it, banishing the chill of the midwinter day. Sophia had added a stick of sandalwood to the fire—an expensive whim but one that Jessica approved. Perhaps the sweet aroma would cheer the English prelate—or whatever he really was. A clean linen sheet covered the high-legged padded divan and a soft wool blanket lay folded across the end. A number of pots containing Jessica's oils and creams were laid out on a side table. A thick scented candle flickered in its wrought-iron candlestick. She closed the door behind him.

The Englishman glanced around the room. "No windows?"

Jessica cleared her throat. "To keep out the drafts—and the unpleasant odors from the canal." She smoothed nonexistent wrinkles from the sheet. She must stop trembling or she would never be able to work on him. "And to insure privacy."

He touched one of the green walls. "Felt?"

Jessica ran her tongue across her upper lip. "To muffle the sounds of the city and to keep in the warmth. It is all for your comfort, *messere,* I assure you. I will leave now so that you may disrobe. Please remove your outer clothes and shirt. You may hang them on those pegs." She pointed to a row of varnished knobs opposite the door. "Then lie down on the divan and cover yourself with the blanket so you will stay warm."

She lifted a thick black blindfold from the table and held it out to him. "I fear I must beg your further indulgence. Please blindfold your eyes before my return."

As he took the ebony silk from her hand, his fingertips brushed against her skin. The spot burned and tingled as if it had been caressed by both fire and ice. Jessica drew in her breath. *What power does this man have that I quake, yet I yearn for him to touch me again?*

He examined the blindfold then glanced at her. "Cosma also told me of this, but why is it necessary?"

Jessica was prepared for this question. All her new

patients asked it. "In order to work on your body without hindrance, I remove my mask. Yet I wish to protect you from the sight of my face. Therefore, I humbly beg that you wear it while I treat you."

He dangled the cloth between his thumb and forefinger as if it might turn into a live eel at any moment. "And if ·I do not?"

Jessica lifted her chin a notch. "Then I will not treat you. The choice is yours." She held her breath.

He studied her for a long moment, then he flashed her a sudden smile that disappeared before she could savor it. "You have me at your mercy, Signorina Leonardo. I will bow to your edict. In faith, you are the most intriguing woman I have yet met in Venice."

Jessica didn't know if he had just paid her a compliment or insulted her but she opted for the compliment. With a quick smile in return she let herself out of the room. "Please call me when you are ready, *messere*."

He held up his hand to stop her. "By which name shall I call you?" he asked. A faint twinkle lit the depths of his eyes.

Her mouth went dry. Her heartbeat increased. "I am known as Jessica," she answered softly. Then she shut the door, stumbled to the nearest chair and collapsed between its welcome arms.

Is this man a wizard? He has cast my wits under his spell.

Francis Bardolph gave the room another swift inspection before he unfastened his cape. Small confines made him uneasy, especially when there were no windows. No quick exit in case of trouble. He shook his head to banish his misgivings. His suspicious nature stemmed from too many years traveling abroad in the service of the crown, first for

old King Henry VIII and now for his young son, King
Edward VI. He jumped at mere shadows these days, Francis
thought ruefully as he hung his cape and outer coat on the
pegs. It was a nerve-racking job gathering secret intelligence for England's clever Secretary of State, Sir William
Cecil.

The muscles in his shoulder protested every movement.
He kneaded the sore area with his fingers. Then he unbuttoned his garish doublet while he mused upon the intriguing
Signorina Jessica. Unlike the majority of the Venetian
women whom Francis had encountered during his five-
month stay, Jessica did not dress her raven hair with sticky
wax pomade but she allowed it to lie in a braid down her
back. Delightful, he silently applauded. Most provocative.
*I wonder what she looks like with it unbound? Is it as soft
to the touch as it appears?*

Wincing a little, he peeled off the tight jacket. Francis
chided himself for dwelling on the *signorina*'s tresses. He
had enough female worries on his mind as it was. Lately,
Cosma had become more demanding, not for the glittering
baubles provided by Lord Cecil's generous purse, but for
Francis's body and soul. Last night she had all but suggested that he marry her. Francis rolled his eyes at the low-
beamed ceiling. He could just imagine the reactions of the
Cavendish family if he returned to England with that piece
of painted baggage.

What a difference between these two women—Cosma
and Jessica! Francis paused before untying the laces of his
silken shirt. Cosma's hair was that red-gold color favored
by practically every woman in Venice. On sunny days
droves of fashionable ladies could be seen on hundreds of
flat housetops sunning their henna-streaked locks in crown-
less broad-brimmed hats. Young gallants often climbed to

the top of the campanile in Saint Mark's Square just to admire the rippling ocean of gilded tresses.

But Jessica's hair was black as midnight. It beckoned Francis to weave his fingers through it, though his sense of propriety and good manners forbade his hands to follow his lusty thoughts. He wondered why Jessica didn't use cosmetics to mend her looks, as Cosma and the other votaries of Venus did, instead of hiding behind that blasted mask. He had seen only her mouth and yet it hinted of richer beauty above. Jessica's unrouged lips were as lush and full-ripened as any courtesan's skill could render. What would it be like to kiss lips that did not taste of paint? Francis snorted. He had wallowed too long among the fleshpots of the Continent to recall the simple pleasures of an innocent maid in a flowering meadow.

He wondered if Jessica was still a virgin as he pulled his shirt over his head. He guessed that she was past her twentieth year, and most women had been bedded by then unless they were locked inside high-walled convents at an early age. He grimaced. Why should the state of Jessica's maidenhead matter to him anyway? The pain that coursed down his right arm reminded Francis that this visit to a woman was strictly business of a medical nature.

He stepped out of his shoes and pushed them against the wall with his foot. He glared at the nodding pom-poms. Ridiculous footwear! How Belle would howl with laughter if she ever glimpsed her somber brother arrayed in these gadabouts! His favorite sibling would never let him forget this indignity.

Sitting on the divan, Francis picked up the blindfold. Small goose bumps prickled his bare flesh. Once he donned this innocent-looking scrap he would become extremely vulnerable. He would literally be in the hands of a woman who was a lovely eccentric. For all he knew, Jessica

Leonardo could be in the employ of Venice's notorious secret police. The Republic would not take kindly to an English spy prowling the dark corners of their unique city. England's expanding merchant fleet already threatened Venice's near monopoly of trade with the fabulous East. The merchant princes of the Republic would be exceedingly glad to end Francis's nefarious career. The mysterious Signorina Jessica could easily stab him with a stiletto while he lay placidly on her couch like a fish on a cutting board.

His shoulder throbbed. He flexed his stiff fingers. The devil take it! He had been in worse spots than this. This woman was said to be a notable healer. He would chance his life—once again. Francis tied the mask firmly in place then gingerly lay down and pulled the blanket up to his neck. His feet hung over the edge of the divan.

"Signorina Jessica!" he called. "I am ready as you have commanded me."

The door opened behind him. He instinctively tensed; his fingers curled under the blanket. His rapier hung within arm's reach. He caught the aroma of her perfume, a heady scent that whispered Arabian mysteries.

"I thank you for your trust," she said in that thrilling low voice of hers. "Please relax now."

Someone else entered the room—a man's soft tread drew nearer to the divan. The hairs on the back of Francis's neck prickled. He jumped when she placed her hand on his brow.

"Pray be at ease, *messere*," she murmured, once again addressing him as if he possessed a noble title. "It is only Gobbo, my lutist. He will play for us while I work. If the mind is soothed, so will be the body."

Her invisible accomplice tuned his instrument and began a gentle ballad. An accomplished musician himself, Francis admired the talent of the unseen fingers that conjured such sweet beauty from his strings. The enchanting melody hovered over him and sank into his very pores.

A pungent odor filled his nostrils. He flinched when Jessica stroked his forehead. She clicked her tongue against her teeth. "Tut-tut, *messere,* it is only a little camphor mixed in a light oil base. Pray forgive its aroma but it does wonders for aching joints and pounding heads."

She massaged his temples. Her touch was the most exquisite thing that Francis had experienced in a long time. Sensual, beguiling. He drew in a deep breath. His imagination wandered into a lush-appointed bedroom—with Jessica waiting for him between silken sheets. What those knowing fingers could do to a man if she—

She interrupted his wanton reverie. "Before I begin, I must examine the area that afflicts you."

He cleared his mind. "The right shoulder," he muttered hoarsely.

She lifted the blanket. The cool air stung his skin.

"Ah, I see." She traced her finger along the track of the ancient scar. "It was a deep wound. How did it happen?"

Visions of that long-ago midsummer's morning crowded into his memory. A sunny, warm day. Astride the huge warhorse of his…his master—and presumed father, Sir Brandon Cavendish. Belle's childish laughter in his ear. The cry of a startled bird, then literally a bolt out of the blue sky. "I was shot by a crossbow," he answered with a snap.

Jessica lifted his shoulder and touched the larger scar on his back. "Clean through," she observed.

"My, uh…the knight I served pulled out the shaft." He swallowed with the memory of that excruciating pain.

Her fingers gently prodded the area. "How old were you at the time?"

"Nine years and a few months."

She sucked in her breath. "What evil creature would shoot so young a boy?"

Francis curled his lips with disgust. "One who sought my...master's life." He couldn't call Brandon his father even though Brandon informally considered him as his son. "I took the arrow meant for my lord."

"*¡Dio mio!*" she murmured. "So young and yet so brave."

Poor aim was more like it, he thought, but said nothing aloud. He liked the way she called him brave.

She continued to prod the scars as if she sought to find the path of the bolt. "Did the wound fester? Did you have a fever?"

"*Sì*," he replied. "There was a wisewoman who sewed me up and fed me herbs. They told me I was delirious for over a day. I was weak for a long time after that."

She traced her fingers down the length of his arm and took his right hand in hers. "I am going to test your range of motion," she told him. "Tell me when it hurts or pulls. And please, *messere,* do not mince your words. I must know exactly where the pain lives in order to help you."

In my heart where there is no cure for it.

Aloud, Francis said, "Begin, but I warn you, I might bellow like a bear." Despite his words, he knew he would rather die than admit that such a gentle creature as Jessica could hurt him.

Supporting his elbow, she slowly raised his arm straight up. With habit born of long suffering, Francis tensed when she lifted his arm above his head. The knotted muscles and battered flesh screamed in protest.

"There?" she asked, returning his arm to his side.

"*Sì*," he replied through his teeth. The pain eased away. She moved his arm out from his body in a long, slow arc. Again he tightened when she reached the level of his shoulder. "There again?" she asked.

He nodded. He hated to admit his weakness but since he was now committed to this path, he would endure it. Cosma swore Signorina Jessica could heal him. In any case, Jessica now stood between him and his clothes.

She stroked his hand. "Please make a fist for me," she asked.

His long fingers protested as Francis folded them against his palm. "It is more difficult on days like today," he apologized. No doubt she would think him the gaudy fop he pretended to be. "Cold and wet," he added.

She lowered his arm to the divan. "Just so," she murmured. "I am surprised how firm your muscles are in spite of the pain."

A little warning bell jangled in the back of his mind. This sweet-voiced minx could be the agent of his destruction if he wasn't careful. Venice literally crawled with secrets and informers.

"I have no desire to grow fat and ruin the line of my clothes, *signorina,*" he replied in the languid manner of his dandy's role. "I usually exercise by riding when I am not living on an enchanted island that floats in a lagoon. Since I have been in Venice, I have taken lessons from one of your renowned sword masters." True enough. Furthermore, the man had taught Francis a great many new and lethal techniques that the brigands in England had not yet envisioned.

Jessica said nothing for a few minutes while she massaged his neck and shoulders. Then she remarked, "You must enjoy your swordplay very much for I see that you fight left-handed although you naturally prefer your right. Please try to relax, *messere,*" she added. "Your muscles feel as if they are tied in knots."

Her keen observation twanged Francis's already taut nerves. He took several deep breaths and forced himself to remain as calm as possible. Would Jessica Leonardo slip a piece of paper with his name on it into the nearest *bocca di leone,* denouncing him as a traitor to the Republic of Venice? Francis had never felt so vulnerable as he did at this moment while he lay half-naked and blindfolded in the house of a strange woman. He should never have come.

And yet how wonderful he felt as the melodic strains of the lute washed over him and the fingers of the lovely sorceress kneaded away his pain! Even his heart, that stone-cold organ, did not feel quite as heavy as it usually did. And his loins? They were on fire. He hoped that the blanket covered the evidence of his desire.

"Buono," Jessica murmured as she worked deeper into his scar tissue. "Good, let your mind and body be at rest. Here there is nothing but peace and tranquillity."

With a deep sigh Francis drifted on the gentle tide of relaxing sensations. His body felt as if he floated above the divan.

"Breathe deeply," Jessica whispered. "Draw in God's pure light and healing presence. Breathe out the vile humors that give pain and disquiet. In…out…in…out…"

The desire to sleep crept over him. Francis knew he should fight the urge but his body craved the blissful peace. The notes of the lute grew fainter.

"Messere?" Jessica laid a warm hand on his arm. "The sands in the hourglass have run their course. I have done for today."

Francis pulled himself back into the wakeful world. Jessica placed one hand on his good shoulder and the other on his opposite hip. She rocked him in a soothing manner. Then she laid her hands lightly on his chest. A healing warmth seemed to flow from her fingers into his body, rejuvenating him. Fire licked between his legs.

A groan escaped his lips.

"How do you feel, *messere?*" she asked as she stepped away from him. The lutist concluded his concert with a long final note.

"In paradise," Francis murmured.

"And your pain?"

He lifted his right shoulder. His muscles moved without protest. He flexed his fingers. They operated smoothly even when he balled them into a fist.

"Tis a miracle!" he whispered in English, then said in Italian, "You have done a wondrous deed, sweet sorceress."

"Oh, no, *messere,*" she answered in a rush. "I have no special powers. I am only a simple woman. Please believe me, my lord."

Francis pulled himself into a sitting position on the divan. For the first time in months, perhaps even years, he felt strong and full of…joy. "I am new-made indeed. What spell did you cast?"

She gasped. "I did no magical thing, my lord. I only loosened those hard knots. But," she cautioned, "the good feeling is temporary at first. I worked your muscles hard today. When you wake tomorrow you may be as sore as if you had been fighting the Turkish army single-handed."

He curled his lip. "Those words bring me much cold comfort."

She moved further away from him. "It will pass, I assure you. Understand this, *messere,* I have not cured you—only time and *il Dio* can do that. If you wish for a lasting effect, you will need many treatments such as I have given you.

"Think of your body as a fine *palazzo,*" she continued in her delightful voice. "One day, a gang of *bravi* took possession of your beautiful house. For years and years, they lived there, destroying your fine furnishings, drinking your prize wines and fouling your gorgeous paintings. Then one day, a little woman enters your house armed only with a broom.'' She laughed again. ''A big broom, of course.''

''Of course,'' Francis agreed, enchanted with the story-teller as well as her story.

''She sweeps the evildoers out into the canal, then begins to put your house in order. But the *bravi* do not like this new state of affairs. They want their comfortable life back, so they return.''

''And she must sweep them out again?'' he ventured.

''Exactly so,'' Jessica replied. ''The *bravi* have dwelled within you for a very long time. It will take many sweepings to expel them forever. Do you understand?''

Francis drew in a deep breath, thinking of the darker devils that plagued his soul. ''More than you realize, little one. When may I come again? Tomorrow?'' What a delicious way to spend each day!

''Tomorrow is too soon, *messere*. You must allow your body to rest after the work I made it do today. Even the Good Lord had a day of rest. But you may come on the next.'' She shyly added, ''If you wish.''

Francis placed his hand on his chest where hers had so lately lingered. ''With all my heart. At what hour will you receive me?''

''Is ten in the morning too early for you?''

Francis shook his head. ''I would be here at dawn, if you commanded me, *madonna*,'' he replied with heartfelt truth.

She laughed once again. ''Then you would be most un-usual, my lord, for no gallant in Venice is abroad before noon, unless he is still awake from the night before.''

Francis allowed a smile to form on his lips. ''But I am

English and practice my strange ways even in your civilized city."

Jessica opened a door. A sudden cool draft brushed his bare skin.

"At ten of the clock on the day after tomorrow. And your name, my lord?"

Without his usual caution, he replied, "Francis Bardolph at your service, Madonna Jessica. I will count the hours until then."

She gave a little cough. "You may leave my fee on the table after you dress, Messere Bardolph. Good day." With that, she closed the door.

Francis untied the blindfold and looked around for the musician, but the lutist had also disappeared. Francis's clothing and accoutrements still hung undisturbed as he had left them, including his heavy money pouch on his sword belt. He pulled his shirt over his head, wondering anew at the unaccustomed ease he experienced when he pushed his arms into his sleeves. As he buckled his shoes, someone knocked on one of the doors.

Francis's heart skipped a beat. The enchantress had returned! "Enter," he called. He wet his lips with expectation.

Instead of the fair Jessica, her elfish maid appeared. "Feeling better?' she asked, giving him an appraising look.

Francis resisted the urge to laugh at the officious little woman. Instead he swept her a bow—and marveled how smoothly he accomplished the maneuver. "I am indebted to your mistress. She has made me a new man."

The dwarf crossed her arms over her ample bosom. "Good!" She eyed his purse. "Be sure to show Madonna Jessica your appreciation by paying her in full. My mistress is not a rich woman. We cannot live on credit as the wealthy do."

Francis grinned down at her. He fastened his cape around his shoulders, then untied his purse. "A ducat, I believe you told me?"

"*Sì,*" the woman nodded. "And it is money well spent, I assure you."

Francis said nothing. He placed two shining gold pieces on the table. He noted with pleasure the maid's startled look. He handed her a third ducat. "Please give this to the musician. He is most gifted." Then he bent far down and kissed her pudgy hand. "And you, *signora,* are the light of the world."

Leaving her gasping with astonishment, Francis settled his hat on his head and let himself out the front door into the narrow street. An old English country song hummed in his head. By the time he crossed the little *campo,* he was singing the words aloud—something he never did.

As he approached the boat landing on the canal, he spied, out of the corner of his eye, a furtive shadow move behind him. Grasping the hilt of his rapier, he whirled to face his pursuer. Except for several old men sunning themselves by the wellhead in the center of the square and a woman hanging out her wet linen on a pole from her second-story window, the *campo* was bare. Francis gave himself a shake. *Now I jump at shadows and alley cats.* Still warm with the afterglow of his visit to the peerless Donna Jessica, he banished his misgivings. Why ruin a perfectly lovely day?

Launching into the second verse of his childhood song, he hailed a passing gondola.

Chapter Two

Cosma di Luna cast a glance over her creamy white shoulder and asked, "After the Englishman left the house of the healer, where did he go?"

In her dressing-table mirror, she observed her young informant gaping at her near-naked beauty with an ill-concealed hunger. Jacopo was such a pliable youth. The merest flash of her breasts was enough to enslave him to her command. She knew she could save herself many ducats if she paid for his information with her favors.

Cosma leaned closer to the mirror to apply a line of sooty kohl to her eyelids. She reveled in her position as one of Venice's premier courtesans who entertained in her bed noble senators, sons of the aristocracy and wealthy merchants. She had no need to stoop to servicing a low-born, would-be *bravo*. Her coin and a well-chosen glance or two of her charms would suffice for the likes of Jacopo.

"Well?" she prodded the stupefied young man. "I presume that you *did* follow Messere Bardolph as I asked you?"

Jacopo ran his tongue over his lips. "*Sì*, Donna Cosma. First he went to the Rialto, where he drank wine with some acquaintances. He stopped by the beggar that sits on the

steps of San Giacomo church and exchanged a few words
with the man. Lord Bardolph gave him alms, as is his custom. Then he went to the bookbinders where he stayed a
quarter of an hour or so if one can rely on the bells of San
Giacomo." Jacopo scratched his head in thought. "After
that he visited the apothecary shop at the corner of Calle
del Spezier and the Campo San Stefano."

Cosma paused in her cosmetic applications. "What did
he purchase?" she asked lightly, though her breath caught
in her throat. Pray God, Francis had not caught the French
pox. "You *did* ask, did you not?"

Jacopo grinned. "*Sì, madonna,* I know my duties. He
procured a vial of an elixir for…that is…" He blushed and
coughed into his sleeve. "To render him impotent, or so
the apothecary swore to me."

Cosma's fear gave way to anger. Her fingers gripped the
ivory handle of her brush until her knuckles turned white.
What a villain with a smiling cheek! Though she had been
his mistress for nearly four months, Francis had yet to complete the act of love with her. Usually he withdrew himself
before the moment of truth. Other times, he claimed to
be…uninspired. Was it any wonder that she had resorted
to having him followed? If he slaked his appetites with
another woman, Cosma knew she could soon remedy that
situation. But why use a potion to deliberately deflate his
desire?

The more she dwelled on Francis's perfidy, the angrier
she grew. His fear of impregnating her was truly an obses-
sion, not merely a whim as she had first thought. Cosma
narrowed her eyes at her reflection. Was she not the reigning Venus of the city? How dare he use her in such a
fashion! Or, more to the point, *not* use her as any sensible
man would.

"Madonna?" Jacopo intruded. "Do you wish to hear the rest?"

Cosma drew herself upright. "Of course," she snapped. "That is why I pay you. What *else* did the canal rat do this afternoon?"

Jacopo started to laugh at her remark, but choked instead when she glared at him. "He visited a wine shop where he dined and played at cards with several young gentlemen. I recognized Messere Niccolo Dandelli and his younger brother."

Cosma nodded. The Dandelli brothers were notorious rakes with full purses and empty time to fill—two of her favorite patrons. In fact, Niccolo had introduced her to Francis last November. She saw no problems in that quarter. "Go on."

The youth rubbed his nose. "Then he returned to his rooms at the Sturgeon where he napped, as is his custom. His landlord told me that Messere Bardolph is not used to the late hours we Venetians keep. He must prepare himself for night sport—and for you, *madonna,*" he added with a fawning look.

And drink his kill-love liqueur, Cosma thought. A plague of fleas upon Lord Francis Bardolph! Aloud she asked, "Where is he now?"

Jacopo folded his arms across his chest. "Still sleeping at the Sturgeon. I took this opportunity to report to you." He gave her another hungry look.

Cosma pretended not to notice his lust though she enjoyed her power over the callow boy. Opening a small casket on her dresser she took out a scudo. "Come, Jacopo," she purred, holding out the money to him. "Come take your fee."

He all but ran across the distance between them. Just

before he could grab the coin, she closed her fingers over it. "Kneel," she commanded with a smile.

He immediately dropped to the floor before her. His slavering obedience soothed her ruffled vanity. Leaning over, she allowed him to view a generous portion of her bosom. "Kiss my foot."

With a huge smile displaying a set of white teeth not yet stained with too much wine or missing from decay, Jacopo smothered her right slipper with his loud kisses. When he tried to pry off her shoe for further adoration, she dropped the scudo in front of his nose. The silver coin clinked on the cold tiles.

"Enough for now, dear boy," she murmured, pulling her foot free of his grasp. "Too many sweets will dull your appetite."

"Never," he replied with a low groan of despair.

Waving him away, she gave her attention to her mirror. "Be off! Return to Lord Bardolph's inn and continue your vigil. Hurry before he wakes from his nap."

Jacopo stood, pocketed his wages, and tossed her a shrug. "He will sleep till five. He is a man of habit." Casting her one final look of longing, the youth left the chamber and clattered noisily down the stairs.

As soon as her minion was gone, Cosma put down her comb and the jar of hair pomade. Her toilette could wait a bit while she attended to a more pressing matter. Still fuming over Francis's dishonesty at the apothecary's, Cosma decided to raise the stakes a notch. If her so-called lover intended to use artifice to cool his ardor, she would employ the same method to bring him to her bed. This English lord was too fine a prize to let him slip away just because of some addlepated notion of his to not father a child. A baby was exactly what Cosma needed to bind herself permanently to Francis, his noble title and his fortune. Then it would be farewell to the exciting but extremely hazardous life of a courtesan.

Cosma rose and crossed her bedchamber to her library next door. She surveyed her four shelves of precious books with pride of ownership. She possessed one of the finest private collections in all of Venice: books of poetry, romance, history, philosophy—and the arts of love. She ran her finger along the ribbed leather spines until she found the one she sought—a new addition to her store of erotic knowledge. *The Perfumed Garden,* written with exquisite detail by a Muslim sheik. She flipped through its pages until she came to the section dealing with aphrodisiacs. She chuckled to herself. Francis's potion would be no match for the delicacies she would prepare for him tonight.

I shall be a titled English lady before Easter!

The great bell of Saint Mark's Basilica tolled six in the evening when Francis put down his quill and rubbed his eyes. Another report completed for Sir William Cecil. Francis blew on the ciphers to dry the ink. He flexed his fingers after an hour of laborious writing in code. Then he raised his right hand and admired the way his fingers still moved without stiffness. God bless the black-haired healer! He wished he had learned of her months ago. What a delightful creature she was! Fresh—and so intriguing behind her mask. Not like Cosma, he reflected with a frown. She hid behind a mask of cosmetics, artfully applied, of course, but false all the same. He massaged the bridge of his nose. Cosma! How was he going to solve that problem?

Initially she had been amusing and full of helpful gossip. Francis had enjoyed her company and taken the pleasure he allowed himself when sporting with a woman. At first she had only laughed at his precautions against conception, applauding him for his thoughtfulness. He had been happy enough to let her think her protection was his sole concern.

Since Christmastide however, their easy relationship had undergone a change. Cosma demanded more from him than he was willing to give—and her font of information about the various members of Venice's Great Council had decreased. Her usefulness now gone, Francis discovered that he had grown tired of her nagging personality. Recently she spoke of marriage in an offhand manner, but Francis had heard those words and seen that same calculating look in a woman's eye before. The time had definitely come to end the affair, but he knew Cosma well enough to realize that she would not let him go peaceably. The break would be loud and messy; possibly dangerous if she sought revenge. He dreaded the confrontation.

He stared at the green glass vial on the table. What sort of witch's brew had that dog of an apothecary sold him? Francis hated the idea of drinking something foreign, but he hated even more the idea of succumbing to Cosma's seductive wiles. He vowed to never father a bastard as he had been fathered. His mind comprehended this deepest fear but he could not yet discipline his body's lustful inclinations. Only this morning, the mysterious Donna Jessica had stirred the desires that he thought he had banked against the assaults of Venus. Jessica's fingers ensnared him when he had least expected it and her voice entranced him into a state of near bliss. Worst of all—he had enjoyed the entire experience and he looked forward to its repetition in two days' time.

Closing his eyes, he groaned aloud. His passionate nature ran too deep for him to completely subjugate it. He should not be surprised, considering the lusty histories of both his natural parents. Their fires flowed in his blood. Francis reached for the vial, uncorked it and sniffed.

Hoy day! If the devil has an odor, this would be it. He grimaced. Church bells tolled the half hour. He dragged himself to his feet. At this rate he would be late to Cosma's house and she did not take kindly to his tardiness. Best to keep her content for as long as possible. Only a few more weeks until the spring thaw made the roads passable; then he could kiss Cosma—and Venice—farewell.

Taking a deep breath, he lifted the bottle to his lips and tossed its vile contents down his throat. Sweet Jesu! The taste alone was enough to convert a man to life-long celibacy.

Three-quarters of an hour later he was in Cosma's lemon-yellow house on the Rio di San Cassiano canal. Her second-floor solar was lit with many fat, sweet-scented candles in black iron holders. Her little handmaid, Nerissa, plucked a pleasing tune on her beribboned mandolin. Cosma herself rivaled the Goddess of Love in her diaphanous gown of pale yellow silk. Her perfume wafted across his nostrils with intoxicating invitation. Though the elixir did not sit well in his stomach, Francis was glad he had drunk it. Cosma had obviously woven her gilded web for his complete downfall tonight.

"Come, let us sup, my love," she murmured after recovering from his cool greeting. "Tell me the news of your day."

He glanced at the table set for a feast. Wine sparkled in pink glass goblets and silver-covered dishes crowded the nearby sideboard. His stomach growled with a mixture of hunger and revulsion. He swallowed. "My day was nothing but loud talk among half-wits." He dismissed his activities both innocent and subversive. "I had much rather feast upon your conversation, *gattina mia*—my little kitten."

Cosma flashed a wide smile as she pulled him toward

her repast. "Then I will not deny you the pleasure of satisfying your appetite—all your appetites," she purred.

With a resigned sigh, Francis lowered himself onto the padded leather armchair. He had absolutely no appetite for anything—food or otherwise. Cosma seated herself opposite him. Outside her window a creeping fog swathed the lantern lights of the houses on the opposite side of the canal in a soft damp glow. The misty gray vapor muffled the singing of the gondoliers as they plied their slim black boats through the still water. With graceful movements born of practice, Cosma uncovered a dish.

Francis's stomach roiled at the aroma of the savory eel soup. "I fear I am not very hungry," he muttered. He took a sip from his brimming goblet. Hopefully the wine would settle the discontented humor of his digestion. Damn that poxy apothecary!

Cosma's brown eyes sparkled in the candlelight. "A taste here, a bite there, *caro mio.*" She allowed a small pout to cross her rouged lips. "I had this meal prepared *especially* for you."

Francis picked up his spoon. "Then I shall eat it especially for you," he replied. It was a shame that he felt so out of sorts since Cosma employed one of the best cooks in Venice.

Lifting her goblet, she toasted him. "You do me honor, my lord." She took a spoonful of the soup. "And how was your visit to Signorina Leonardo?" she asked in a light tone.

At the mention of Jessica, a smile creased Francis's lips. The memory of her voice and her touch gave him delight despite his current discomfort. "A most welcome one, I assure you, *gattina.*"

A small frown knotted between Cosma's delicately drawn eyebrows. "Indeed? I should think you would find her affectation for the mask a bit…how do I say it? Bizarre.''

Francis sipped more wine to ease the eel down his throat. His ruffed collar felt very tight. "Not in the least. In fact, I found it added to her charm." He glanced at the groaning sideboard. Spikes and nails! How many more of these covered dishes was he supposed to consume?

Cosma blotted the corner of her mouth with her damask napkin. "Did you know that her parents were Jewish? The Spanish Inquisition forced them to convert—or so I have been told." She poured him more wine from a beautiful pink glass decanter. "One cannot help but wonder how far from the tree the apple falls."

Francis concealed a burp behind his napkin. "Are you implying that Donna Jessica is a Jew?" His belly filled with wind of a most disagreeable sort. He unbuckled his belt and allowed it to drop to the floor.

Cosma lifted her shoulders in a sketch of a shrug. The action bared her flesh down to her breast. "I merely relate the gossip of the city, my love, as I know it entertains you."

He gently pushed away the half-eaten soup. "Donna Jessica appeared to be as Catholic as I am."

A lie since he had very little interest in religion. The rift between old King Henry and the pope had squashed most of Francis's interest in spiritual matters. He came from a Catholic household that had been forced to practice their faith in secret now that the young King Edward pursued with zealous fervor the propagation of the Protestant creed throughout England. Whatever her religion, Jessica was probably more devout than Francis had ever been.

Cosma shrugged again, baring her other shoulder. "It matters not to me in the slightest."

Francis mopped his damp brow. "Nor to me. Jew or Catholic, Jessica is a wonder and that is God's own truth."

Cosma pouted. "Indeed," she muttered. Then she lifted the lid of the largest platter. "Perhaps these will titillate your fancy."

Francis gulped down the bile that threatened to rise in his throat. "What are they?"

"A dish of doves," she cooed.

He rolled his eyes to the gilded vaulted ceiling. "Oh, me, pigeons again? It is well that so many of them flutter in the Piazza San Marco to fill your larder, Cosma."

She placed one of the tiny golden fowl on his plate then sucked on her fingers in a provocative manner. "Prepared with hot spices from the East and roasted with onions."

He groaned inwardly. He should have guessed that Cosma's supper would harbor an ulterior motive. Lady Katherine Cavendish, Brandon's wife, was well versed in the lore of aphrodisiacs. Years ago she had taught Francis the hidden properties of many an innocent-looking meal. Onions for a man's virility; hot spices and peppers to excite sexual impulses; eels to stimulate motion in bedsport—and those blasted doves? The special pets of Venus herself. Francis gulped more wine, but instead of settling his much-distressed stomach it only made things worse.

Cosma, ignorant of Francis's gastronomic turmoil, pulled off some of the succulent pigeon breast with the tips of her white teeth. She curled her long pink tongue around one of her fingers and languorously suckled it. "My food is not to your liking? Oh, dear! I have displeased you—and after I tried so hard to make this meal a warm one. To heat you after a day spent in the cold air outside." A tear shimmered in her eye.

Francis blew out his breath with exasperation. "Don't weep!" he snapped. Weeping women completely unnerved him. On the one occasion when his mother had wept in his presence, Francis thought he would die. "Your supper surpasses all delights." He stuffed a whole roasted onion into his mouth and chewed it with loathing.

Cosma immediately brightened. "I hope not *all* delights," she hinted. "There are others yet to come."

Francis's stomach lurched. His gorge rose in his throat. Clapping his hand over his mouth, he bolted from the table. Grasping the nearest chamber pot, he emptied the contents of his tortured innards.

"I crave your pardon," he said hoarsely before retching again. *I will flay that apothecary by inches if I live through this night.*

With a stricken look, Cosma rose from her chair and came toward him. "I had no idea, my lord...that is to say, I should not have spiced the soup so much."

"Stay back," he gasped before he was sick again. *Into your hands, oh, Lord, I commend my spirit. Pray take me soon!* Clutching the reeking pot for dear life, he sank to the cool floor.

Cosma wrung her hands. "Mayhap it was the wine, but I only seasoned it with a little ginger, cinnamon and vanilla."

Francis retched again. "Enough! Speak no more of food! Can't you see that I am dying?"

From her corner, Nerissa shrieked and dropped the mandolin.

Cosma's eyes grew even larger than her cosmetics had made them appear. She pressed her hand against her lips. "Do not say that! You can't possibly be! I swear upon the crocodile of Saint Theodore I have not poisoned you!" She fell to her knees. Wailing, Nerissa joined her mistress.

Francis clutched his heaving stomach. "Stop that caterwauling and fetch me another pot—quickly! A plague take that scurvy knave," he added in English.

Nerissa dashed into the next room and returned with two

more receptacles. She practically threw them at Francis. "Please do not die, my lord," she whimpered. "I am much too young to go to prison."

Despite his agony, he managed to give her a weak smile. "Fear not, little maid. I shall not haunt you in this life or the one to come." He pulled himself to his feet and staggered around the corner where Cosma kept her closestool. "Your pardon, my dears," he gasped.

Francis had never felt so ill in his life—not even when he had made the rough sea voyage from Marseilles to Genoa. Now his head ached, his throat was raw and his skin felt hot and clammy at the same time. *Truly methinks that charlatan did poison me.* He gritted his teeth until the spasms finally receded, leaving him weak as a newborn calf.

When he emerged, he found Cosma and Nerissa still on their knees and praying—a sight he would have found highly amusing had he not felt so wretched. "Arise, *gattina,* and take me to your bed," he attempted a feeble jest. "Unfortunately, it is sleep I crave and not pleasure. Be of good cheer. I believe I will survive after all."

With many soothing words, the women helped him toward Cosma's wide bed that stood in regal splendor on its platform in the middle of the adjoining chamber. He fell amid the feather pillows and lay as a corpse while Cosma and Nerissa dragged off his clothing. The bed linens smelled faintly of lavender.

Francis emitted a low groan. *The chit would have seduced me past all my restraint tonight if it had not been for that hellish elixir.* He drifted into a heavy sleep still wondering whether he should kiss or kill the apothecary on the morrow.

Chapter Three

Morning came far too early. Francis felt as if he had barely closed his eyes before Nerissa shook his shoulder.

"Please, *messere*." She shook him again. "Awake!"

Cosma stirred next to him. "What is it, Nerissa? Go away! The dawn has not yet showed her face."

Francis rolled onto his side. If his stomach muscles weren't so sore and his mouth didn't taste so full of chicken feathers, he would have sworn he had slept through a nightmare. "How now, little Nissa?" He scrubbed his face with his hand.

The girl clutched her dressing gown closer about her thin trembling form. "There is a man downstairs to see you." She bit her lower lip. "A very large man."

Cosma frowned at her maid. "You mean to say that I have a guest at this unholy hour? What barbarian would seek the company of a lady so early in the morning? The sky is dressed in wisps of the night."

Nerissa shook her head. "No, *madonna*, the visitor is not for you but for Lord Bardolph and he said it was most urgent." Bending closer to the bed, she whispered, "He is a blackamoor."

Francis tossed back the covers. "Did he give his name?"

he asked with mounting excitement. He had not seen Jobe the African for over a year.

Nerissa held out the parti-colored hose of green and gold that she had peeled off Francis last night. "He gave no name but yours, *messere*. But he *did* ask me mine," she gulped. "He has very large teeth!"

Francis grinned at her. "I promise he will not bite you."

"A pity!" Cosma pouted from the midst of her pillows. "I need a diversion since you are so sluggish. Tell me, Nerissa, is this Moor a handsome man? Well proportioned? Is he able to keep his dinner inside his stomach?" She wrinkled her nose at Francis.

Despite her fear, the little maid giggled. "He wears a golden earring and has a great many knives across his chest."

Francis hurried with his dressing. "That is Jobe to the letter!" He had no idea how much he had missed a friendly face that bespoke of England.

Cosma motioned for her dressing gown. "Ah! Our early visitor grows more interesting by the minute. Is he rich?"

Francis laced up his shirt. "That depends upon the wealth of the most recent ship Jobe has plundered." He chuckled to see both women blanch. "Do not look so pale. Jobe is a very lamb when among ladies."

"Now I *am* intrigued," Cosma declared, rouging her lips and cheeks with quick deft movements. "Show him up immediately, Nerissa. And, mind you, do not gawk!" After the maid departed, she asked, "Just how are you acquainted with such a fascinating man?"

Francis assumed his pose as an English dandy. "It is a passion of mine to collect interesting objects whilst on my travels, *gattina*. A Roman sculpture, a piece of the True Cross, even a wily African or two."

She gave him a penetrating look. "Indeed? It seems to me this man is more than one of your passing whims."

Francis pulled on his padded velvet doublet. "Indeed," he agreed.

As Jessica had forewarned him, his shoulder ached this morning as if he had exercised too much. More than ever he looked forward to his visit with her on the following day. Now that Jobe had arrived in Venice, the next twenty-four hours promised to pass less tediously. He grinned at the thought. Just then Nerissa reappeared with the giant African looming behind her like an avenging ghost.

Cosma's eyes widened. *"¡Madre del Dio!"* she breathed, taking in the African's amazing height, the width of his powerful shoulders and the dozen tiny knives that crisscrossed his broad chest. "Welcome to my home, Black Apollo." She retreated to the protection of her elevated bed.

Jobe looked first at Francis in his state of semidress and then at the sleek-limbed woman in her state of near nakedness. He swept Cosma a flourishing bow. "I wondered why there was no fair moon last night to guide my ship into port, but now I understand. Diana of the silvery orb came down to earth and reclines before me. *Madonna,* I am your humble servant," he said in passable Italian.

Francis smiled behind his hand at his friend's lavish compliments. Always the master of surprise, Jobe's cupboard of skills was never empty. Cosma allowed her dressing gown to slip a little, revealing a snowy portion of her thigh.

"How charming!" she replied in a voice like silk. "I forgive your early arrival when you come with such sweet words on your tongue. Francis, pray tell me, who is this god?"

Francis gave her a wry look. *She already plans to seduce*

him out of his purse or to make me jealous. Oddly enough, he found he wasn't the least disturbed by Cosma's fickleness. "Allow me to present Jobe of Africa. My family calls him our guardian angel as he has often proved to be so."

Jobe beamed at his introduction and bowed again, this time including the awed Nerissa in his attentions. "Do not dislike me for my complexion, I beg you, sweet ladies. I have been burnished by the fierce sun of my homeland. But who is this flawless pearl, Francis?" he asked, nodding to Cosma. "Now I see why you do not spend much time in your own lodgings. Your landlord wondered when I asked him where you were."

Francis rolled his eyes at his friend. Jobe could butter the bread of compliments very thick. "I have the pleasure to present to you Donna Cosma di Luna, one of the peerless beauties of Venice."

Jobe advanced to the thronelike bed, dropped to one knee and kissed Cosma's bare foot. "The pleasure is all mine, I assure you."

You may have her with good riddance.

Jobe turned to the little maid who stood on tiptoe in order to see him better. "And it is only fitting that Venus should be attended by such a delicate nymph as you, sweet Nerissa," he added in his deep voice.

The girl nearly fainted with shock while a dart of anger flashed from Cosma's eyes. She hated any competition. "Nerissa," she snapped. "Some wine and bread for our guest and hurry…you slug!"

With a squeak, Nerissa darted away.

Francis addressed his friend in English, "A pox on you, Jobe! How can you utter such honeyed phrases at this sober hour? You will need a cask of wine to cleanse your mouth.'' He clapped the huge man on his shoulder. ''Sweet Jesu! My eyes are glad to see you, you old pirate!''

Jobe enveloped him in a bear hug. ''And you! Though I must confess that I did not expect to find you costumed like a jester.'' With a chuckle, he pointed to the wide green bows on Francis's shoes.

Francis gave him a rueful look. ''Tis a counterfeit pose, Jobe, and a long story best saved for when we are alone.''

Before the African could reply, Cosma spoke up from her cloud of lace, lavender and goose down. ''Fie, gentlemen! It is not polite to speak in a language I cannot understand. Are you plotting the downfall of Venice?''

Jobe grinned at her. ''Not so, lovely dove. We were discoursing upon *your* downfall. I fear you have quite overcome me.''

Cosma simpered in reply and flashed a little more bare leg. Francis tugged at his friend's sleeve. ''Please wait until after I leave before you ravish her. In the meantime, tell me what brings you to Venice to seek me out before even the pigeons are awake?''

At that, Jobe's expression changed to a somber one. ''I bear a heavy duty, Francis, but one that had to be done.'' He withdrew a thick letter from inside his leather jerkin.

Francis stared at it, recognizing Lady Katherine's handwriting. Icy fingers squeezed his heart. ''Bad news from...from Wolf Hall?''

Jobe nodded. ''I am sure that good Lady Kat has written her sad tidings with a gentle hand. I will amuse yonder lady while you read it. Take your time, my friend.''

Francis turned away from Cosma's bed. Clutching the letter close to his chest, he crossed into the antechamber. Seating himself on one of the armchairs, he drew in a deep breath before he broke open the sealing wax. His sudden hot tears blurred the words before him.

Dearest Francis,

Tis with a heavy heart and hand that I take up pen to write such doleful news. Two weeks ago, on the twelfth of November, Sir Thomas Cavendish was taken suddenly from this life. He died as he had lived—in the saddle. The day had been cold and bright with frost. Sir Thomas together with Brandon and Guy and many of the men from the estate went out into the forest to hunt a boar for the coming Christmastide feast. During the afternoon, at the height of the chase, the heart of his great horse burst with the strain, throwing Sir Thomas to the earth. Alas, his neck broke upon landing against a tree trunk. Death was immediate, I am told, and without pain. Dear Lady Alicia bears her sorrow well. She said to tell you that it is a comfort for her to know that Sir Thomas and his beautiful black horse rode posthaste to heaven together and that was the way you know Sir Thomas would have wanted it. I fear that Brandon has taken his father's loss most heavily, as has Guy. It is hard for me and the children to realize that Sir Thomas is indeed gone from this earth. He seemed to be one of those men destined to live forever. Please remember him in your prayers, Francis. You were always his special pride. He often praised your love of language and poetry— gifts you both shared. In his will he has left you his library…

Francis wiped his streaming eyes with his sleeve. Only yesterday, he had arranged for a beautiful copy of Sir Thomas More's *Utopia* to be especially bound in red leather and embossed with a silver wolf's head—the Cavendish family symbol. It was a belated New Year's gift for the man who was his beloved grandfather. Now it was too late! Francis covered his face with his hands. After the first wave of raw grief had receded, he continued Kat's letter.

...of books. He knew that you most of all would appreciate them. I am sorry to be the bearer of such sad tidings. Know that I hold you close to my heart in your sorrow. Brandon joins me in sending you our love. Dear Jobe is here and will give you further details as you require. We look forward to the day when you will return to us. Come home soon, Francis! Written this 28th day of November 1549 at Wolf Hall, Northumberland.

Your loving Katherine Cavendish
Countess of Thornbury

Francis reread her signature and title several times as her message sank into his brain. How quickly the world turned and turned again! Of course Lady Kat was now the new countess just as his...as Brandon became the tenth Earl of Thornbury the instant that the breath of life had left his father.

Gripping the paper in his hand, Francis laid his head down on the table. His silent tears soaked into the green velvet cloth that covered the top. He had not felt one tenth this sorrow when he had learned of his mother's death three years ago. Francis had barely known her in life and he had liked her even less.

His emotions were quite different with Sir Thomas's passing. Francis had lived under Wolf Hall's roof for over fourteen years. Though a big man, as all the Cavendish men were, and blessed with a powerful voice, Sir Thomas was a gentle friend to the young and weak. On the other hand, the earl was a fierce competitor in the jousting arena and a ferocious foe in combat. Francis remembered the many hours they had spent together in his library studying the plays of Plautus and the writings of Erasmus. Sir Thomas had patiently taught his bastard grandson the joys of Greek and Latin and he had championed the boy's bent for study when Brandon wanted Francis to spend more time handling a broadsword and lance. "The pen is mightier than the sword," Sir Thomas had often told his eager pupil.

Now that grand old man was gone forever.

Francis read the letter a third and fourth time. He barely noticed the goblet of watered wine and a small loaf of honey bread that Nerissa placed by his hand. He stared out the window at the gloom of the breaking day. As if heaven mirrored his sorrow, rain fell lightly from the leaden skies and rolled like teardrops down the wavy panes of glass. In the distance, he heard church bells calling early worshipers to Mass.

Francis dragged himself to his feet. *I must go to church.* He could not remember the last time he had stepped willingly inside a place of worship. Though he believed in God and the existence of a heaven and hell, the daily practice of religion meant very little to him. *But it meant all the world to Sir Thomas.* Francis must pray for his soul. It was the only thing left he could do for that wonderful old man. He strode into the bedchamber where Jobe sat on the bed's carpeted platform and conversed with Cosma in low tones. Spying Francis, the African stood and came toward him.

"How now, friend?" Jobe asked in English.

Francis held out the letter now wrinkled by his grief. "These are the most loathsome words that ever blotted paper," he told Jobe. "To think that he has lain cold in his grave for these past three months and I never knew…never knew. I have been drinking, singing and dancing—aye, and wenching while the worms dined upon my…my grandfather." He could not continue. His shame overwhelmed him. He had never told Sir Thomas how much he loved him.

Cosma took his hand in hers. For once, there was no artifice in her eyes. "Jobe has told me of your loss and I am sorry to hear it."

Francis bowed his head with his wordless thanks. Grief choked him.

Cosma turned to the African. "His grandfather was a great man?"

Jobe nodded. "One of England's finest. Now he takes his place among his noble ancestors and leaves his earthly cares to his son."

Cosma's expression changed subtly. "And his son is…?"

Jobe hooded his dark eyes. "Sir Brandon Cavendish, the tenth Earl of Thornbury."

Francis crumpled the letter. The earl was Sir Thomas— it had always been. Francis could not yet imagine Brandon filling those large shoes.

Cosma flicked her tongue between her teeth. "Then you are now an earl's son, Francis," she whispered. She did not add, "And one day you will be the next Earl of Thornbury." Francis heard her unspoken words inside his head and it sickened him. *She* sickened him.

"Guard that rash tongue of yours, *madonna,*" Jobe told her in a deceptively gentle tone. "One day it will be your downfall."

Cosma ignored the warning but Francis heard it. "Heed him," he snapped at her. Jobe possessed a rare gift—the ability to see events in the future for everyone except himself.

"The Earl of Thornbury is a very important title in England?" she prodded.

Francis pulled on his overcoat and grabbed his cloak, hat

and doeskin gloves. "God rest his soul, he was the most important man in my life," he told her as he stalked toward the wide staircase. As he spoke the words, he realized how true they were and his sorrow doubled. "Come, Jobe," he called over his shoulder in English. "We must hie ourselves to Saint Mark's. Mass has already begun."

Cosma recognized the name of the great basilica that stood in the heart of Venice. Running after Francis and Jobe she asked, "You are going to church, Francis? Now? I thought you and God were in disagreement."

"It is time I made some amends," he shouted back up the marble stairs. "My grandfather deserves it."

"Then return to me soon, *caro,* and I will comfort you."

Jobe clapped his hat on his head. "Hold, woman! Can't you see that his mirth has fled?"

Cosma opened her mouth but Jobe held up his hand. The fire in his eyes silenced her. "Remember the words I have told you, mistress." Then he followed on Francis's heels.

Rather than take a gondola to the *piazza,* Francis and Jobe hurried through the sinuous narrow streets toward the great church. The mist-draped *piazza* already teemed with masked revelers celebrating the pre-Lenten season of *Carnevale.* Francis ignored them just as his grief blotted out Cosma's unashamed avarice. When he had the fortitude, he would deal with her later. For now, he would pray for his grandfather's soul in the afterlife and remember the great man who had loved him—like a son.

A reedy-voiced priest droned the Latin ritual as Francis and Jobe slipped through one of Saint Mark's massive doors. The huge vaulted domes high over their heads gleamed dully with gold-spangled mosaics depicting biblical tales. The white faces of the painted saints looked strained and pouchy under their eyes, as if they had been carousing all night. The hundreds of candles flickering before altars and shrines did little to dispel the pervasive gloom of the massive building's interior. When Francis's eyes adjusted to the dimness he noticed that very few worshipers attended the divine services.

Francis sank to his knees on the cold marble paving and folded his hands in prayer. The geometric pattern of the floor made him light-headed so he closed his eyes. While he half listened to the familiar words of the Mass, Thomas Cavendish flashed through his memory. Dredging up long-forgotten prayers, Francis whispered them in the chill air. Never had he felt so desolated as he did at this moment. His anger at himself for missed opportunities in the past joined his regret for a future now empty of Sir Thomas's imposing presence.

Francis roused himself from his meditations when Jobe tapped him on the shoulder. "The priest has finished," the African whispered. "And my bones are chilled."

Blinking away the vestige of grief, Francis rose heavily to his feet. He had no idea how long he had knelt on the hard floor but now his knees ached. Even inside his gloves, his fingers felt like icicles. He rubbed warmth back into them.

"I pray your patience a moment longer, my friend," he said to Jobe. "I must buy a taper and light it for Sir Thomas."

Without waiting for his friend to reply, Francis made his way to the church's porch where an ancient nun presided over a tray of beeswax candles. Selecting a long one, he paid for it and returned to the main aisle where he searched for a place to light it. Jobe followed him in respectful silence. Francis realized that the Catholic rituals were completely foreign to the African, and he appreciated Jobe's faithful company all the more. In the small Chapel of the

Cross, Francis pressed his candle into a vacant holder, lit it with a waxen spill, and whispered one final prayer.

A faint but familiar scent wafted on the cold air. Francis lifted his head and sniffed. A rich Arabian perfume filled his nostrils and stirred a pleasant memory. Signorina Jessica? He spun on his heel and peered into the huge dark body of the church.

Jobe moved to his side. "What is it?" he asked in a low tone. "Danger?"

Still scanning the interior, Francis shook his head. "Nay, tis an angel, methinks, and one that I long to see soon again." Never was he in more need of Jessica's healing touch than now. His heart beat faster.

Jobe lifted his dark brows. "A woman?" he asked with surprise.

Francis stepped into the yawning nave. "Aye, but more than that. You will understand when you meet her. Ah! There she is!" He spied a slim cloaked figure at a side door.

He broke into a trot across the undulating, uneven floor. If she managed to slip away before he could reach her, he would lose her among the holiday crowd in the *piazza.* "Signorina Jessica," he called softly as soon as he dared.

The woman turned. Her white-painted mask shone starkly from the folds of her dark hood. Francis called her again. "Signorina Leonardo? I crave a word or two."

Placing her hand on the large brass doorknob, she paused like a startled deer in a wooded glen.

Francis drew to her side. Jobe lingered in the shadow of one of the stone pillars.

"Donna Jessica?" Francis asked again, though he was sure it was she. Her perfume enveloped him with its enchantment.

"*Messere,*" she murmured, drawing her hood lower over

her hidden visage. Her hand trembled. "I hope you are feeling better this morning."

He placed his hand on his chest. "In body yes, but my heart is broken in twain."

She stepped closer to the door. "Pray do not jest with me. It is not seemly to play trifling games inside God's house." She turned to go.

Francis touched her arm. "Forgive me. I do not sport with you, Donna Jessica. I have just learned that my grandfather is dead. Do you have a healing potion for a grieving heart?"

She looked up at him. Her eyes shimmered behind the mask. "Your pardon, *messere,* I mistook," she whispered. "You have my deepest condolences."

Francis took her hand in his. "May I escort you back to your home? Just hearing your voice is balm to my sorrow."

Her trembling increased. "It is already daylight outside and I am late. I beg your pardon, Lord Bardolph, but I must hurry away."

He refused to relinquish her hand. "Then I shall attach wings to my feet and fly with you."

"Like Mercury?" A half smile brightened her lips below the mask. "But it is not possible. You are a great personage and I am a nobody. We should not be seen together. My company demeans you."

"Never," he protested. He longed to shed the disguise of his garish clothing and his pretense of nobility. "I swear upon yon Holy Cross that all my wealth runs in my veins, not in my purse or position."

She lowered her head so that he could not see her eyes. "You speak in riddles that I do not understand. Pray, let me go now. I must be away from here. There are too many prying eyes and wagging tongues." She glanced up at him.

"For your loss, I am sorry, and I will remember your grandfather in my prayers. What was his name?"

"Thomas," he replied softly.

She nodded. "A fine name. I will remember him—and you," she added. She glanced over to the pillar. "I see you are attended by a friend and so I will leave you with better company than I. Good day, *messere,* until tomorrow."

Francis looked over his shoulder at Jobe. *"Sì,"* he answered with feeling, "he is a wealth of friends rolled into one, but you—" When he turned again, he found that she had slipped away without a sound.

Jobe stepped out of the shadows. "You spoke the truth," he remarked, putting his hand on Francis's shoulder. "The maid is a very pearl among the swine of Venice."

"She seemed afraid of me, yet I meant her no harm. Did you hear the music of her voice? Oh! She is sweet and brings a ray of sunshine into the cold vault of my heart."

"Tread softly lest you lose her forever," Jobe whispered.

Francis gave him a penetrating look. "What do you see in the mists of the future? Do you see her?"

Jobe stared beyond Francis, past the bright candles and the holy statues into the dark recesses of his inner vision. "Aye, I do, but tis murky. That little one will save you or she will condemn you. She carries joy in one hand and sorrow in the other. Because of her, you will die, be reborn and new baptized."

Chapter Four

Sophia looked up from her kettle of thick soup as Jessica entered the tiny kitchen at the back of the house. The savory aroma of simmering chicken and onions comforted the young woman. Still out of breath from her dash through the maze of alleyways and squares between the great *piazza* and the safety of her little home north of the Rialto Bridge, Jessica sank onto a short-legged wooden stool. Tossing back her hood, she plucked the mask from her face.

Sophia planted a hand on her ample hip. "How now? I thought you went to church?"

"I did," Jessica replied. Her heart still raced within her bosom.

"Then why have you returned looking as if you were pursued by a demon?"

Drawing in a deep breath, Jessica leaned back against the cool plaster wall. "He was at Saint Mark's."

The little woman's eyes widened. "Who? *Il diavolo* in a house of God? Tell me, does he truly have horns and cloven feet?"

Despite her recent fright, Jessica smiled. "No, Sophia. I speak of the English lord from yesterday." She sat up straighter. "He was there and he stopped me as I was leaving."

"And?" Sophia cocked her head like one of Venice's gray-feathered pigeons.

Jessica twisted her fingers in her lap. "How did he know I would be there?" she whispered. "Unless he had me watched. Did he station a man outside my door to see if I consorted with Jews? Perchance he hopes to trap me, to prove that I am not a good Christian woman."

"Mayhap he expects you to fly over the rooftops on a broomstick," Sophia remarked wryly. "Or invite nine or ten alley cats to a dance."

Jessica glared at her. "Tis no laughing matter. Why do I feel that I tread upon eggshells when Lord Bardolph is near? He frightens me."

Sophia snorted. "Only that? Are you sure there is nothing *else* he does to you when he is standing next to you?"

Closing her eyes, Jessica allowed herself to explore the myriad unfamiliar feelings that had assailed her when Sir Francis had held her hand. Though he had worn gloves, she felt his heat penetrate her skin. Setting her blood afire. Leaving her breathless. Making her giddy with a strange emotion that she had never experienced.

"He is not like other men," she responded lamely.

Sophia turned back to the soup that threatened to bubble over into the fire. "Agreed. He is as tall as a ship's mast."

Jessica rolled her eyes. Sophia could be so annoying at times. "I mean he is not like the others who have sought my help. I know how to slip away from the searching hands of those Lotharios old and young who seek to press their advantage upon me. They laugh and shrug and tell me that there will be another day. And I know how to listen to those sad-faced men who complain of their aches and pains when it is really their wives and their dull marriages that make them feel ill. They leave happier and call me sweet names that they will not remember by the time they reach the canal. But *this* man…''

Shivering, she hugged herself as she recalled his low gentle voice and the infinite beauty of his face. "He is so different. He dresses as if he had not a care in the world, yet he bears a weight inside of him greater than all the henpecked husbands of Venice." She caught Sophia's gaze. "He told me this morning that he had just learned of his grandfather's death."

The little woman paused in her soup stirring and sketched a hasty sign of the cross. "Poor man!"

Jessica stared at the glowing red coals in the hearth. "And I think that is the truth, yet he was sad yesterday when he did not know of his grandfather's passing. Is he sad because he must disguise his true self? Sophia, I cannot banish the fear that he is really a secret agent of the Holy Office."

Sophia tasted her concoction and added a pinch of salt. "And yet?"

Jessica massaged her temples. "I swear I must be going mad for I cannot wait until he returns here tomorrow. Just thinking about him makes my heart pound. Do you suppose I am coming down with a fever?"

Sophia turned slowly around and surveyed Jessica. She crossed her arms over her breasts with an odd gleeful look in her eye. "Just so, *cara mia.* I think you have been bitten by a strange malady that usually comes in the springtime."

Jessica gasped. "The plague? Please, Sophia, tell me it is not so!"

Sophia chuckled. "No, my sweet girl, you are safe from that scourge. Let us speak no more about it today for I could be wrong and I do not wish to alarm you further. Wait and see. Perhaps tomorrow I can better tell."

Jessica felt her forehead and cheeks with her palms but found that she was not unusually hot. "Is it a fatal illness?"

Sophia laughed behind her hand. "Not usually. Enough of this idle prattle. Go attend to your business and allow me to tend to mine. Little Miriam is due to arrive at any moment and she needs all the soothing care that you can give her." The small woman shook her head. "If you ask me, fourteen years is too young to have a baby, no matter what her dolt of a husband thinks. Bah! Men!"

Jobe regarded his young friend with a keen interest. He was heartened that the most serious member of the Cavendish family had finally given evidence of his passionate nature. "Be of good cheer, Francis. You said you will see your elusive dove on the morrow. For today, let us walk about this delightful city and share goodly talk. I confess I am consumed with curiosity. Why these gaudy garments that are better suited to a rake than to a man of intelligence and somber wit?"

Francis curled his lips. "You do not approve of my rags? They are the very last word in fashion, I assure you."

The African arched his dark brow. "If those are the last words, then put a period to end their sentence."

A ghost of a smile hovered on Francis's lips. "'Tis for the future of England's foreign trade that I play the fool. I am dressed to blend into the background."

Jobe snorted. "Aye, as the red nose of a drunkard blends in with his green face."

Francis waved away this observation. "When I was in Paris, I played the part of a roving *jongleur*. Thank God, Lady Alicia insisted that I learn how to play a lute and recorder! That disguise served me well for over two years. In Padua, I became a dense medical student. In Pisa and Rome, a stuttering cleric. The stutter spared me from having to say a Mass, hear a confession or to answer probing questions.''

He continued, ''In Genoa, I worked as a dockhand until my muscles screamed in protest. In Florence, I pretended to be an artist. That was a mistake of the first order for I discovered that I could not draw to save my life. When I came here I adopted the guise of an English rake who is somewhat addled in his wits.'' He kissed the back of his hand with a flourish. ''Naturally I was accepted by the ruling class as one of their own.''

Jobe chuckled. ''Belle would die laughing if she could see you now.''

Francis grimaced. ''Don't remind me and I pray you, never tell her. She would tease me for a lifetime. How fares my sister and her rogue of a husband? Are they well? And her children? Tis an odd thing to think of Belle as the mother of two boys.''

Jobe guided their steps toward the Rialto Bridge where he hoped the bustle of early morning commerce and gossip-mongering would lighten their mood. ''All are in most excellent health and pine for your return. Tis seven years since you last set foot in Wolf Hall. Do you intend to roam the wide world forever?''

Francis avoided Jobe's gaze. ''I am needed abroad in the service of the king,'' he replied without emotion.

''Belle's son Thomas needs his godfather to give his young mind direction toward books instead of pranks. And your father yearns for your company again.''

''Which father is that?'' Francis mumbled into the collar of his cloak. ''I had several.''

The African narrowed his eyes. Since Jobe had last seen Francis in Rome the previous year, the young man's melancholy had grown worse and the canker in his soul had festered. If it were not lanced soon, Jobe feared that his friend would not live to see his fortieth birthday. And yet, this morning had given the African a spark of hope. He vowed he would not leave Venice or Francis until that spark could be ignited into a blaze of joy. "Tis the season of mirth," he remarked aloud.

Francis cast him a glum look. "I am too heavy for sporting tricks."

They entered a crowded square near the Rialto Bridge. Vendors of vegetables and fish did a lively business with the early rising housewives of the district. The mouthwatering aroma of fresh bread took the chill off the day. Even the sun's watery eye seemed to burn brighter. Clusters of bearded men in bright yellow hats spoke among themselves in low tones. The Jews who controlled the intricate web of international financing discussed the price of gold and the rates of interest on the cargoes of rare spices from the Turkish empire: nutmeg, cloves, cinnamon and peppercorns. The paving stones of the square and the stucco walls of the surrounding houses reverberated with the pulse of life.

Clapping Francis on the back, Jobe pointed to the marketplace. "My purse is full and these goods entice me. Let us lose ourselves in some wanton shopping."

Francis surveyed the cheerful scene. "Methinks I should buy a mourning band for Sir Thomas."

Jobe nodded. "Aye, that as well, but first you must help me select some fripperies for my wives."

Surprise etched Francis's handsome face. "I never knew you were married."

The African laughed. "Four times and each one is a priceless jewel."

The young man shook his head. "Methinks there is something unholy in that arrangement."

Jobe disagreed. "Not so, my friend. You forget that I am not a Christian and so am not bound by your laws, though my Portuguese captors did their best to beat the word of the Lord into my head. At least I learned how to swear most religiously in a number of tongues."

Francis rewarded him with a grin. The boy should laugh more often, Jobe thought. A man with such a face as his commits a grave sin against the Creator by not enhancing his good looks with a smile.

"Very well, my dear pagan, what sort of gifts have you in mind for your women?" Francis asked.

Jobe steered him toward one of the goldsmith shops that edged the *campo*. "My darlings come from Africa, Alexandria and Cyprus, but they all have one thing in common. My delicate flowers adore jewelry. I shall deck them in gold necklaces, copper bracelets and those colorful glass beads. Come, help me choose!"

Francis ducked through the shop's low door. "Your last voyage must have been a profitable one."

Jobe grinned. "Aye, both legal trade of English wool and some conveyance of goods courtesy of several unfortunate galleys belonging to the sultan."

Francis nodded a greeting to the eager shopkeeper. "One of these days you will find yourself dancing on the point of a scimitar."

Jobe placed his forefinger against his nose. "But not yet and tis only today that counts." Then he turned his attention to the glittering wares that the goldsmith displayed for them. "You have all the wealth of the world," he complimented the snaggletoothed little man in Italian.

By the time Jobe had completed his purchases, the weak sun had managed to dispel the last of the morning's dank mist. The African was pleased to note that Francis's mood had also warmed, especially after a mug of spiced red wine and a repast of juicy roasted fowl from the wine shop. The sounds around them increased as masked merrymakers ebbed in and out of the square leaving laughter and music in their wake.

"Ah! I love carnival time!" Jobe exclaimed. "Especially in Venice. Tis the only good reason to have Lent for—"

At that moment his inner sixth sense told him that a pair of secretive eyes watched them.

Without altering his cheerful expression, Jobe said in a low tone, "We have interested a shadow." He touched one of the knives he wore in a bandoleer across his chest. "Shall I tickle him to see how well he squeals?"

Francis glanced over his shoulder, then shook his head. "You mean that thin whipster in the stained brown cloak? He has been with us since we left Saint Mark's. He is one of Cosma's lapdogs." He gave Jobe a rueful grin. "Methinks my mistress does not trust me to be faithful to her."

Jobe's intuition scented an undercurrent of danger. "Are you sure this dog has no teeth?"

Francis shrugged. "Tis but a pup—all ears and tales. Trust me. I have seen him skulking around Cosma's house on several occasions."

"Pups can grow into vicious jackals," the African muttered.

Jobe spent the rest of the day in Francis's company helping him to ease the pain of his loss. While the young Englishman paid their shadow no mind, Jobe kept a wary eye on the sallow-faced boy who hovered behind them at a short distance. The guttersnipe needed to learn a thing or two about the art of concealment and pursuit, Jobe decided. He almost pitied their dogged follower.

In midafternoon, Francis surprised Jobe by announcing, "What a dolt I am! I have an appointment that almost slipped my mind."

Thinking that his companion meant that he had a meeting with an informant, Jobe turned to go. Francis put his hand on his arm. "Nay, do not leave me now. You must accompany me and keep me entertained for one more hour at least."

Mystified by Francis's sudden animation, Jobe nodded. "I am yours to command for this whole day. Do we visit a house of pleasure, perchance?"

Francis shook his head. "Surely you jest, my friend. Donna Cosma is all I can manage as it is. I speak of something that you will find infinitely more amusing—I am having my portrait painted by one of Maestro Titian's pupils."

Laughter bubbled up from Jobe's broad chest. "You? I did not realize that a rivulet of vanity ran through your veins. Tis rich news indeed."

Francis's ears turned red. "Tis not for vanity's sake but as part of my false persona. All wealthy travelers to Venice must have their portraits painted. Tis expected. I had barely been in the city a fortnight when I received at least a half dozen invitations to visit the studios of the city's famous painters."

He turned down a *calle*. "Titian's studio is at the far end of this street. The *maestro*'s work is superb but very costly. His pupils are apt enough for Lord Cecil's expense account. Is our fledgling still with us?"

Jobe did not need to turn around to know the answer. "Aye, though he grows weary."

Francis grinned. "A pity he cannot come inside. I fear he will have a long cold wait."

Jobe chuckled. Francis knocked upon a door that was in desperate need of a fresh coat of green paint. After a few minutes' wait and a second rap of the knocker, a harried young boy admitted them. With scarcely a nod of recognition, the child ushered the two tall men up a narrow flight of stairs and into a large chamber filled with the most amazing jumble of clutter that Jobe had ever seen. Half-finished paintings of every size leaned against the walls in haphazard formations. More paintings sat on easels that stood at random angles on the wide bare floor. A dozen or so young men, most of them covered with daubs of paint and all of them looking intense, worked at various projects. The odor of turpentine, paint and rotten eggs hung overhead. Jobe sneezed.

Their page interrupted the most frazzled member of this fraternity and pointed to Francis. By way of greeting, the Englishman executed the most outlandish court bow. Jobe covered his snicker with another sneeze.

"Signor Bassanio, a thousand pardons," Francis gushed. "My dear friend Jobe, standing here before you, arrived quite unexpectedly this day and we have been gamboling about *La Serenissima,* Venice the most Serene, enjoying its delights. I fear that I have overstepped my time. I beg your forgiveness."

Jobe hid his grin. If he punctured Francis at this moment the boy would spew treacle instead of blood.

Bassanio wiped his hands on his smudged smock. "No apology is necessary, my lord. It is always a pleasure to wait upon you." He pointed to the high-legged stool set in a spot that caught the faint glow of the afternoon's playful light. "Please take your accustomed seat, *messere.*"

Francis doffed his cloak, shook the dampness from the plume on his hat and fluffed his sleeves. With a wide smile and graceful movements, he approached the humble stool and perched his hip upon it. He winked at Jobe.

Despite his mummery, Jobe liked like him better for the pose. Francis should adopt it as his own—in moderation.

Bassanio selected a covered canvas, screwed it into place on his easel and removed the cloth. *"¿Signore?"* He gestured to Jobe. "You may wish to see what I have done while I prepare my palette." He stepped away with an expression of shy pride on his round face.

"My pleasure," replied Jobe, advancing closer to view the nearly completed portrait. He drew in a quick breath at the sight.

"Tis that bad?" Francis asked in English. "I had planned to give it to Belle. Mayhap she should use it as a target for her archery practice. Well? What do you think of it?"

"Tis a wonder to behold," Jobe replied.

Why had he never marked the resemblance before? The tilt of the head was the same. So was the merry sparkle in the blue eyes that Francis usually shielded from public view. The long legs, the tapered fingers and the easy set of the shoulders mirrored those same attributes of Francis's true paternity. Unknowingly, the Venetian artist had set in paint a study not of Sir Brandon Cavendish but of his brother Sir Guy, the most handsome member of that illustrious family.

Staring at the canvas, Jobe experienced a rare flash of hindsight. As if he were an invisible onlooker, he observed a scene in his mind that must have taken place thirty years beforehand. As clearly as he saw Francis perched on the stool before him, Jobe saw Guy as a young man glowing with good health and the pride of his victory in the day's tournament. A ripe beauty with nut-brown hair sauntered into view, smiled and beckoned to the too handsome youth. With a lusty but silent laugh, Guy followed her into a colorful pavilion. The image shimmered in Jobe's brain for a final moment before it shattered into the present.

"Heigh ho, Jobe!" Francis called. "Have you wax in your ears? Tell me what the devil do I look like."

The African gave himself a shake. Clearing his throat,

he smiled at his bewildered friend. "You have not seen it for yourself?"

Francis made a face. "Bassanio has strictly charged me not to view my visage until he gives me leave to do so. Methinks he fears I will be displeased and refuse to pay him. Well? What say you?"

Bassanio came up behind Jobe. The young painter eyed the bandoleer of knives. He gulped. "Does my work please you, *signore?*"

Jobe smiled at him. "You have a true gift. You have caught his very soul." And much more, Jobe realized as his prophetic insight once again took hold of him. A secret, greater than anyone suspected, lay hidden over the shoulder of the painted Francis.

Bassanio grinned like a schoolboy. "*Grazie, signore.* Now, my Lord Bardolph, wipe away your doubts and do not move a muscle. I have much work still to do." He dipped his brush into a golden hue and mixed it with a light brown color. "It is the highlights in your hair that elude me and I must work quickly. The daylight fades even as we speak."

Francis sighed with exasperation but said nothing while Bassanio commenced to paint. While Jobe watched him, he mulled over the scant knowledge of Francis's birth that he had learned from Belle's husband, Mark Hayward. It was no shame among the Cavendish family that both Belle and Francis had been conceived out of wedlock in June 1520 during the near legendary meeting between the kings of England and France that the chroniclers now called the Field of Cloth of Gold. Belle was the love child of Brandon Cavendish and a French vintner's daughter while Francis was born to a noblewoman of infamous reputation, Lady Olivia Bardolph.

When seven-year-old Francis was fostered to the Cavendish family, his distinct Viking looks bespoke of his true parentage. Since Brandon had also slept with the lascivious lady, he presumed Francis to be his own, as well. But Brandon had never claimed Francis, not even when Lord Richard Bardolph, Francis's father of record, had died.

Studying the portrait, Jobe willed his vision to appear once more but it did not. No need. Under the light strokes of Bassanio's brush, Guy returned Jobe's penetrating look. The African wondered if he should tell Francis now or wait to see if the young man would notice the resemblance himself. Jobe decided to remain silent on the matter. Francis had suffered enough shocking family news for one day. The time of this latest reckoning—and its hidden secret—would come soon enough.

Francis longed to scratch his nose but he did not dare move. Why was it that his nose never itched until he sat for this poxy portrait? He hoped that Belle would appreciate Bassanio's labors. To distract himself from the annoying tickle, he stared into middle space and listened to the idle chatter of the other apprentices in the chamber. Since he had first sat for Bassanio, he had overheard several interesting tidbits of news that he had passed on to Sir William. This mindless exercise turned out to be well worth the ducats and tedium.

He tried not to let his mind wander back to his grandfather's demise. That wound in his heart was still too raw to allow much thought in such a public place. He was deeply grateful that Bassanio had not asked the meaning of the black armband that Francis now wore in Sir Thomas's memory. Instead, Francis cast furtive glances at Jobe's serious countenance. *He has that look he gets when he sees the future.*

Bassanio clicked his tongue against his teeth. *"Per favore, messere,"* the painter pleaded. "Do not roll your eyes so. You try me to the quick."

"Your pardon," Francis replied, barely moving his lips.

He wished he could read Jobe's inscrutable mind. There was something about the portrait that had surprised the African. Yet he did not seem displeased. Francis prayed that the painter had not given his skin that greenish tinge that appeared on some paintings he had seen during a covert trip he had made to Madrid. It was bad enough that he would be preserved in these gaudy clothes for all time. In any event, Belle would have a good laugh at his expense.

Bassanio stepped back and cocked his head. *"Fine,"* he pronounced.

With relief, Francis got off his stool. "Finished? May I see it now?"

The painter shook his head. "I only meant that I was finished for today. The good light is gone." He dropped his cloth over the easel. "You can come next Wednesday?"

Francis hid his disappointment. Portrait-sitting was indeed a rare form of torture. *"Sì,"* he agreed. He retrieved his cloak and turned to Jobe who still appeared to be lost in the forest of his own thoughts.

"Have you seen enough art for the day?" he bantered.

Blinking, Jobe nodded. He placed a ducat in the hand of the surprised painter. "My thanks, *signore,* for a most excellent afternoon."

Bassanio's face lit up with a wide smile. "Come again, *signore!* Come often. Indeed, it would be an honor to paint *you!* I am your humble servant." With more drivel of the same sort, Bassanio showed them out into the narrow street.

Francis drew in a deep breath of the early evening air. Another light mist from the lagoon curled around the house corners. "Tell me, Jobe, what did you see in there?"

The ebony giant chuckled. "I saw a painted fool."

Francis knew there was more. "And what else? Come now, I saw your face. You had another vision. Tell me."

Jobe gave him a searching look before he answered. "Very well. I beheld a dangerous secret, one that is bright-shining like the sun in splendor. For many years it has lain hidden deep amid the roots of your family. Soon it will be revealed but how or when, I do not know."

Which family, Francis wondered, Bardolph or Cavendish?

Assuming a lighter mood, Jobe draped his arm over Francis's shoulder. "Where away? Do we sup with the delectable Donna Cosma?"

Francis stared up at the chimney pots across the way. He had no desire to see his husband-hunting mistress. "Not I tonight, my friend, though I would not deny *you* that singular pleasure if you wish it."

Jobe stroked his beardless chin. "How now? Surely the wench expects you. Your landlord gave me the impression that you always spent your evenings at her establishment."

Francis thought of the sweet, mysterious, fascinating Jessica. "'Tis time for a change, methinks. Let us repair to my inn where mine host serves a passable meal, and we shall have a long talk in private. I am anxious to hear all the news of...of home."

Jobe nodded with a grin. "Then I am your man. I will purchase a bottle of sweet wine and then I will fill your nighttime hours with so many tales that you will cry 'enough!'"

"Good!" Francis savored his pleasant thoughts of Jessica. "The morrow will come more quickly."

Jobe's laughter rumbled up from his throat. "Methinks I scent *l'amore!*"

Francis snorted. "When pigs fly."

Chapter Five

The bells of the nearby church chimed ten melodic strokes. Using a pair of wooden tongs, Jessica laid a thick piece of toweling over the pile of hot stones that hissed with clouds of steam when she ladled a dipper of water over them. Sophia rushed into the kitchen and shut the door behind her as if all the demons of hell had arrived by gondola.

"He's back!" she told Jessica, her eyes wide with fright.

Her little companion's demeanor unnerved Jessica. She swallowed. "I presume you mean the Englishman. He promised to come this morning at ten." Jessica's hands trembled. "What is amiss?"

Sophia glanced over her shoulder at the closed door. "*Sì,* the sad lord is in the antechamber but he is not alone." She lowered her voice to a hoarse whisper. "He is accompanied by another who is even taller."

Jessica experienced a sudden sinking feeling in the pit of her stomach. "*¡Madre del Dio!* They have come to drag me before the Inquisition. But I have done nothing wrong, Sophia," she protested. "Though my parents have returned to their former religion, I have always obeyed the Holy

Church of Rome. I have done nothing wrong," she repeated under her breath like a prayer.

The little woman did not hear Jessica's plaintive words. She stared fixedly at the door. "The new one is black as midnight. An Ethiope, I warrant." She made a face. "And he smiles exceedingly much!"

Jessica blinked. An African in company with Lord Bardolph? Could such a one also be a member of the Holy Office? She discarded the very notion. She had seen a few blackamoors in the *piazza*, especially during the *Carnevale* season, but never one inside a church. And yet—yesterday, the English gentleman had been accompanied by a tall man, one who lingered in the shadows. Like a dark shadow himself.

She gave herself a shake. She could not hide in her kitchen for the rest of her life. "Come, Sophia! We must not tarry or they will grow restive and knock the house down with their elbows."

Sophia crossed her arms over her tight bodice. "This is not the time to jest, child. We must look to our safety. I shall tell Gobbo to be armed with his stiletto as well as his lute."

Jessica refrained from pointing out that the little man's dagger would be as effectual as a mouse's tooth against a lion. "Prepare a tray of sweetmeats and pastries for the African. Pour him a generous goblet of wine—our best vintage, Sophia, and…do not water it too much. Perchance we can lull him with food until we learn their true intent."

Sophia snorted as she bustled about the small chamber. "I vow that Ethiope could drink a full keg of thick wine and still keep a sober head. Wait until you see the size of him!"

Jessica nodded, then donned her mask. It wasn't her curiosity to meet the giant African that caused her heart to pound against her rib cage and her skin to tingle. Her thoughts centered on the handsome English lord. She squared her shoulders just before she lifted the latch of the door. "Be quick," she whispered to Sophia.

Both men swept her courtly bows when Jessica entered her waiting room. Sophia had not exaggerated. Their physical size filled the antechamber almost to bursting. She faltered a step.

"Good morrow, Madonna of Mystery." Displaying a surprising grace, the African greeted her in good Italian spoken in a deep rolling bass. "Your fame is exceeded only by the beauty that you try to hide."

I wonder where he acquired such a silky tongue? Under her mask, Jessica returned his infectious smile. "You are welcome to my home, *signore.*"

She glanced at his silent companion. Her breath caught in her throat. Though grief rimmed his blue eyes, the gentleman appeared ten times more handsome than when she had last seen him. *Must be a trick of the light.*

She cleared her throat. "Good morrow, *messere.*" She tried to smile at him but her lips trembled too much. "Everything is prepared for you, if you are ready."

Before the lord could answer, the African chuckled. "Francis has been ready for you since yesterday morning, *madonna.*"

His friend muttered something in his own language. The African laughed again but said nothing else. Then the gentleman replied in Italian, "Forgive, Jobe, Signorina Jessica. My friend speaks more nonsense than any man in Venice."

Jessica made a fluttering motion with her fingers. "There is nothing to forgive, *messere.* It is I who must beg your pardon for I see that you are not well. I fear that my cure was not as effective as I had hoped. I will gladly refund your fee. Indeed, you overpaid—"

The blond man unfastened his cloak and tossed it to the African. His blue velvet bonnet followed. "I paid you a mere pittance and your healing did me a world of good, though I must confess that I did ache a bit as you had warned me." A tiny smile flitted across his lips before it disappeared. "It is my recent sorrow that adds bitter pangs to the old hurt. Like a pilgrim on a holy quest, I have come seeking your solace, *madonna*."

Jobe whistled through his teeth. "My friend speaks the truth, fair mistress. He is much sicker than I suspected."

The gentleman glared at the blackamoor. Just then Sophia barged through the doorway laden with a large wooden tray that was piled high with the sweet provender that Jessica had requested. Setting the platter on a small Turkish table, Sophia fixed a stern eye on the African.

"You, Signore Treetop, sit!" She pointed to the larger of the two chairs in the room. "I'll not stretch my neck out of joint so that I can see you clearly."

"Sophia!" Jessica gasped. What had gotten into her companion that made her speak so rudely, especially to a man who wore a brace of wicked-looking daggers across his chest?

The African broke into rolling laughter as he sank down onto the chair. "Most excellent!" he rumbled with delight. "By my beard, if I had one, I think I have met my match!"

Sophia cocked her head. "I am already married!"

The Englishman cast her a wry look. "So is he, *signora*. Four times!"

"Truly?" Jessica eyed the grinning giant. If he practiced such a heathenish custom he could not possibly be a cleric. Relief relaxed the knots in her stomach.

The African popped a sugared almond into his mouth. "Indeed, *madonna*. Now go to, Francis. I know that I leave you in good hands." He turned his merry eyes on Sophia.

"Meanwhile, little pigeon, draw up the other chair and tell me your whole life's history and I will tell you mine." He winked at his friend before returning his gaze to Sophia. "Methinks you and I will be spending a goodly amount of time in each other's company."

Jessica led Francis into the warm treatment room. A bushy-haired little man sat on a stool in the far corner and tuned his lute. Though he did not hide his bold scrutiny, the little fellow inclined his head to Francis with a sign of respect. He must be the husband of Jessica's companion, Francis thought.

Under her mask, Jessica smiled at her accompanist. "This is Gobbo, *messere*," she introduced him.

Though Francis was almost twice the man's height, he returned the other's bow with equal gravity. "Your music is a feast for the ears, *signore*. I have not heard such skill in a long time."

Gobbo gave him a gap-toothed grin. "You do me honor, my lord," he replied. Then he returned to his strings.

Jessica held out the blindfold as before. "Pray disrobe to your waist, Messere Bardolph, and once again, I must ask you to wear this."

Francis started to protest but saw, out of the corner of his eye, that Gobbo opened his vest to reveal that he wore a wicked-looking stiletto on his belt. Francis suppressed a grin at Jessica's protector. The little man would no doubt defend her with his life, if necessary.

"I am at your command, *madonna*," Francis replied, though he wished otherwise. Her pale mask teased him to distraction.

"Gobbo will call me." Jessica flitted through the far door. Unbuttoning his doublet, Francis eyed the musician. Perhaps he could learn a thing or two about her from her minion. "Mistress Jessica is a gifted healer, is she not?" he began in a casual tone. "Where did she learn her art?"

Gobbo considered the question for a long moment before he answered. "Her father is a doctor."

Francis peeled off his shirt. His shoulder ached with the effort. "Ah! And does the good doctor also reside here?"

Gobbo took even longer to reply. "Father and daughter disagreed. Her parents live...not far." His dark eyes glittered in the light of the fat candle on the sideboard. "Why do you ask?"

Francis gave him a disarming grin. "To make idle conversation. In truth, I am not used to undressing before an audience."

Gobbo's expression did not change. "Unless your audience is Signorina di Luna?" he inquired.

Francis's mouth went dry. *Hoy day! Have I blundered into a nest of informants?* He cocked an eyebrow at the lutist. "You are singularly sharp, Master Gobbo. Is it your habit to spy upon your mistress's clients?"

Gobbo grinned. "*Sì,* my lord. Jessica's welfare is my greatest concern. And," he added with a note of triumph, "this is Venice. In our city, a mere cat cannot sneeze without a hundred people knowing within the hour when and where and what color was the cat."

That unruly hair hides a clever mind. I had best watch what I say to the bewitching lady. The Council of Ten has many eyes and ears about this city of secrets. Aloud, Francis said, "I thank you for your advice."

Gobbo plucked a chord on his lute. "Consider it a warning, my lord." He pursed his lips, then added, "There is one who follows you."

Francis nodded. Cosma's young spy was singularly inept. "I will keep your words in mind." He lay down on the padded table. "Tell your mistress that I await her magic."

Gobbo cleared his throat. "The blindfold," he reminded Francis.

Francis sighed as he tied it over his eyes. "Surely an angel with such a sweet voice should not fear to show her face. I have roamed enough in the world to know that true beauty resides below the skin."

"Then you claim to be wiser than most men, my lord," the lutist replied. "Nevertheless, it is Jessica's wish."

"Tell me, friend Gobbo," Francis said softly. "Have *you* seen her without her mask?"

"I have known her since she was in leading strings," he answered with fondness in his voice.

Francis's heart increased its rhythm. "Is she truly so…deformed as she claims?"

Silence answered him. He chided himself for pushing Gobbo's patience. The man's loyalty to the mysterious Jessica was commendable.

Without warning, Gobbo snapped, "She is a peerless pearl and one beloved by many. Woe to the man who insults or harms her!"

Francis exhaled slowly. "Do not fear me, Gobbo. I am the chiefest of all her admirers."

The other man sniffed loudly. "False words often fall from handsome lips, my lord." Then he raised his voice and called to Jessica.

"Trust me," Francis asked him before the healer returned.

Gobbo's only reply was the first chord of an old ballad. The door again opened. Jessica's spicy perfume announced her presence even before she spoke. Its heady scent bathed him. His skin tingled with the expectation of her touch. When her knowing fingers glided across the old scar, his heart beat faster. A sudden flame seared through his veins, catching him by surprise. Then Jessica tucked a cloth around his shoulder.

"I have a towel that I have steamed for you, *messere*," she told him in that voice that reminded him of gentle breezes and singing birds. "Moist heat softens the tightness under the skin and helps to relieve pain. May I place it on your shoulder? I warn you, it is very warm."

"I would go into hellfire itself, *madonna,* if you held my hand," he replied with more truth than charming prattle.

She chuckled. "I do not think it is *that* hot, my lord." Without further ado, she laid the heat pack over the cloth. Its warmth quickly seeped through the thickness of the material into his flesh. Then Jessica moved behind his head. She placed the fingers of both hands on his forehead and stroked his skin as if she sought to smooth away all the faint lines that years of apprehension and tension had formed there.

"Think of nothing, my lord," she murmured as she massaged his temples. "Let your mind float on a cloud of peace."

Francis drew in a deep breath. "What is peace?" he muttered. "Where can I find it?"

"In your heart," she answered, running her thumbs along his neck.

He quivered under her touch. "My heart is a barren place, *madonna.*"

Though he would never have admitted that truth to any member of his confusing family—not even to Belle who was closest to him—it seemed right to open himself to Jessica. Beguiled by the warmth that suffused his body, the soft music, her heady perfume and her delicate touch, Francis relaxed his customary guard.

She worked her fingers through his hair and began to slowly massage his scalp from the crown down to the base of his neck. "Tell me about this pain that gnaws your heart. When two share a burden it grows lighter," she whispered.

Francis inhaled deeply. "I...I have always been a stranger among my family," he confessed, not understanding why he wanted to reveal his hidden anguish to this near stranger.

Jessica smoothed her palms across his forehead. "Yet I perceive that you loved your grandfather deeply."

He took another deep breath. "*Sì*, he was my one true anchor."

"Your parents?" she murmured. "What of them?"

The blurred image of his wanton, feckless mother rose in his mind. "My mother is also dead," he said in a cold voice.

Jessica made a soothing sound in the back of her throat. "It is a true tragedy when a boy loses his mother."

He grimaced under the blindfold. "She was dead to me long before God took her. The true tragedy is to know that your mother was a whore."

Jessica's hand stilled in midstroke. "*¡Dio mio!* How can you say such a vile thing about your own mother? She must have been a fine lady since you are nobly born."

Francis winced inwardly. He was a bastard without land or a title, but he knew he couldn't tell her that glaring truth. He must maintain his disguise of nobility for another month at least.

He cleared his throat. "You speak the truth. My mother was indeed a lady but her morals would have shamed an alley cat. After she gave her husband two sons to insure the family line, she left him in his country manor among his beloved cows and horses. My lady mother went to court where she disported herself with every man in sight—including the kings of England and France, or so I have been told."

Jessica removed the cooling towel. She ran the heel of her hand along the scar tissue. "Surely you have mistaken her. Perhaps she was merely full of high spirits."

Francis snorted. "I wish that were so for my, um…father's sake. He was a good man, though he had the spine of an eel. No, the truth of the matter was that Lady Olivia opened her quiver to every arrow. She reveled in her pleasure." His throat tightened with the shame of the memory. "Once a year, she returned to Cloverdale, her husband's home, and there delivered herself of another child."

Jessica's hands trembled against his warm skin. "I have never heard of such a thing."

Exhaling deeply, Francis wished he could expel the stain of his birth as easily. "My mother apparently enjoyed being pregnant but disliked the fruits of her labor. She left her children with her husband and assorted wet nurses while she returned to the pleasures of the court as soon as she could ride a horse."

He pressed his lips together. He had already told Jessica far more than he had intended. She kneaded his shoulder in silence, no doubt shocked by his frank revelations. Her touch, though firm, soothed him. Gobbo continued to play as if he had not overheard a single word.

Jessica worked her way down his arm. "How very sad for your father," she murmured.

Francis gritted his teeth.

"Ah," she murmured. "I have hit the sore point of your tale."

He moistened his lips. "*Sì, madonna,* you have." Only Francis knew the real truth of his paternity now that his mother had gone to her cold grave in that faraway convent.

After adding more ointment to her fingers, Jessica worked on the long muscle between his elbow and wrist.

"Do you wish to speak of this painful thing?" she asked with the gentleness of a dove. "I assure you, I am discreet."

Francis groaned from the depths of his soul. "Oh, sweet Jessica, if only you could erase the days of my childhood."

Chapter Six

Jessica stared down at the handsome man lying on her table. She wished she had the courage to enfold him in her arms and kiss away the hundred hurts that had been inflicted in his youth. Instead she took his right hand between hers and began to gently stretch the long fingers. A man with such a hand as his possessed both a great heart and a great pride to go with it. He would disdain any show of pity. Perhaps his loneliness was why he had sought the solace of the church—if he was a priest, that is.

Pressing his lips together in a hard line, Francis turned his head to one side away from her. Jessica knew that he had revealed as much as he could bear. She worked the muscles of his chest—his very broad chest. What would it be like to pillow one's weary head on his shoulder, even the injured one? Jessica allowed her hand to caress the smooth skin at the base of his collarbone. She bit her lower lip. Very unprofessional, she chided herself. He would think that she was one of Venice's infamous strumpets—until he saw her face, of course. She worked her thumb deep into his scar tissue.

Lord Bardolph grunted with surprise. "Hold, *madonna!* I am not a quintain to tilt at."

Jessica lightened the pressure. "Your pardon, *messere*," she murmured. "I think *you* have tilted at quintains many times," she added.

A wry smile tinged his lips below the blindfold. "Too many," he replied. "My...my mentor was determined to make me into a proper knight."

"From the looks of your body, I would say he succeeded," she observed lightly, though her mouth was dry. This handsome man was the very devil come to tempt her virtue—or to send her to the stake.

"I joust more with my head, than with my arm. My grandfather taught me the wisdom of that," he added softly.

Jessica covered him with the blanket and laid her hands over his heart to speed the healing force through him. "A most wise man," she observed. "No wonder you mourn him."

He sighed. "Though my mother was not honest in her virtue, my grandfather was indeed true of heart. He treated me as one of his sons and I...I loved him for it."

Jessica rocked his body with a gentle motion to balance his humors. "You are most fortunate indeed."

He pursed his lips. "How so, *madonna?* Fortunate is not a word I would use to describe myself."

Laying her palm on his forehead, she murmured a prayer to Saint Luke, patron saint of physicians, for the efficacy of her work. Then she observed, "Such a man as your grandfather comes only once in a person's lifetime. You are fortunate to have recognized his greatness."

The Englishman turned down his mouth. "I never told him that I loved him."

Jessica trailed the backs of her fingers down his cheek. "He knows that now, *messere*."

A hot ache burned in her throat. She turned to her sideboard and covered her pots of ointments. The desire to kiss those enticing lips had become too strong. What had happened to her sense of decorum? No other man had ever affected her in this way. It must be his sorrow that appealed to her maternal heart.

Jessica wiped her hands on her apron. "I have done for today, my lord," she said, backing toward the door. "Please dress and rejoin your friend. I will be with you anon."

She slipped through the welcome portal with Gobbo right behind her. Once safely in the back hall, Jessica sagged with relief.

Gobbo touched her elbow. "Are you unwell, *madonna?* I thought for a moment in there that you might faint."

Jessica patted her flushed face with her hands. "It is nothing, dear friend. The room was too warm. I worked too hard. In faith, the English lord will be quite sore by tomorrow morning's light and speak most ill of me."

Gobbo cast her an arched look. "I think not, child. That man will bless your name at morning Mass." Leaving that observation nestled in her ear, he walked down the narrow hall with his lute under his arm.

Jessica leaned against the cool plaster wall for a few minutes until her quickened pulse subsided. Closing her eyes, she inhaled a few deep breaths. What had come over her in there? Why should that handsome stranger cause her mind to flutter and her skin to burn? She again wondered if she were coming down with some dread fever.

Common sense warned her to have little to do with the enigmatic Lord Bardolph. Intriguing rogue! Though she was more sympathetic to the melancholy that he bore in his heart, she still did not trust the man's motives toward her. *They say the devil has a handsome face and speaks with a honeyed tongue.* She harbored no further doubt that his garish clothing and outward manner of a pleasure-bent gentleman was nothing but a sham—as much a disguise as the mask she wore to face the world.

On the other hand, she wondered if he was indeed a priest—he seemed far too much a man of the world for that role. She massaged her temples. Yet Venice teamed with clerics who overate, overdrank, slept through confessions, missed Mass and disported with lewd women. If the *messere* was not a priest, he could still be in the pay of the Holy Office. The mere thought of the Inquisition filled her with icy dread. She had been weaned on the tales her parents had told her of the horrors they had endured before they fled from Spain. Late last year, the pope had sent the Holy Office to Venice with its dreaded instruments of torture.

Jessica shivered. She was a good Catholic girl. She attended Mass nearly every day, fasted and prayed at the appropriate times and led a chaste life. And yet that might not be enough to save her from the flames. In recent weeks, spies of the Inquisition had made it their special business to observe the activities of the *marranos* like her parents— Spanish Jews who had converted to Catholicism in order to save their lives. By one false look or word, Jessica knew she could be the downfall of her family who lived close to their friends inside the Jewish Ghetto.

No, the somber Englishman in the gaudy clothes was a man to be watched but never trusted—not with her family secrets and certainly not with her heart. She heard Lord Bardolph reenter her antechamber. With a sigh, she slipped on her mask and then opened the door just as Sophia hopped off her chair and planted herself squarely in front of the Englishman.

"You are looking better, *messere,*" the little woman observed. "Pray do not forget to pay the fee for such good health. We have to eat in this house, you know." She shot a wry glance at Jobe. "Indeed, your giant has consumed enough provender for a week!"

Before Lord Bardolph could reply to this brazen speech, Jessica intervened. "Hush, Sophia! You insult these gentlemen to the quick with your blunt words." Do not ruffle their feathers, she silently begged her friend. They could do great damage to us in return.

Instead of growing angry, the Englishman threw back his handsome head and laughed with real mirth. The sound and sight of such a surprising display rendered Jessica speechless. Opening his money pouch, he smiled with added brilliance at her. Her knees weakened.

"Fear me not, little Jessica. The good service you have done for me this day is worth a Turk's ransom!" He took her cold hand in his and counted out ten ducats into her palm.

She trembled at his touch and at the sight of the pile of money.

He closed her fingers around the coins. "Take these paltry pieces of gold, *madonna.* You have lightened my heart, so I shall lighten my purse."

She backed against the door. The coins shivered against each other in her hand. "You are too generous, *messere,* but I cannot keep such a fortune." It was blood money! She would rue it later when she would be forced to confess to the Inquisition that she had received a great deal of gold from this man for...for... She couldn't think what but she knew the Inquisition would turn this outrageous gift to their own hideous purposes.

Sophia tottered on her tiptocs to see the sum that Jessica held. "Do not be overhasty, *madonna,*" she cautioned. "Gentlemen enjoy being generous."

The African chuckled in the back of his throat. "My wives know the truth of that."

Jessica shook her head. She handed back nine of the ducats. "My fee is only one, my lord. To accept any more would be wrong."

Sophia muttered something under her breath. The great Jobe chuckled again.

With a show of regret, Lord Bardolph pocketed his rejected gold. Then he held out his hand to her with another one of those heart-stopping smiles. "If you will not allow me to pay you for making me into a new man, come walk with Jobe and me to the Rialto where I can purchase you a frippery of your choice."

Jessica shook her head, though the pleading in his eyes nearly melted her resolve. This could be a trap. The officers of the Inquisition could be waiting for her in the marketplace.

She swallowed hard before she replied. "I am greatly honored by your offer, *messere,* but I cannot. I rarely go abroad in the daylight." She touched her mask.

He did not lower his hand. "It is carnival time, *madonna.* Everyone in Venice wears a mask these days. In fact, Jobe and I must purchase masks of our own so that people will not gawk and point at us. We desire your expert advice on this matter."

"Most excellent idea!" Jobe agreed.

Jessica refused to listen to the pleading of her heart. She must remain firm in this matter. The sooner the Englishman left her home, the better. "I am sorry, my lord. I pray that you pardon me, but I cannot accompany you. I am unworthy of the honor and—" She hurried her speech before he could object again. "I am expecting another patient within this hour." Thank heavens her mask covered the blush that her lie had brought to her cheeks!

The gentleman dropped his hand to his side. "Of course! In my gratitude for your healing art, I had forgotten that

mine is not the only body or soul whom you solace. I envy
your next patient, *madonna,* for he will enjoy the company
that we will lack. When shall I come again?''

Jessica tried not to look at him. He was too charming by
half. ''In two days, *messere,*'' she replied. Her voice shook
a little. ''At ten in the morning?''

He again took her hand in his. She trembled at his touch.

''I shall be on your doorstep by the tenth stroke of yon
church bells.'' He pressed his lips against the backs of her
fingers.

Her flesh prickled at his gentle touch. The shock of the
brief contact ran through her body, making her flushed and
chilled at the same time. A fluttering arose at the base of
her throat.

''Pray, excuse me, *messere,*'' she murmured, snatching
her hand away. ''I feel suddenly—'' She pushed open the
door and fled to the gloom of the hallway. She sank in a
heap on the cool floor tiles.

¡Madre del Dio! I have a fever in truth!

Jobe settled himself against the gondola's plump red
cushions. ''Methinks the little healer has bewitched you,''
he remarked in English. ''How came these sudden merry
spirits of yours?''

Francis turned his face toward the winter sun's rays and
basked in their golden gleam. ''Tis a puzzlement, I trow. I
know not why or how but while the sweet Jessica plied my
shoulder with her balm and healing fingers, she also
touched my soul.''

He glanced down the canal behind them in time to see
their ever-present shadow descend into a gondola. Francis
almost felt sorry for Cosma's hireling.

Jobe cocked his shaven head. ''How now? By what
magic did she coax away your melancholy?''

Francis stretched out his long legs. Gondolas were eminently practical boats for long-limbed men such as Jobe and himself. "She asked me about my parents—and, God help me, I told her."

The African knotted his dark brows. "Everything?" he asked, casting a quick look at the impassive gondolier.

Francis chuckled then lowered his voice. "Nay, I have not lost all my wits. She still believes that I am a noble gentleman. But in the brief telling of my tattered background, I felt as if a great weight was lifted from my chest—a weight that I didn't even realize had been there until it vanished. Is that not truly remarkable?"

A slow grin spread across Jobe's face. "Not at all, *meo amigo*. You are indeed a true Cavendish."

With a frown, Francis pushed his bonnet further back on his head. "Explain yourself, Jobe. I am not in the mood for your riddling answers. My brains are too light today for heavy thoughts."

The African laughed. "I mean to say that tis no surprise you have finally discovered the hot blood of your heritage. Tis been a long time coming."

Francis refused to allow Jobe's darts to puncture his good mood. "Posh! I have always had a passionate nature. Ask any maid in Rome, in Pisa, in Florence!"

His friend snorted. "I do not speak of mere lust. *That* is commonplace."

Francis crossed his arms over his chest and closed his eyes. "What else is there?"

"Love," Jobe replied.

Francis did not open his eyes. Love? How little he understood of that foreign emotion! Only yesterday he had realized too late how much he had loved his grandfather. Love a woman? Francis snorted. Brandon and Guy had been most fortunate to find the pearls of their wives amid all the chaff those two had reportedly enjoyed during their salad days.

On the other hand, Francis's youth had been spent inside Oxford's great library. The women he had known were good for a dalliance or witty discourse but not for something more permanent. He had learned that with rare exceptions, a man couldn't trust the species. Just look at the example of his own mother!

Yet he had trusted Jessica with a quick look into his closely guarded past and the experience rewarded him with a lighter heart. There must be something in that. Francis refused to mull over the matter. Not today.

A gentle thump jostled him from further musing. "The Rialto, my lords," announced the gondolier.

The day's pleasant weather had attracted many citizens to the great marketplace in the quayside and nearby *campo* that was the center of commerce for the Republic. Francis and Jobe strolled amid the late morning's crush of people. A babel of a dozen languages filled their ears. The aroma from the hundreds of cheeses, fresh fish, fruits and spices assailed their nostrils. Colorful garb of the Venetian dandies and their paramours, the Arab traders, the visitors from Paris and Utrecht mixed with the red shoulder sashes and pom-poms on the hats of the city's senators.

Francis clapped Jobe on his back between his massive shoulder blades. "Truly tis a gladsome day, my friend."

Before the African could respond, Francis spied a wooden booth sagging under a load of glistening dark dates.

"Fresh yesterday from the Holy Land, *messere*," the fawning vendor assured him.

Jobe and Francis each took a fruit, split it open and tasted the sweet pulp. "You speak the truth," Francis nodded.

Jessica would like these, he thought. She missed too

much of the sweetness that life offered by hiding in that little house of hers on a watery backstreet. She needed a taste of the sun in the middle of winter. Francis snapped his fingers to one of the ferret-quick young boys that lounged about the marketplace.

"Is this one a trusty soul?" he asked Jobe while pointing to the eager lad.

Jobe gave the youth a penetrating look into his eyes. "Aye, *meo amigo,* if sufficient silver crosses his palm."

Francis dug into his purse. Both the vendor and the boy wet their lips with anticipation. Francis sprinkled scudos into their outstretched hands. "Take up the best basket of this delectable fruit, my boy, and be like winged Mercury. Fly hence to number sixteen Fondementa di San Felice— do you know the area?"

The youth nodded with a wide grin.

"For such a fortune, methinks your messenger would say 'aye' even if he didn't," Jobe observed behind his hand.

Francis laughed aloud. The sound pleased his ear. "Deliver these dates to Signorina Jessica Leonardo. Now be off with you!" He waved the boy away.

The lad gripped the brimming two-handled basket. "Whom shall I say sends this gift?"

Francis grinned down at the reed-thin youth. "Tell the *madonna* it is from one whom she has lately saved."

The boy repeated the message under his breath, then raced away in the direction of the Rialto Bridge. Francis clapped his hands together with satisfaction. "Tis little enough, Jobe," he explained. "Indeed, the fair Jessica has eased my heart wondrous much. Mere thanks is not enough. Ah! Look there!"

He pointed to a nearby purveyor of sweetmeats. "Sugared almonds! She will need to replenish her store after your gorging, Jobe. A scudo's worth, do you think?"

Jobe whistled through his teeth. "Tis four times the amount I ate," he protested with a grin.

"Good!" Francis replied, again pulling out his purse. Jessica must have almonds to accompany the dates. Sweets for the sweet!

A small pushcart stood nearby filled to overflowing with the first flowers of the year—deep purple violets. Francis needed no second thought. Jessica struck him as the type who loved flowers. He chose the largest bunch.

No sooner had he dispatched his third gift clutched in the hands of another eager messenger, than his attention was attracted by a table laid with colorful ribbons and laces. Scarlet, emerald green, deep butter yellow—how beautiful such colors would look entwined amid Jessica's raven tresses! She needed color in her sheltered life. She must have ribbons woven from the rainbow.

A fourth messenger quickly followed after the other three, bearing a wealth of ribbons and a fine piece of lace to trim her gown. Jobe only smiled wider as the spending fever ensnared Francis. They roamed through stalls of perfumery, drapers and goldsmiths—all of whom Francis rejected with a sigh.

"Twould be unseemly to give the maid such costly gifts upon so short an acquaintance," he told Jobe as he tore himself away from a tray of colorful glass bead necklaces. "She would think I sought...um, unholy favors."

Jobe lifted one of his dark brows with amusement. "What about one of those for Donna Jessica?" He pointed to a swarthy man who held a number of red leather leashes in his hands. At the end of each one, a tiny long-tailed monkey gamboled on the paving stones. "There is a merry creature to make her smile."

Francis eyed the playful pack. "God shield the fair Jessica! I seek her golden opinion of me, not to raise her ire."

Jobe squatted and picked up the nearest monkey. It wound itself around his neck. "Women like silly furry things. Twill give her many hours of delight."

Francis cocked an eyebrow at the brown monkey. "That frolicsome beast would turn Jessica's ordered household into a fur-flying chaos. Nay, put down the creature, Jobe, and think upon a more proper gift."

Francis cast a look around the marketplace for a better alternative. He smiled when he saw it. "Ah! The very thing! Beeswax candles to banish winter's dark hours." He picked up a thick taper for closer inspection. It had a faint scent of jasmine. "*¡La perfezione!* The perfect thing! She likes to surround herself in perfume. I'll send her two." He tossed a ducat at the pleased candle-seller.

Jobe held his tongue until a fifth young messenger was despatched to number sixteen on the Fondementa di San Felice. Then he rumbled, "I liked the monkey more better."

Francis glanced at Cosma's henchman huddling over a nut-seller's brazier. He chuckled as a wicked idea formed in his mind. "Very well, Jobe, you have prevailed upon me. We will indeed buy one of those hairy creatures—and send it to Donna Cosma. I should not forget my dear mistress amidst my sudden generosity."

A wide smile wreathed Jobe's lips. "Most excellent sport!"

Chapter Seven

"Another one?" Putting down the petticoat she was hemming, Jessica stared at the wrapped bundle in Sophia's hands. "From Lord Bardolph?"

Smiling, the little woman nodded. "*Il Dio* in His infinite wisdom has finally sent you a very rich patron."

"Who is very foolish with his money," Jessica added, though she couldn't dampen her flutter of excitement as she accepted the Englishman's latest gift. She unrolled the piece of muslin that held two fat candles. Jessica lifted one to her nose and inhaled its fragrance. "This is far too rich a gift—even more than the lace. Surely it is wrong to accept so much."

Sophia sat on a stool next to the bowl of sugared almonds. She popped one into her mouth. "Too late! The messenger has gone. Besides it would be rude to return such bounty to the giver—especially when he displays good taste in his offerings." She savored another almond. "Very good taste indeed!" She smacked her lips.

Jessica ran her fingers over the smooth wax of the candles. "Gaudy gold proved to be hard food for King Midas. I do not require a surfeit of trifles."

Sophia frowned at her. "*¡Silenzio!* You chatter like a

parrot! It is high time that you enjoyed the attentions of an admirer. Twenty-four and nary a suitor? It is a scandal! Enjoy the moment now.''

Returning to her sewing, Jessica shifted uneasily on her chair. ''Give over your prattling, Sophia. The gentleman is merely grateful for a few hours of blessed relief. His pain will return soon again, I fear,'' she said, searching for a plausible explanation for Lord Bardolph's sudden largesse. Perhaps he hoped to assault her virtue.

Sophia folded her hands over her round stomach. ''Then *he* will return soon again.'' She chuckled.

Jessica's fingers tensed. Her thread snapped in two. Thoughts of the handsome, mysterious yet melancholy foreigner caused the fragile shell of her composure to quiver. She took her time to thread the needle. Her hands shook. The Englishman disturbed her in every way. Each time they had met, his attraction grew stronger.

Giving herself a shake, she attempted to concentrate on her stitching. What a ninny she was to allow her emotions to rule her head! Not only was the gentleman far above her station, but he harbored some secret that frightened her. She should distance herself from him, not look forward to their next encounter.

''Besides,'' Jessica said aloud. ''When the weather turns hot and the fever season comes, he will go back to his homeland.'' She would be living in a fool's paradise if she considered any permanent relationship with Lord Bardolph. He was her patient—nothing more.

Sighing, she touched the unsightly birthmark on her face. Sophia might talk of courting admirers, but long ago Jessica had resigned herself to spinsterhood. ''I will die as chaste as the goddess Diana. Mayhap, I will become a nun in my later years,'' she mused.

Sophia made a rude noise with her lips. ''You? Ha! The

daughter of *marranos*? Your vocation would be instantly suspect. Besides, you cannot hide from your heart—not even within a convent's walls."

Cosma's pretty lips puckered with supreme annoyance as she watched Lord Bardolph's gift climb up her red silk draperies. Before Jacopo could capture it, the little beast leaped to the top of her cupboard where it scampered back and forth. Nerissa giggled into her apron. Cosma boxed the chit's ears, then she turned her full wrath upon Jacopo.

"This?" She pointed at the capering monkey. "No necklace? No ivory comb? No pretty bauble for me? This filthy animal is what my lord sends as a token of his esteem?"

Jacopo backed away from her righteous ire. "His very words, *madonna,* to the letter." He struck his hand against his forehead. "*¡Stupido!* I nearly forgot. He sends you this letter as well." He pulled out a scribbled missive from inside his wool tunic.

Cosma snatched the paper out of his grimy hands. "I do not pay you to lose your wits but to use them! Now catch that disgusting thing and remove it from my house! Throw it into the canal for all I care."

Leaving Jacopo and Nerissa to coax the monkey down from its perch, Cosma went into her bedchamber to read Francis's letter in private. His brief message did not soothe her ruffled feelings but inflamed them. She crumpled his note and tossed it onto a glowing brazier. The paper caught fire immediately and curled into black ash.

Cosma stared at her reflection in her looking glass. "He begs my pardon but he cannot come tonight," she snarled at herself. "He has made other plans with that blackamoor pirate."

She slammed her fist down on her dressing table. Her pots of cosmetics rattled against each other. "Other plans without me! For the first time in over four months that preening English peacock disdains my company. *Me?* The greatest courtesan in all of Venice!''

Cosma moved closer to the mirror. She searched her features for any sign of a blemish or a wrinkle that heralded the onset of middle age. She smoothed her hand across her peerless complexion achieved by daily applications of pigeon's milk and cream of cucumbers. How could that fop not yearn for her? Why didn't his desire for her burn between his legs? Could she be losing her allure?

''Never!'' she snapped, though she trembled at the possibility.

She must wed long before that dread day when a new Venus of the city was proclaimed. Cosma had enjoyed that hallowed position for five years and the sands of time slipped faster through the glass now. Francis would be leaving Venice soon. He had already spoken of his departure and the news of his grandfather's death no doubt hastened his thoughts of home. He might be a passive lover but his wealth more than made up for that deficiency. One day in the future, Francis would be an earl. If Cosma intended to become the Englishman's lady wife, she must not dally now.

She sat at her table and opened her writing portfolio. She dipped her quill into the ink bottle and held it poised while she considered her wording. Her invitation must intrigue— entice—beguile. Tomorrow she would wear her most seductive gown no matter how cold or wet the weather was. She would take Francis on a most memorable picnic on the nearby island of Sacca Sessola. And they would leave that damned blackamoor in the middle of the *piazza*.

''Dearest Francis,'' she wrote. She smiled as she filled the page with flattering words.

* * *

Jobe drained his wineglass and eyed his silent companion across the weather-beaten table in the Sturgeon's public room. Francis's jovial spirits of the afternoon had now given way to a reflective silence. His glassy eyes stared into the flame that danced on the wick of the oil lamp. Jobe pelted him with a nutshell left over from their supper. The missile bounced off Francis's chin.

He scowled at the African. "How now? Am I a stuffed man to be taunted by a crow?"

Jobe raised his eyes and his hands to the low ceiling. "Praise be! He speaks!"

Francis grumbled a mild curse, then returned to his contemplation of the firelight.

Jobe regarded his friend with narrowed eyes. The boy had all the signs of being bitten by a poisonous viper—or impaled by the dart of love. The dark-eyed wench of the pale mask had located the key to this Cavendish heart. Jobe shook his head. What a family! They delighted to construct mountains out of molehills—especially in matters of love.

Jobe stretched. "You are boorish company tonight," he remarked with a loud yawn. "I had sooner hold a conversation with a goat."

Francis shrugged. "Are there any goats in Venice?"

The black man grinned at him. "Only one, my friend, and methinks you are it."

Francis did not blink. "I thank you for your compliment. With a honey tongue like that tis no wonder you are so popular among the ladies."

Jobe ignored the gibe. He tossed another nutshell at the sluggard. It clipped him on the ear.

Francis shot him a look of annoyance. "Your game grows tiresome. Go find yourself other company if you wish to target practice."

Jobe merely broadened his smile. "Your game of silence also wearies a man. This night is a fine one. The moon goddess bends her bright bow in the starry sky. We, too, should be abroad in search of fair game instead of huddling inside this smoky den."

Francis frowned. "I have already sent my regrets to Cosma. I have little appetite for her company this evening."

Jobe nodded with relief. "Another prayer answered by heaven! Nay, sickly youth, I speak of a certain mysterious beauty who lives on the far side of the Grand Canal near the Church of San Felice."

Francis sat up straighter on his bench. "Donna Jessica?" He whispered her name.

Ah! He is snared like a hare in a trap! Aloud, Jobe replied, "Well aimed and to the mark. Get up, man! Give yourself a shake. Put on your boldest suit of mirth, string your lute and let us go serenade the wench. Twill make the hours pass more agreeably than lolling in this sty."

Francis shook his head. "My voice is out of tune," he protested though his eyes danced in the candle's light. "Methinks I am coming down with the ague or some such fever. My heart beats in double time and my throat is tight."

Jobe swallowed his laughter. Francis was certainly infected with lovesickness for the first time in his solemn life. He needed gentle prodding, lest the malady wither from lack of nourishment.

Taking Francis by the arm, Jobe pulled him to his feet. "Act the lion instead of the mouse! By the devil, you have put on some weight since we last wrestled, my friend."

Francis allowed Jobe to lead him outside. "You are serious?"

Jobe relaxed his grip on the other's sleeve. "Aye, courting is serious business. First, we must find covering for our faces before we caterwaul beneath the fair Jessica's window.''

He looked around them. Half the citizens of Venice filled the narrow streets; all masked and in holiday moods. Jobe studied the bright-painted visages that surrounded them. Sly cats, long-beaked birds, leering Harlequins and coquettish Columbinas grinned back at him. Christian fools with varnished faces, Jobe thought. He collared the landlord's tapboy.

''You have a merry eye,'' he told the youth. ''Find us two masks of your own choosing and furnish us with torchbearers. Be back here within a quarter of an hour and it will be a golden ducat for your pocket.''

Francis drew in a deep draft of the cool air and shook the cobwebs from his joints. ''I perceive that there is no defeating your purpose, is there?''

Jobe draped his arm around his friend's shoulders. ''None whatsoever.''

''And you mean to make a fool of me in public?'' Francis continued.

Jobe's laughter rose up from his throat. ''Nay, *meo amigo*. Only *you* can do that. I shall merely stand by you and play upon my flute.''

The tapboy returned bearing two red-and-black masks. Several young men holding aloft flaming torches followed him. All were in cheerful spirits thanks to Jobe's generosity. Inspecting the masks in the light, the African whistled. ''Two devils? *¡Molto bene!*''

The tapboy held out a basket of eggs. ''And these, too, great one,'' he panted. ''For *Il Giuoco dell Uovo*. The egg game.'' He appeared very pleased with himself. ''You throw them.''

Jobe gave the youth a stern look. ''We go to entertain a fair maiden, not insult her.''

Francis groaned. "I knew this folly would bring us grief."

The tapboy held up his hands. "No, no, *messere*. You mistake my meaning. The eggshells are filled with perfume. You throw the eggs when the lady appears at her window and she is showered with the scent of flowers. By my mother's soul, I do not lie."

One of the torchbearers nodded. "He speaks the truth, great lords. It is a custom at *Carnevale* time."

Sniffing one of the eggs, Jobe discovered it was filled with rosewater. He grinned down at Cupid's grubby apprentice. "Most excellent! If it works, I will reward you handsomely."

Francis glared at the boy. "But if the lady is displeased, I will skin you alive."

The bells of San Felice church tolled nine o'clock when Jessica heard the muted sound of a lute through her shuttered window. She lay still in her bed and listened intently. Some fortunate girl was being honored with a serenade this evening. Jessica tried to think what maid lived in her *campo* that was the right age for courting. The music grew louder. She detected the high notes of a recorder accompanying the lute. The tune was a lively air that she did not recognize.

Streaks of firelight gleamed through the slats of her shutters and danced along the far wall of her bedchamber. The musicians were very near. Just then, her bedroom door creaked open. Jessica gripped her blanket. Sophia peeked inside.

"Hssst! Jessica? Are you asleep?"

Jessica sat up. "How could anyone be asleep at this moment? Who are they serenading?"

Chuckling, Sophia tiptoed across the small chamber. "Come see for yourself. I promise you *will* be surprised."

Tossing back her covers, Jessica swung her feet to the cold floor. "Tell me who, Sophia. I cannot think of anyone unmarried who lives nearby. Surely it can't be for Signora Spindelli. She's a widow past forty!"

Sophia peered through the gap in the shutters. "Look! Three torchbearers! And a train of urchins in their wake."

Jessica wrapped a soft woolen shawl around her shoulders, crept to the window and peered down to the street. She gasped when she saw that the colorful entourage had halted in front of her door.

"Those men have had too much to drink," she whispered. "They have taken a wrong turning."

Sophia shook her head. "I think not. Look! Listen!"

One of the devilish masquers sang a French ballad in a pleasing baritone. Though Jessica could not understand most of the words, she realized that the song spoke of love and a yearning heart.

"This is a shame!" she whispered to Sophia. "Please go downstairs and tell them they have made a mistake. Some poor girl is even now waiting for her serenade and here they all are—at the wrong address!"

Sophia did not move, but continued to stare through the shutter's crack. "Shh! Listen!"

A second devil, hooded in a black cape from head to toe, stepped out of the shadows and lifted his voice. "Jessica! Fair Jessica! Open your window! Accept our gift of song and music."

The dozen little street boys took up the cry. "Jessica! Open your window!"

Jessica flattened herself against the wall. "What prank is this? They do it to mock me."

Sophia clicked her tongue against her teeth. "*¡Basta!* You are such a coward. That was the voice of the blackamoor." She unlatched the shutter.

Jessica sank to her knees. "Sophia! No!" She held her hand against her birthmark. "Please! I shall be ridiculed. How can you do this to me?"

Sophia folded back one of the shutters. The boys below cheered.

"You have nothing to fear. Those two devils are as tall as Master Jobe and Lord Bardolph. Mark how the moonlight shines on his head, turning his golden hair to silver. Stand here in the shadow and let the sounds of his music creep into your ear. No one will see you."

Despite her fears, a hot joy suffused through Jessica. She pulled herself up to the window ledge and peeked out. The whole *campo* was bathed in the bright torchlight. Many upstairs windows around the square opened as her neighbors looked out to see the cause of the commotion. Standing in the middle of the pack of ragged boys, a tall, gaudily dressed man in a devil's mask sang another song, this time in Italian with a Roman accent.

Before Jessica could stop her, Sophia produced her white handkerchief and waved it out the window. The little boys again cheered, then they reared back and hurled a shower of eggs. Jessica ducked. The shells broke against the house and the aroma of roses filled the air.

Sophia clapped her hands. "The Egg Game! Give them your thanks, child, or the next eggs might not smell so pleasant."

Still keeping within the deep shadow cast by the shutter, Jessica called, "My...my thanks to you all. I am very honored." Her voice shook. "I don't know what else to say to them," she whispered to Sophia. "No one has ever sung under my window before."

Sophia waved her handkerchief. "Sing again, brightplumed devil! Sing again!"

"Hush!" Jessica told her. "You are shameless, Sophia. You will make us the laughingstock of the neighborhood."

"Nonsense!" the little woman replied. "Enjoy it! By my garters, the gentleman has a beautiful voice."

His music filled Jessica with a giddy delight. She pressed her hand against her mouth while she trembled as his loving message washed over her. Against all her common sense, she became completely entranced by the sound of his voice. She closed her eyes, the better to savor the delicious moment.

A trill of the flute ended their concert. A smattering of the neighbors' applause echoed around the square.

Jessica took another glimpse out the window. "Everyone knows he is singing to me," she moaned. "They will laugh at me in the morning."

Sophia shook her head. "Ha! They will envy you for having such a tuneful swain to serenade you. Say something to him, Jessica. Thank him for your pleasure."

Jessica's throat closed up. "I can't," she squeaked.

Sophia frowned at her. "If you do not speak to him, then I will—and you never know what fancy might fly out of my mouth," she threatened.

"Wait! I know!" Jessica scurried to her bedside table where Lord Bardolph's violets rested in a beaker of water. She took several flowers, bound them with her hair ribbon then tossed the posy out the window.

"Thank...thank you, charming devil, for your kindness and for your sweet music," she called from the safety of the shadows.

To her further embarrassment, her neighbors applauded even louder. The urchins cheered and chanted her name. The tall masquer picked up her gift from the paving stones. He kissed the flowers, then tucked them into his doublet's buttonhole. Sweeping off his garish hat, he made a deep bow to her window.

"Fair thoughts, sweet dreams and happy hours attend on you," he called to her. Then the whole company withdrew and disappeared around the corner, leaving the *campo* a much darker and colder place.

Sophia drew the shutters together. "There now," she asked, "was that as bad as a toothache?"

In a daze Jessica stumbled back to her bed. "*Sì*, it will keep me awake all night." His blessing danced in her heart. She released a long audible sigh.

Chapter Eight

The night's passage had almost run its course before Francis and Jobe returned to their room at the Sturgeon Inn. Still humming one of the songs he had sung under Jessica's window and warmed by a flagon of spiced wine, Francis fell backward onto his bed. The walls gently rocked in his befuddled vision.

"Zounds, Jobe! What a night! What merry sport!"

The ebony giant pulled off one of his boots. "Did I not tell you so?"

Francis laced his fingers together behind his head. "Bestrew me, that devilish mask made me bold. I have never in my life thrown an egg—even a perfumed one—at a woman. What would Lady Alicia have said if she had seen me?"

Jobe chuckled. "Knowing your grandmother, methinks she would have approved. Tis high time that you opened that dull brain of yours and let the spirit of carnival romp inside."

Francis made a face. "I am not dull. All my tutors reported that my wits sparkled." He hiccuped.

Jobe unrolled his stockings. "Methinks your tutors were also a dull lot."

Francis hiccuped again. "True. They were never in Venice at carnival time. By the Book, Jobe, she liked our singing, didn't she?"

Jobe unbuttoned his leather doublet. "Aye, she did—but how many other cats has she heard howling in the night?"

Francis ignored him. He extracted the little nosegay from his buttonhole and brushed the violet petals across his lips. "She is sweet, is she not, Jobe?"

The African chuckled again. "I see that Cupid has hit you squarely in the heart."

Francis yawned. "Not so never! I merely make a scholarly deduction after much observation."

Jobe snorted at his answer. Not bothering to remove either his shoes or his outer clothing, Francis rolled up in the coverlet. He nestled his head in his pillow and closed his eyes. The room spun slowly behind his eyelids.

"Heigh ho! Here's something!" said Jobe.

Francis did not move. "Aye, something indeed. You see before you a man dreaming of a fair maiden with dark rippling hair, gentle hands and lips as lush as honey-sweetened cherries. Shh! Go away! You are disturbing my repose." He turned his back on Jobe and the irritating candlelight.

"Nay," his friend protested. "Tis a letter for you. By the handwriting and the scent of the paper, methinks tis from your mistress."

Francis winced. He groaned into his pillow. "I speak of an angel, you speak of a polecat. One delights me, the other wearies me. Tis too late in the night for reading. Put out the light."

Instead Jobe broke open the seal. "Indeed you will need your sleep, *meo amigo*. Your polecat entreats—nay, in plainer words she *demands* your company on a pleasure trip to Sacca Sessola departing from her quay at ten this very morning.''

Francis squinted at his friend. ''Ten? Hoy day! Cosma must be desperate for my company. She never stirs from her bed until afternoon.'' He shivered inside his covers. ''Besides that little island must be a howling wilderness at this unseasonable time. Plainly, Cosma has lost her wits.''

Jobe grinned at him. ''Perchance she was especially pleased with the monkey.''

''Ha! That I highly doubt!''

Jobe ran his finger along the page. ''She also entreats you to leave your midnight friend to his own devices.'' He glanced at Francis with an innocent look in his large eyes. ''Do you think she means me?''

''Aye, Sir Midnight.''

Jobe flashed a wicked grin. ''And I thought I had pleased her right well upon our first meeting.''

Francis yawned again. ''Aye, but *you* do not pretend to have a fortune or titled ancestors.''

''According to this missive, she awaits breathlessly for your reply.''

Francis barked a laugh. ''At this late hour? Nay, she is abed either alone or with some other man to comfort her. If she is breathless, twill be from lovemaking. She is not pining on her landing in a waiting pose.'' He knotted his brows in a frown. ''Though poor Nerissa may be doing just that.'' He pictured the little maid huddled on Cosma's cold pink marble staircase.

Jobe sat down at the plain table between their beds. ''I do not form my letters as well as you, nor can I spell Italian, but for gentle Nerissa's sake, I will pen a reply if that suits you.''

Francis knew he should be the one to answer Cosma's summons but he could not move from his prone position.

He waved his hand at Jobe. "Go to and the devil take your spelling. Be brief. Say I am unwell."

"Tis true enough," Jobe muttered under his breath. "You are sick with love."

"Nay, with too much wine," Francis objected. "Love has nothing to do with me."

Cosma stood amid the shards of several smashed vases. Disarrayed by her angry exercise, her hair fell into her face. Nerissa crept into the room carrying a broom and pan. She flinched when Cosma glared at her.

"How dare he?" the courtesan screamed at her maid. "Just who does this...foreigner think he is? No sensible Venetian would have dismissed my invitations with such flippant notes in return—and all of them poorly written, too!"

Nerissa bent her head over her task. "Lord Bardolph said he has been ill," she murmured. "He certainly was the last time we saw him."

Cosma stamped her foot. "Lies! He is as hale and hearty as any man in Venice. Jacopo has kept me informed of his every move this past week. Oh, no, our wayward Francis has been extremely active for one who claims to lie abed near death."

Nerissa had the good sense to say nothing in return. Cosma stalked to her window and stared down at the green canal water below. A gondola, filled to the gunwales with *Carnevale* merrymakers, glided by. The sight of such mirth made Cosma's teeth ache.

When she had invited Francis to join her for a dalliance on Sacca Sessola, Jacopo reported that the viper went instead to a gaming house in the company of that black pirate. When Cosma had urged her lover to come to an evening's entertainment she had specially prepared, Francis had gone out singing under windows and tossing perfume eggs like a lovesick schoolboy.

She narrowed her eyes. More disturbing were Jacopo's reports of Francis's shopping sprees. Bags of comfits, hothouse flowers, a sweet-singing canary in a cage were only a few of the items he had purchased within the past few days. Obviously presents for a woman—but not for Cosma di Luna, Venice's reigning beauty.

Yesterday, Cosma had lowered herself to write a groveling letter to that wandering wastrel. She begged him to tell her what she had done to displease him and to meet with her for a serious discussion. Not trusting a mere lackey with her message, she delivered it herself to the Sturgeon Inn only to be told by the smirking landlord that the Englishman and his friend had gone for the day to the glassmakers' island of Murano and were not expected back until late that evening.

This morning a sleepy Jacopo reported that Francis had visited several workshops there and had bought a number of pretty things: a necklace of flowered beads, a set of pale green wine goblets decorated with gold filigree and a delicate hand-held looking glass. So far none of these items had made their appearance at Cosma's door. Only more curt notes filled with shallow regrets.

Cosma leaned her forehead against the cool glass of her windowpane. The answer stared her in the face. Francis had found a new mistress. Cosma saw her dream of becoming an English countess disappearing like the revelers' gondola that turned the corner. She balled her hands into fists.

Never! She would not concede defeat so easily. The prize was too rich to be lost without a fight. Cosma would be the next Countess of Thornbury—wherever that was—no matter what the cost. Jacopo must learn the identity of Francis's new interest. If the girl was sensible, Cosma would introduce her to several handsome sons of the Republic's nobility. Those lusty youths would provide any fortunate courtesan with wealth and merry pastimes.

If the chit refused to give up her Englishman—well, many unpleasant things could happen in Venice to a lady of pleasure. A scarred face to mar her beauty—a word here and there about the presence of the dreaded French pox—or a sudden attack at night and a watery grave in the morning. All things were possible in *La Serenissima* if one had enough ducats.

In the end, Francis would be glad to seek Cosma's favors once more. Maybe she would make him suffer a little before she welcomed him back into her bed. Make the handsome *bastardo* pay for the hot tears she had shed over his current perfidy.

Cosma smiled at her reflection in the window glass. How she would enjoy making Francis grovel!

Jessica massaged Francis's shoulders, savoring the strength and warmth of his flesh under her hands. After a fortnight of her ministrations, his muscles responded to her skilled fingers. By a silent, mutual agreement, neither of them spoke of Francis's nocturnal wooing nor of the plethora of gifts he continued to shower upon her. Jessica feared to say anything while she worked on him lest she sever the thin thread of trust and affection that had formed between them.

At least she knew that she was attracted to him, though her instinct of self-preservation continually fought against the wiles of her heart. She prayed that Lord Bardolph had grown to admire her. She ignored the unsettling idea that he might be wooing her only to entrap her later on. She could not abandon herself to his gentle seductions no matter how weak he made her feel. She must not play the wanton or she could find herself burning at a stake.

Jessica applied more of her ginger and rosemary ointment to her palms before beginning the long, deep rolling strokes that she knew he liked. She allowed her gaze to wander slowly over him, appraising each naked contour of his chest with approval. The sight of his golden body made her heart beat more rapidly. She fought her almost overwhelming desire to enfold him in an embrace...to brush her lips across his sensuous mouth that grinned at her from under the blindfold. Even at complete rest on her table, Francis radiated a vitality that enticed her.

Gobbo struck a discordant note on his lute, interrupting her pleasant musing. When she glanced over to him, he frowned and shook his head at her. Jessica nodded her understanding. Her ever-watchful servant knew exactly where her thoughts drifted and he highly disapproved. Gobbo was right, she scolded herself. She rolled back her shoulders, gave her head a little toss and proceeded to knead the Englishman as if he were a large mound of bread dough.

Francis made no sound save for an occasional grunt when she hit a sore spot. At length, she drew the session to a close before her good intentions slipped out the door.

"Very well, *messere*," she said, breaking the silence. "I have done with you today. You should sleep well tonight."

Quick as an eel, his hand caught hers before she had a chance to turn away. Rising silently from his stool, Gobbo fingered the hilt of his stiletto. Jessica shot him a look that commanded him to be still.

"You require something more, my lord?" she asked. A spark of excitement danced through her.

His lips smiled at her. "*Sì, madonna,*" he replied in a near whisper. "Come walk with me. Jobe will be our chaperone."

Regret choked her. "I cannot," she whispered in return. She tried to free herself from his gasp but he held her tightly. Gobbo stepped closer. Again, Jessica stopped him with a frown.

To Francis she added, "You know I never go out in broad daylight. Please do not ask me again." Her heart wept with her words.

Francis brought her hand to his lips and kissed it with infinite tenderness. Gobbo's shoulders relaxed somewhat.

At the touch of his kiss, Jessica's pulse skittered like a mouse before a cat. A delightful shiver swept through her. She felt light-headed and breathless as if she had run up and down three flights of stairs too fast.

His thumb moved across the back of her hand in a slow, extremely sensuous circle. "Then come out with me tonight when only the moon casts her silvery eye upon us mortals."

She licked her lips. "Please, my lord, you know I do not like to be seen in public."

He threaded his long fingers between hers. "Lent comes quickly apace. The streets fill with masked revelers. Who will know that the reclusive Donna Jessica Leonardo is among their company? All are *mascheras* until Ash Wednesday arrives. There is dancing in the *piazza*," he added seductively.

Jessica swallowed. How she would love to go! She had never seen Venice's great square except by dawn's pale light when she hurried to hear a special Mass at Saint Mark's. What would the *piazza* look like when it was filled with colorful revelers?

"I...I do not know how to dance," she murmured.

Gobbo snorted at her falsehood. Often he had played sprightly tunes while she and Sophia capered around the kitchen. Crossing his arms over his chest, he glared at her.

Francis smiled again. "Then permit me to be your dance

master. When I was a boy my good grandmother insisted that I learn the steps to every pavane, branle and galliard. Now I bless her wisdom. Your sweet company will be my reward for all those tedious hours I spent partnering my rebellious sister Belle.'' He kissed her hand again. ''Come out with me tonight.''

Jessica swayed against the side of the table. She cast a frantic look at Gobbo but instead of coming to her aid, he grinned and nodded his head in agreement.

She took a deep breath. ''Very well, my lord, you have prevailed upon me. I…I will dance with you but I will never remove my mask.''

He chuckled. ''What of that? Neither will I. In faith, sweet *madonna,* you will be dancing with the devil to-night.''

She trembled at his choice of words. *God save me, I hope not!*

Jacopo's latest report shocked Cosma.

''Are you *sure* of this?'' she snapped at the ashen-faced youth.

''*Sì, madonna,* I swear to it upon my mother's soul,'' he replied, gathering in his arms the monkey he had saved from his mistress's wrath. ''It is Signorina Leonardo who receives Lord Bardolph's attentions. So say the neighbors whom I questioned. And I saw with my own eyes a market boy deliver a basket of fruit to her door. When I asked him who had sent the gift, he told me it was a giant Englishman wearing a hat with many colorful feathers. Who else could that be?''

Cosma chewed her lower lip while she considered these ill tidings. Few Englishmen were in Venice at this chilly time of year. Even fewer were unusually tall and sported such a glaring taste in fashion. Yet how could this news be true? Jessica Leonardo was not only a mere commoner but possibly a secret Jewess. Such a liaison between a noble lord and a woman of her ilk was ludicrous. Now that the masters of the Inquisition were in the city, the relationship could also be dangerous.

Cosma inspected her fingernails. "Lord Bardolph visits the Leonardo person for her healing only. I need further proof, slug."

"True enough," the boy replied, "but when he bid her farewell on her doorstep this morning, I heard him plainly say that he looked forward to dancing with her under the moon tonight. My own ears do not lie, *madonna*." Taking a step backward, he lifted the monkey to his shoulder.

Cosma curled her lips. "So, Francis is well enough to dance under the moon tonight yet an hour ago he sent me word that he was still fevered? The man is a dolt. He throws away *my* beauty and prefers a strumpet who dares not show her ugly face to the world? Ha! I will not be mocked. I am Cosma di Luna—and a force to be reckoned with. Signorina Leonardo will soon learn this to her everlasting sorrow."

She whirled on her heel and strode into her bedchamber. "Nerissa! Fetch my mask, hooded cloak and *zoccoli*," she ordered, referring to the high platform clogs that fashionable women wore out of doors. "Jacopo, stop playing with that wretched beast and hail me a gondola. I will nip this harebrained dalliance in the bud before it has a chance to blossom. At once, do you hear me?" she shouted to her minions.

A half hour later found Cosma in the northern section of Venice. She drew her cloak tighter around her, adjusted her mask and prayed that she would not meet anyone who might recognize her. She wrinkled her nose at the disgusting smell of fried onions and fish that hung over the area.

She had spent twelve years escaping from this sordid background and she had no intention of ever returning to it. Choking back the bile that rose in her throat, she gave Jessica's blue door a sharp rap.

After a second knock, the dwarfish maidservant answered her summons. "Good afternoon, *madonna*—" the little woman began but Cosma pushed her aside.

"Where is your mistress?" she demanded.

Instead of being properly cowed, the woman crossed her arms. "Who wants to know?" she dared to reply in a voice that dripped disdain.

Cosma raised her hand to strike the insolent creature but thought better of it. There was no point wasting either her time or soiling her gloves with this piece of baggage. Pulling off her mask, Cosma brushed past her and flung back the inner door that led into a long hall.

"Hold, madam!" the dwarf shrieked behind her.

Cosma paid her no more mind than a flea. She marched down the hallway following a noise she heard in one of the back rooms. She would flush out the cowering chit from her rat hole.

Just then her quarry stepped into the passageway. "Sophia? What is amiss? Oh, no!"

Recognizing Cosma, Jessica turned away but it was too late. Cosma had already seen the girl's naked face. Teetering on her elevated *zoccoli,* the courtesan gripped a doorjamb for support.

"*¡Madre del Dio!*" she gasped, making a hurried sign of the cross. "Now I see why Francis is no longer interested in me. You are a *witch!*"

Chapter Nine

Cosma's shrill denunciation chilled Jessica to her marrow. Panic threatened to sweep through her, taking her wits with it. Though her terror at her discovery gnarled her stomach into knots, she fought to preserve her fragile control of the situation.

Jessica lifted her chin a notch and stared into the glittering eyes of the enraged beauty. "How now, Donna Cosma?" she asked as coolly as she could manage.

The courtesan backed up a step but did not flinch. "No wonder you hide your face! You bear the devil's mark. You are Satan's creature."

Jessica moistened her trembling lips. "It is only a birthmark. I hide it to preserve myself from the very emotions you now feel. I am a good Catholic," she added. *Better than you, I suspect.*

Cosma rallied from her initial shock. She curled her lips with contempt. "Oh, really? You have used your potions and incantations to bewitch Lord Bardolph. Why else would a man forsake my good company for...yours?"

A stunning realization shook Jessica. Jealousy had driven Cosma to her door and jealousy proved stronger than her fear or revulsion. Spurred by that powerful emotion, the courtesan could become more dangerous than a wounded lioness.

Fighting her instinct to run and hide, Jessica nodded toward her antechamber. "Let us sit and discuss this problem, Donna Cosma."

Without giving her unwanted visitor a backward glance, Jessica brushed past her. She took the more comfortable of the two chairs and arranged the folds of her skirt while she waited for Cosma to join her. She prayed that her calm exterior would cloak the terror that thundered inside her chest. All the dread she had harbored during the past two decades enveloped her.

Cosma followed at a short distance as if afraid that she would become tainted if even so much as her hem touched Jessica. She refused the offered seat. Staring at Jessica, her eyes burned with hatred and loathing.

Cosma wasted no words. "Leave Francis alone. He is mine. We are engaged to be married."

Jessica concealed her shock behind a smile. "Indeed? Then I wish you both much happiness—when you are wed. In the meantime, Lord Bardolph is a free man to come and go as he pleases. Remember, it is *he* who visits me. I do not run after him."

"How can he possibly find you so attractive?" Cosma snarled.

Tread softly now. Jessica lifted a shoulder in a shrug. "I am only a simple healer. All I did was to help his injured shoulder feel better."

Cosma's face grew red. "Witchcraft!" she spat. "You used your unholy spells to enchant poor Francis."

Jessica gripped the arms of her chair for support. "Not so! I say holy prayers not incantations. My ointments are made from olive oil, beeswax and wholesome herbs."

"Has he ever seen your face?"

Jessica turned her head away from her accuser. "I swear before God that I am not a sorceress."

A wicked smile wreathed Cosma's scarlet lips. "The truth of that is not for *me* to judge."

Jessica's breath seemed to solidify in her throat. She opened her mouth but no words came out. She could barely breathe. A tense silence filled the tiny chamber. Jessica's heart pounded loudly against her breast. Would Cosma denounce her as a witch to the Holy Office? Jessica's worst nightmare threatened to come true.

Cosma chuckled in a vile manner. "I will say nothing— *if* you henceforth reject all of Lord Bardolph's advances, return his tokens—" She glared at the pretty yellow canary that trilled in his gilded cage by the window. "And undo your spell. Once I am safely married to Francis, this unpleasant matter will be forgotten."

Made more bold by her threat, the courtesan ventured closer to Jessica. "If you do not—" She allowed the horrible thought to hang in the air between them. "I understand that they drown witches in the lagoon on moonless nights. They say that the wicked creatures sink without a trace. They return to their demonic master on that watery highway to hell."

Cosma's beautiful face contorted with malice. "No one will shrive a witch of her sins. There are none to mourn their passing. The condemned merely slip away. Green water muffles their last screams. Think on it."

With that parting shot, Cosma donned her mask, pulled her cloak tighter around her trim figure and let herself out of the door. Jessica sagged against the back of her chair. Sophia, who had hovered in the hall, rushed to her side with a glass of wine.

"There now, child," she soothed. "Sip this slowly. It will strengthen your blood."

Jessica wiped her cold hand across her fevered brow. "God defend me! I fear that the sins of my parents have visited me at last." She touched the dark stain on her face as if it burned. "What evil did my mother and father commit that God would brand me thus?" Tears rolled down her cheeks.

Sophia put her short arm around Jessica's heaving shoulders and hugged her. "Hush, my sweet! You prattle nonsense. You have listened to the ravings of a jealous woman."

Jessica drank a little of the wine. "Cosma di Luna has nothing to fear from me. Lord Bardolph has no intention of marrying me—or her, for that matter. For all we know, he could already be married to some lady in England." Jessica shut her mind against that idea.

Sophia nodded. "Pay Signorina di Luna no mind. She may be a beauty of renown but inside her heart, she is as rotten as last year's pears. She is nothing but a whore."

Jessica inhaled a fortifying breath of air. "But she called me a witch. Of the two of us, the laws of Venice and the Church would go harder against me." She drank more of the wine.

Sophia held her tighter. "Do not let that piece of painted filth frighten you. Who would believe her? She wears her jealousy like a great green snake around her neck for all to see. It is clear as glass that she only desires the Englishman for his wealth and his title. She would not care a fig if he were ugly and a lecher in the bargain."

Francis's face appeared in Jessica's imagination. What woman could resist such a handsome man, even if he did dress in the worst of taste? "Lord Bardolph has a good heart though prone to melancholy."

"Exactly!" Sophia agreed. "And that is why you must help him to lighten his burden."

"But Cosma—"

Sophia dismissed the worrisome woman with a wave of her hand. "Fie! Fie, Jessica! Listen to me. *You* have given the greatest beauty of Venice cause to be jealous of you. Think what power you possess!"

Jessica sipped more of the wine while she pondered this startling truth. "Cosma could do me grievous injury."

Sophia leaned over and whispered, "If you let her! The time has come, Jessica, for you to cease living in the shadows. Let the daylight into your life. Ignore Signorina di Luna with all her fine clothes and sparkling jewels. Seize what this moment offers you."

The wine warmed the blood in Jessica's veins. She rested her head against Sophia's ample shoulder. "You mean that I should go out dancing tonight with Lord Bardolph?" she asked.

"*Sì*, now you have caught the right pig by the tail!" Sophia replied, draining the remainder of the wine in Jessica's glass. "Take what pleasure you can. Life is far too short as it is, even without that whore's threats."

Doctor Stefano Leonardo strolled among the people who thronged the streets near the Rialto Bridge. Nodding to his many acquaintances, he basked in their open approval. As one of Venice's most respected physicians, Doctor Leonardo savored the wealth and social status he had achieved. Unpleasant memories of the hunger and hiding in his youth had dimmed with time. Spain with its terrifying Inquisition was long past. Here in Venice no one suspected that the most trusted physician—one who enjoyed the patronage of the Doge himself—had returned to the religion of his forefathers. Pleased with the success of his deception, Doctor Leonardo stroked his snowy white beard as he inspected a platter of purple grapes fresh off a boat from Damascus.

"*Messere* Doctor?" said a low voice in Stefano's ear.

He glanced over the heaps of produce at a short, anxious man with a curly brown beard and bushy eyebrows. Though he did not wear the yellow cap prescribed by Venetian law, Tubal was a Jew. Stefano inclined his head a fraction, then pointed to a shadowed alley. The little man darted away. Adjusting his handsome black bombazine robe with red-velvet facings, the eminent doctor sauntered after him.

"¡*Buon giorno! Tubal.* And a lovely day it is, too," said Stefano. "Does something ail you? Your wind, perchance? More aches in your joints?"

Tubal shook his head. "I am sick with fear, good doctor."

Stefano stepped further into the shadow cast by the buildings that enclosed the alleyway. "Speak softly, Tubal. Venice is alive with listening ears," he whispered.

"The eyes and ears of the Holy Office," Tubal agreed. He spat on the ground. "A pox on them all."

Stefano tossed a quick glance over his shoulder, but no one appeared to be watching them. "Smile as you tell me in case we are observed. Many daggers are hidden in a smile. What is the matter?"

Tubal clasped his hands together. "I think that someone has mentioned my name to the officers of the Inquisition."

Stefano felt a sudden chill. Though Jews were openly accepted in Venice, provided that they obeyed the city's laws concerning their dress, residence and occupations, re-canted *marranos* such as Tubal and himself were harshly punished if they were discovered. The physician hunched inside his costly robe.

"How do you know this to be true?" he whispered.

Tubal gnawed his lower lip. "Yesterday, several Franciscan friars visited my street. They asked my neighbors about me.'' He lowered his voice even more. ''They asked how often I went to hear Mass.''

Stefano wished he was far away from this unfriendly alleyway. He wished he had never met Tubal. He wished it were yesterday again. ''This is indeed unsettling news,'' he remarked through his weak smile.

The little man laid his hand on Stefano's arm. ''You must help me and my family, good doctor,'' he pleaded.

Stefano shuddered inwardly at Tubal's touch and his request. Instead of coming to his aid, the doctor wanted to distance himself as quickly as possible from this dangerous person. Though Stefano had remained true to the faith of his fathers, he was also a man of the world. It had taken him half a lifetime to build up a golden reputation here in Venice. He did not wish to have his comfortable life come crashing down around his ears now. Yet Tubal was doubly dangerous since he knew the doctor's secret heart. Tubal was a weakling. Under torture, he would betray everyone, especially if he held a grudge against Stefano Leonardo.

Stefano lifted his palms to the heavens. ''What would you have me do?''

Tubal wiped his mouth with his sleeve. ''Take my Talmud and hide it away in your house. Hide my gold, as well.'' His eyes narrowed. ''I have saved over five hundred ducats.''

Stefano choked at the enormous sum of money. ''It is foolish to have so much coin under your roof. Why not give your fortune to one of the goldsmiths to keep for you? That is their business and I am sure that their interest rate would be generous.''

Tubal snorted. ''Generous to whom? Themselves—not me! No, doctor, I do not trust them with my life savings. No one but you. Will you do it?''

Stefano stroked his beard while he pondered this

disagreeable situation. Tubal was right to hide his fortune and the incriminating books from a possible search by the Inquisition officers. On the other hand, the doctor had no intention of being caught in this net. Why compromise the safety of his own fortune as well as his own life for Tubal? A less risky option formed in his mind. Jessica! A good Christian girl who went to daily Mass. Completely above reproach. Beloved by both her neighbors and by her patients high and low. No one would suspect the doctor's sweet pious daughter of recanting her Catholic faith. Many people considered her practically a saint.

Doctor Leonardo nodded to his companion. "Meet me at nine o'clock tonight at the Campo de San Felice. Bring those things you wish to hide."

Tubal cast a shrewd look at him. "That is not your address."

The doctor again nodded. "True enough. It is where my Christian daughter keeps her establishment. She will be our safeguard."

"Can the wench be trusted?" the man wheezed.

Stefano drew himself up. "Though Jessica is as Catholic as the pope in Rome, she is still my daughter. Blood will prove true. She will do as I say. Now let us part with a cheerful countenance. Until nine this evening."

Tubal tossed a corner of his dark cloak over his shoulder. "Until the clock strikes nine." He scurried away from the bustle of the marketplace.

Doctor Leonardo followed Tubal's retreat with a soft curse.

Jacopo took up his familiar position across the *campo* from Jessica's door. He rubbed his nose under his black *dottore* mask and wished that its leather didn't itch him so much. With his black cloak wrapped snugly about him and his head covered by its inky hood, Jacopo melded with the shadows around him.

The boy yawned. He was tired of trailing the Englishman day after day. What was the point? The *messere* knew that Jacopo dogged his steps. In fact, Lord Bardolph had even taken to waving at him. On one cold evening, the Englishman had sent him a mug of spiced wine to ward off the chill of his lonely vigil. If Madonna Cosma knew how poorly her hireling had concealed himself, she would have flayed him alive by now. Across the small square, Lord Bardolph and his black friend, attended by several jovial torchbearers, rapped on Jessica's door. The whole company were masked and dressed in colorful attire. Jacopo grumbled under his breath. He longed to have a few free hours for his own *Carnevale* amusements.

The fat dwarf answered their summons with cries of delight and she ushered the lords inside the lighted house while the torchbearers waited in the street. Jacopo rubbed his itching nose again. By the look of things, tonight would be a long one—and cold, as well. The boy hunched against the wall and wished he had brought along his new pet monkey to entertain him.

The door opened again; golden light from a lantern spilled into the *campo*. Jacopo stifled another yawn. Lord Bardolph led out a young woman who wore a white *volto* half mask and a full-length black cloak. The blackamoor followed close behind them. The spy straightened up. By Saint Mark's book, they had flushed out the elusive Signorina Jessica Leonardo after all! Jacopo didn't think they could have persuaded her to leave her nest—especially after Donna Cosma's visit this afternoon. He whistled through his teeth. Though he could not see her face, the girl appeared to be comely and her laughter sounded like silver bells. No wonder Donna Cosma was worried!

"¡Volare!" the blackamoor called to the lounging torch-bearers. "We have enticed a beautiful dove from her cage, now let us fly away with her!"

Lord Bardolph added, "To the *piazza!*"

Signorina Jessica laughed again. "I am yours to command, *messere.*"

The torchbearers fanned themselves around the trio. "To the *piazza!*" they chorused.

Jacopo slipped further back into the shadows as the merry band passed within ten feet of his hiding place. Lord Bardolph looked over his shoulder. "Ho, young *bravo!*" he called to Jacopo. "Come join us in our sport. It would be more pleasant than skulking in the corner all night."

Jessica looked across the empty *campo.* "To whom do you speak, my lord? I see no one."

The blackamoor chuckled. "We have a little shadow that follows us. He is somewhere nearby. I can smell him. Do not fear, *madonna.* That alley cat is harmless," he added with a laugh.

Jacopo pressed his spine against the wall. The blacka-moor's disdain pricked his ego and compounded his shame at his discovery. The boy in him wished he could accept the Englishman's invitation to pleasure but the man in him rejected the offer. Donna Cosma would carve him into dog meat if he joined that happy crowd. He stared up at the slice of the night sky that was visible between the two houses where he hid. Tomorrow he would tell Donna Cosma that he had found other employment—then he and his monkey could enjoy a bit of the carnival season before Lent came.

When he looked back into the *campo,* Jacopo saw his quarry disappear down the Fondementa. He pushed himself away from the wall and stretched his chilled muscles. No need to rush after them. They had made it plain where they were going. Jacopo had just stepped into the square when he saw a short, round man enter the *campo* from the side street that led to the canal. The newcomer's furtive haste and the large pouch that he hugged to his chest immediately drew the boy's interest. Jacopo slipped back into dark alley and watched.

Just as the church bells of San Felice began to toll the hour, a second figure appeared in the square. This man was taller, wore the gown of a physician and had a white beard. He, too, acted in a surreptitious manner, looking over his shoulder several times. He carried an intriguing chest under his arm. Jacopo wet his lips. *What sport is this?*

As fortune would have it, the two men met each other within earshot of Jacopo's hiding place. With the African's words still burning his pride, the boy pulled his stiletto from its sheath at his belt. He was not a whelp to be dismissed with a sneer but a *bravo* to be feared. Perhaps he could make a little profit on the side—to repay himself for his long hours of watching. A bold, swift strike could make him a very rich man—if that pouch contained coins as he suspected. He heard it clink when the short fellow moved. Flexing his fingers, Jacopo pressed himself against the wall and listened.

The first man greeted the second with a kiss on each cheek. Then they spoke quietly in a foreign language. Whatever it was they said, the meaning was obvious from their demeanor. A stealthy, perhaps unlawful game was afoot. The boy wiped his sweating palms on his cloak.

The short man handed his pouch and several books to the physician who deposited them in the chest. The tall man then murmured something to the other who nodded and scuttled away. The whole mysterious transaction had concluded in less time than it took the church bells to toll the nine strokes. Jacopo tightened his grip on the hilt of his dagger. How easily fate had played into his hand! One man was certainly easier to kill than two, especially since he was burdened with a heavy chest. Jacopo planned to attack after his prey had passed by him. He tensed and waited.

Instead of returning from whence he had come, the physician moved further away from the alley where his death lurked. He crossed the *campo* with quick strides and stopped in front of Donna Jessica's house. Jacopo ventured a step or two closer to observe what would happen next. The physician rapped on the blue door, waited for a few moments, then rapped again. Once more, the dwarf answered the summons.

Her eyes widened with surprise when she recognized the visitor then she dropped a bob of a curtsy. "*¡Buona sera! Doctor Leonardo,*" she greeted him in sour tones. "It is late for you to be abroad."

"I wish to speak with my daughter," the physician snapped.

The maid shook her head. "She is not at home."

"Have her wits slipped askew?" he asked even more sharply. "It is dangerous for her to be out in public."

Jacopo tucked this little piece of information in the back of his mind. It might be worth his while to investigate this nugget at a later time.

The maid laughed. "Curb your fears, sir. She is accompanied by several friends. They have gone to enjoy the sights and sounds of *Carnevale.*"

"Wanton gambols!" the father snorted. "Jessica will rue it later, I vow. Well, woman, do not stand there gaping at me! Am I not allowed inside my own house? Do not forget who pays for my daughter's privacy. Go to, go to!" He tapped the chest. "I have something to give her."

The maid held out her hands. "I will relieve you of that, sir. I will tell Jessica that—"

"No!" the man almost shouted. "This chest is too heavy for such a snail mite as you to hold. I will put it in her room myself. Stand aside, Sophia. I am in no mood to banter with an ape."

The little woman did as she was told, but she glared at him in return. "Nor am I, Doctor Leonardo." She shut the door with a bang behind them.

Jacopo released his pent-up breath. He tried to make sense of the scenes he had just witnessed but could not see a connection between the two men who acted as if they feared their own shadows and the physician declaring that he had a present for his daughter. A few minutes later, the door reopened and the doctor stormed out into the *campo*. He no longer carried the chest.

"In the future, Sophia, remember who buys your bread," he warned her. He drew his gown around himself and stalked off in the dark.

Sophia shook her fist at his departing figure before she again shut the door. Jacopo waited for a few more minutes to see if anyone else would come, but the only sign of life in the square was a lean cat that stalked around the rim of the wellhead. Relaxing his shoulders, Jacopo returned his dagger to its sheath. His near attempt at murder left him weak and shaking. He took off his hot mask and mopped his face with a corner of his cloak. When he thought of what he had almost done, his stomach lurched in shame. *The blackamoor was right. I am the poorest excuse for a* bravo *in all of Venice.*

Jacopo donned his mask again. Though he had gained nothing for the time being, he had learned two interesting things for possible future profit: that Donna Jessica had a dangerous secret and that a chest of money was now hidden in her room. He promised himself to wait for the right opportunity to steal it. Certainly not now with that miniature she-dragon guarding the house. Pulling his hood lower, Jacopo crossed the square and headed toward the *piazza*.

Patience is always rewarded, his father had once told him. The boy would bide his time.

Chapter Ten

Gobbo sat up in bed and pushed his nightcap out of his eyes. "Who was at the door?" he asked his diminutive wife.

Sophia set down the lantern on the coffer at the foot of their bed. "Doctor Leonardo." She made a face.

Gobbo yawned. "Strange time to visit his only child. Was he afraid that someone might recognize him if he came during the day?"

Sophia shook her head. The mystery of the doctor's box pricked her curiosity. "He had no desire to see Jessica. He carried a cedarwood casket. He claimed it was a gift for Jessica, but I think not."

Gobbo curled his lip. "When was the last time the good doctor remembered to send a gift to her? New Year's Day? Ha! Her birthday? Hardly! Had it not been for his wife's tender heart, I warrant Jessica would not have lived past her first day on this earth."

"That is what confounds me," Sophia agreed.

Gobbo tossed back the featherbed and struggled into his mules. "Where is this marvel?"

Sophia picked up the light. "As always we are of one

mind, my love. The doctor wedged the box under Jessica's bed. Come.''

Holding the lantern as high as her short arm allowed, Sophia led him down the hall to Jessica's chamber. She mounted the bed's platform and lifted the coverlet hem. A corner of the intriguing chest protruded from under the bed frame.

With a low grunt, Gobbo hunkered down next to it. "It is well made," he remarked as he pulled it out from its hiding place. "And heavy, as well."

Rubbing her finger across the lid, Sophia noted the smoothness of the grain and the high polish of the wood. "Dare we open it?"

The two of them looked at each other for a long moment. Sophia and Gobbo regarded Jessica more like the child they never had than their employer. Any hint of danger to Jessica enkindled a fierce reaction in the hearts of the little man and his wife. They did not love nor owe any allegiance to Doctor Leonardo, no matter what the man boasted.

Gobbo tapped the box. "This night visit bodes no good, I vow. The doctor is a selfish man. This is not so much a gift for Jessica but a profit for her father." He pushed the clasp but discovered it was locked.

Sophia snorted with her frustration. "Have you lost all the skills of your youth? Surely you can pick the latch." She held the light closer for his inspection.

He studied the problem for several minutes before finally shaking his head. "This is no ordinary lock but one fashioned with cunning skill. Therefore, I think it must be a treasure chest." Frowning, he pushed it back under the bed. "I think it best that we have nothing to do with it, sweetheart. I have escaped the gibbet for so many years now that I have grown cautious in my old age."

Sophia bit back her disappointment but could not disagree with Gobbo. She, too, had known the hard hand of the law in her salad days and she had a healthy respect for it now. "I will tell Jessica about it in the morning."

Gobbo rose and hugged his wife. "That's my good girl! Let us return to our bed. Perhaps you can help warm these chill bones of mine." He gave her a hearty kiss.

Sophia giggled like a woman half her age. "Perhaps I will at that."

Jessica felt as if she had entered another world; one of firelight, color, music and laughter. She had heard of the merrymaking that took place during the carnival season but never before had she witnessed it for herself. As a child she had been forbidden to leave her parents' house lest someone denounce her as a spawn of the devil. Once on her own, Jessica continued to hide her shameful secret within the little world she had created for herself. The excitement of tonight's revels opened her eyes and heated her blood. At each turning of a street corner, a new sight and sound greeted her.

A troop of actors had set up their impromptu stage in the middle of a tiny square where they entertained whomever stopped to watch the antics of the sly Arlecchino and the befuddled Pantalone, two time-honored characters from the Commedia dell'Arte. Holding tightly to Francis's arm, Jessica laughed until tears formed in her eyes and her stomach ached with mirth. She had never seen a play enacted and she loved her first experience. With a cheer for their performance, Jobe tossed a shower of silver scudi at the delighted actors.

Still breathless from her laughter, Jessica was not prepared for the fire-eater who swallowed an amazing number of flaming brands while the crowds at the foot of the Rialto Bridge gasped and applauded.

"*¡Dio mio!* How can he stand the pain?" she murmured.

Francis patted her hand. "I suspect that he has drunk a good deal of wine earlier today and now feels nothing but giddy happiness."

Jessica winced as the man consumed another ball of fire with apparent relish. She worried that his throat would be sore in the morning. Francis dropped a coin in the little box that the fire-eater's young assistant held out to him.

Jessica leaned over to the urchin and whispered, "Tell your master to drink honey mixed with myrrh and he will feel much better."

"*Grazie.*" The child thanked her with a twinkle in his dark eyes and a snicker in his voice.

Growing larger by the minute, the cheerful crowd surged across the bridge taking Jessica and her entourage with them. Looking at the sea of masks around her, she realized that Francis had told her the truth. No one knew who she was, nor did anyone care. Everyone was masked with the most outlandish painted faces. Men and women alike dressed in rainbow-hued ribbons, colorful satin rosettes, gaudy tassels, golden bells on their ankles and strings of glass beads around their necks. Tambourines, tabors, recorders and mandolins filled the air with their music. Francis's torchbearers started a rowdy song that was quickly taken up by everyone nearby. The lusty lyrics both shocked and titillated Jessica. She felt delightfully wicked.

Conducted by the song and laughter through the maze of winding narrow streets, the merry company came suddenly upon the huge central *piazza* that throbbed with hundreds of people in the frenzy of enjoyment. Jessica's eyes widened. Never in her wildest dreams had she imagined such a sight. In the huge square, light from a thousand torches had turned the night into day. Lithe acrobats clad in green-and-red-striped tights tumbled and cavorted on the porch of the great basilica. Nimble jugglers tossed balls into the air so quickly that they became a whirl of color. Another man had dressed several small white dogs in red ruff collars and golden ribbons. To the delight of the onlookers, the little animals capered on their hind legs, dancing in time with the music.

Francis dismissed his torchbearers. They needed no extra light in the *piazza*. A band of rough-looking men, their leering masks askew, pushed their way through the crowd. Jessica froze when one of them pointed directly at her. Fear and anger knotted together in the pit of her stomach. Had it come to this—a betrayal in the midst of such good cheer? Had Lord Bardolph lulled her misgivings and lured her to this sea of pleasure only to cast her into the hands of those who meant her harm? She glanced at the English nobleman but she could not read the look in his eyes behind his devil's mask. Would he give the order to drag her away to the chapel of Saint Theodore where the Officers of the Inquisition held their dread court?

Instead, the leader of the motley band roared with laughter. "What ho, *capitano!*" he cried. "Think you could hide that great body of yours?"

Jobe answered with rolling laughter of his own. "Sebastian! You look as if you have been drinking since I last clapped an eye on you!" He smiled down at Jessica. "Have no fear, little one. These men are members of my crew— and the finest blackguards that ever skewered a Turk!"

Jessica had no idea if she should be relieved or more fearful. Jobe's sailors looked extremely dangerous. Francis put his arm around her trembling shoulders and drew her closer to him.

"It seems your fellows have frightened the lady, Jobe.

Away with you and amuse your friends with saltier company. I will take good care of Jessica.''

Leaning against his tall body, she relaxed and reveled in the strength he exuded. She chided herself for doubting his intentions. His warmth enveloped her; his scent of cloves comforted her.

Jobe looked at them both and his eyes took on a distant smoky glaze. Then he spoke in English to Francis. Jessica had no idea what he said but she felt her protector tense beneath his satin and damask costume.

Francis recognized that look of Jobe's. The African's strange gift of prophecy had often proved true in the past.

"Give the little dove a night she will long cherish in her memory, *meo amigo,*" Jobe told him in a deep, faraway tone. "This is her first and will be her last carnival in Venice."

Francis held her tighter against him. His throat had gone dry. "What do you see?"

"Danger," Jobe murmured in his ear. "It draws nearer with each passing hour."

Francis swept his gaze around the square crowded with the multitudes that hemmed them on every side. He fingered the hilt of his rapier. "Should I take her home straightway?"

Jobe's expression softened. "Nay, the danger will not come tonight. Though I cannot make out its face or form, it hovers in the distance. But trust me, Francis, it is very real. Tonight, all will be well. Be merry. Let the coming hours overflow with pleasure for both of you. I will carouse with my men. Come the dawn, I will make due preparations."

Francis narrowed his eyes. "Of what nature? Do not

leave me in this quandary, Jobe. Your words chill me to the very marrow.''

His friend laid a large hand on Francis's shoulder. "Heed me. Cast aside all worry for tonight. Enjoy this pleasant time that the Creator has given you. On the morrow, I will ready my ship to leave Venice at a moment's notice. Now smile, my young friend, for I see that we have frightened your dove.''

Francis grimaced in return. "Blast your second sight, Jobe! You are like a raven croaking on a stile. Your vision has drained the mirth from my heart.''

Jobe smiled at Jessica and spoke to her softly in Italian. "Do not tremble, *madonna*. I merely told my friend to guard you well. Your beauty will attract many men like honey draws a thousand bees.''

She pursed her lips before replying, "Though I could not understand your language, I think you spoke of more serious matters.''

He cocked an eyebrow then nodded. "*Sì*, you are a marvelous reader of minds, *madonna*. Chiefly, I have commanded this wooden head to make it his first business that you enjoy this night, so smile for us both. Let it fill our hearts with your sunshine. I will go now, and leave you in far better company than mine.'' Turning to his sailors, he shouted, "Ho, lads! Let us find the largest butt of wine in Venice! Who will drink with me?''

His men answered him with a rousing cheer. Within seconds they melted into the throng. Though disturbed by Jobe's warnings, Francis took heart that the African had seen no immediate trouble. His lips softened when he looked down at Jessica. For her sweet sake, he would banish his foreboding and give her what Jobe had suggested—a memorable night.

He cupped her chin between his thumb and forefinger

and lifted her head so that he could see into those dark brown eyes. "Jobe likes to hear himself talk," he explained. "Pay him no mind. Are you hungry? I spy a purveyor of pastries by yonder pillar."

Though her lips quivered a little, she flashed him a smile in return. "I have always been overly fond of sweets, my lord."

He leaned down a little closer. "Please, Jessica, call me Francis." He longed to hear her say his name.

She bit her lower lip. "I would not presume to do so, my lord. I am not worthy—"

He drew nearer to her, enticed by the lushness of her mouth. "You are more than worthy, *madonna*," he whispered. "You have no idea who it is who asks you this favor. Please, call me by my given name."

Her pink tongue darted out and moistened her lips. "Since you and I have concealed our true identities for tonight, I will do as you ask. But on the morrow—"

"Let the devil take tomorrow, sweet Jessica," he murmured.

Desire fueled by an overwhelming urge to protect her rushed through him like a wildfire. Gathering her into his arms, he held her snugly in his embrace. "What is my name, Jessica?" he whispered into her black silken hair.

Softer than a butterfly's wing, her long eyelashes fluttered against his cheek. "Francis," she breathed. Her rosy lips beckoned his kiss.

Sizzling fireworks exploded within him. His mouth covered hers with a hunger he had not known until this moment. She gasped; her sugar breath filled his mouth. He moved his lips over hers, devouring their soft sweetness. His tongue explored the corners of her mouth.

Jessica tensed; her body quivered in his embrace.

Regaining a measure of control over himself, Francis

raised his head and gazed into the beautiful eyes behind her mask. They were wide with surprise—or fear.

"I crave your pardon, *madonna*," he murmured, though he did not release her. "I frightened you. Forgive me. I have been a man of the world for too long. I am rough and woo not like a lover should."

With her fingertips,. she touched her lips, now slightly swollen from his bruising kiss. "You…you have no need to apologize, my lord…that is, Francis. I wanted you to do it. The fault is mine."

He stroked her hair and wished he had the courage to untie the ribbons that held her wild raven tresses in check. "Impossible! You have no faults, sweet angel."

Jessica's lips burned from his touch. Though the intensity of his action had startled her, she had no desire to leave his arms. When she lifted her head and gazed into his eyes, she beheld a heart-rending tenderness in their blue depths. Her heart skipped in response. An invisible warmth enfolded her.

Jessica trembled though she continued to smile. "I am an unlessoned girl, unschooled, unpracticed in the arts of love," she confessed. Her cheeks flamed behind her mask.

Her answer seemed to amuse Francis. He returned her smile with a wider one of his own. "Pray tell me, *cara*, has no one ever kissed you?"

The beautiful sound of his voice enthralled her. She tried to hold back the dizzying current that raced through her, but failed miserably. She placed her hands on his chest, lest she collapse on the paving stones.

Jessica shook her head. "No, Francis," she replied, savoring his name like a sugar wafer on her tongue. "I have led a very sheltered life."

The heat from his body warmed her, banishing the last

trace of the night's growing chill. The hundreds of revelers that surrounded them receded from her vision. The music, bells, laughter, cheering and songs from hundreds of voices dimmed in her ears. Only Francis was real. Her fingers ached to touch him. Flinging aside her carefully nurtured caution, she rose on tiptoe and slid her arms around his neck, burying her hands in his golden hair.

He chuckled. "Allow me to shelter you now," he whispered as he lifted her into the cradle of his arms. His mouth brushed against hers. This time his kiss was as gentle as a prayer, though she could not mistake the passionate message that throbbed from his lips. Clasping him tighter around his neck, she shamelessly returned his kiss with reckless abandon.

The eagerness of her own response shocked Jessica, but she did not pull away. When his tongue again begged entry, she did not deny him. As if he plumbed the depths of a honey jar, Francis explored the recesses of her mouth. Then he teased her tongue to twine with his in a dance of mutual joy. Her wildly beating heart was the only sound in her ears.

As he deepened his kiss, Jessica's nipples rose and tingled against the soft fabric of her shift beneath her bodice. Blood pounded in her temples. More giddiness washed over her and she was very glad that he held her so tightly. Leaving her mouth burning with his fire, he moved to nibble her earlobe before trailing a series of light kisses down her neck. She sighed with pleasure.

With a final lingering kiss in the hollow of her throat, Francis eased back. "You are as heady as summer wine," he told her in a husky voice. "And the depth of my thirst would frighten you."

He set her on her feet again but did not withdraw his arm from around her waist. "Let us enjoy a cup or two of the juice of the grape and dance away the hours. Bestrew me, Jessica, I am as lighthearted as a schoolboy and that is a wonderment, I assure you.''

Though she missed the touch of his lips on hers, she had to agree with him. This first dip into lovemaking had left her reeling with many unexplored and intriguing emotions. Jessica took several deep breaths to allow her heart to return to its normal rhythm. Then she nodded.

''I, too, am very thirsty,'' she replied. *For you.*

It took less than an hour for Jacopo to locate the Englishman and Signorina Leonardo amid the crush of merrymakers in Saint Mark's Square. Lord Bardolph was literally head and shoulders above the mob and his garish feathered hat made him even more conspicuous. When Jacopo located them, the couple were whirling to the music of a mad *moresca* dance. Bracelets of tiny bells jingled from their wrists.

Leaning against a stone lion carved from red marble that sat in a small square to the left of the great domed basilica, Jacopo watched them with half an eye. His thoughts were back at Jessica's house where her father's mysterious chest lay. In his imagination, he saw the box filled to the brim with gold coins and jewels of great price—enough treasure for Jacopo to buy himself a grand palace on the canal, coffers of handsome clothes, a pliant wife from one of Venice's finer families and a beautiful courtesan to be his mistress. He grunted to himself. Why, he might even buy Cosma's favors!

When the wild Moorish dance concluded, the Englishman caught up his partner in a tight embrace. The two kissed each other shamelessly for several minutes while the people nearby clapped and cheered their display of passion. Jacopo flicked an eyebrow. Donna Cosma would tear that

wench apart if she saw how the girl had charmed Lord
Bardolph. Jacopo pondered how many details he would relate to his jealous employer. He had no desire for Cosma
to box his ears just because he bore bad news. No wonder
the Englishman preferred Signorina Jessica—she had a
much sweeter disposition than Cosma. The choice between
the two women was an obvious one to any sane man.

The hours swept past midnight and still the couple remained in the *piazza*. They laughed, danced, kissed, ate
honey pastries, drank wine, kissed, danced again, enjoyed
the street entertainers, had their fortunes read at the tarot
booth and kissed some more. Jacopo nursed a cup of wine
and hunkered against one of the arcade pillars of the Pro-
curatie, an office building that bordered the north side of
the *piazza*. The semi-enclosed area offered the cold youth
a respite from the wind that blew around the square. None
of the revelers seemed to notice the weather. The two
bronze blackamoors in the great clock tower struck their
bell once, twice, three times and still no one—least of all
the couple that Jacopo watched—showed any signs of going back home to their warm beds.

The late hour surprised the boy. After several weeks of
observation, Jacopo knew that Lord Bardolph was a mod-
erate man in his food, drink and pleasures, despite his at-
tempts to make himself appear the wastrel. Young as he
was, Jacopo was more flagrant in his vices than the Englishman. As for Signorina Leonardo, her behavior tonight
went completely against everything the boy had learned of
her habits and manner. He yawned. It must be the spirit of
the carnival season that had infected them both with a temporary madness.

By four in the morning, Jacopo's feet felt like twin
blocks of ice. He was cold and decidedly out of sorts. From
his new position at the base of the soaring campanile, he

glared at the couple who once again kissed and fondled each other with growing familiarity. His envy had long since been frozen out of his heart. His fingers were icy, his ears ached from the cold and his nose ran without ceasing. Jacopo could not think of another night he had spent in more miserable conditions.

"*¡Basta!*" he growled deep in his cloak. "I have had enough of this wooing for a decade. They can kiss until midday. I am for my pallet."

The youth stamped his feet to get some feeling back into them. Lord Bardolph and his new mistress paid him no mind even when he approached them.

"May your lips freeze together," the young *bravo* snarled at them.

Only then did the couple break apart. The *signorina* turned away from the boy but Lord Bardolph laughed. He drew a ducat from the seemingly inexhaustible supply in his pouch and tossed it to Jacopo.

"Sleep well, my friend," the Englishman said. "May your dreams be as sweet as mine are this moment."

Jacopo did not trust himself to reply in a civil manner. Clutching the gold in his stiff fingers, he hurried away in the creeping fog of dawn. Lord Bardolph's hearty laughter echoed behind him.

Chapter Eleven

The sky already lightened with the dull pewter color of pre-dawn when the *piazza* clock tower chimed six. Its fluted tones were immediately followed and underscored by the deeper peal from Saint Mark's Basilica. Most of the night's revelers had already tottered off to their beds. The diehards shuffled toward the church with many yawns behind their masks, perhaps to seek forgiveness for whatever sinful foolishness they had indulged in during the night hours.

Jessica slipped her small hand into Francis's large warm one. "I must go to Mass," she told him in her lovely low voice.

Francis gave her cold fingers a little squeeze. "Whyfore, sweetheart? You have done nothing wrong. A kiss or two is no sin," he added with a smile. It was a good thing she could not read his mind for he had harbored much more lusty thoughts throughout the night.

Jessica shook her head, then adjusted her hood over her glorious hair, now charmingly disarrayed from hours of dancing. "It is not any wrongdoing of last night that prompts me," she replied, hurrying toward the large double doors of the church. "There are things I must atone for that are far past." She spoke with a quiet firmness that suffered no argument. "You need not accompany me."

Francis adjusted his hat more firmly on his head. "Not so, little one. I will see you safely home. Besides..." He glanced at the black mourning band that he still wore around his left arm. "I should pray for my grandfather."

She looked up at him. "Was he a good man?"

Francis smiled at the memory of his larger-than-life grandsire. "*Sì,* he taught all of his children to love God first—and hunting second." The pain of remembrance did not stab him as sharply this morning as it had a few weeks ago when Jobe had first brought him the doleful news.

Jessica smiled. "I wish I had met this fine gentleman. Come, let us remember him in our prayers."

Francis held open the heavy door for her. He breathed in the odor of stale mustiness, hot wax and lingering incense that seemed to thrive inside every cathedral he had ever visited. He scanned the gilded mosaics above them. Large-eyed saints stared back. Inside this church was a celebration of beauty that had been static and dead for hundreds of years. Outside was the celebration of beauty that lived for the moment. If truth be told, Francis much preferred the open *piazza* to this dark house of God.

Following Jessica's lead, he knelt on the uneven stones and tried to pay attention to the divine service. Fatigue settled over him. His eyes burned from lack of sleep. He stifled a number of yawns and thought of his bed—with Jessica lying naked beside him. He shook himself awake and apologized to the Lord for his weakness.

When they emerged once again into the *piazza,* the new day had already arrived, cloaked in a dank fog that shrouded the far side of the square. Tossing her head back, Jessica inhaled deeply.

"What a wonderful night, Francis! Thank you so much

for showing me such amazing sights. To think—I have lived all my life in Venice and have never known such pleasures existed.'' She looped her arm through his. ''I feel new born, thanks to you.''

Francis smiled down at her. He was glad that he had accomplished what Jobe had suggested. He knew that he would never forget this wonderful night, either. Concern mixed with anger as Jessica's unknown danger rippled down his spine. He drew her closer under his cloak. ''Let us prolong this pleasant interlude a little longer.'' He pointed to the Mole where several dozen sleek gondolas bobbed on the Grand Canal. ''I will return you to your home in the style of a lady—not as a serving maid.''

She stared at the boats. ''In faith, I have rarely ridden in a gondola. We can reach my house faster if we walk through the back streets. You have spent far too much money on me as it is.''

Francis signaled to one of the gondoliers. ''What good is money but to spend? My purse is unlocked for you.'' Thank heavens, Lord Cecil could not see how his money was spent.

Francis helped her descend into the boat. She gripped his hand tighter when the vessel rocked with her weight. The gondolier steadied the craft until Francis joined her on the red plush cushions inside the *felze*.

Francis drew the thick black curtains of the gondola's tiny cabin around them, shutting out the pale rays of the rising sun. ''This will turn day back to night for a little while.'' Then he covered them both with his warm cloak and gathered her in his arms.

Jessica giggled nervously. ''Would you ravish a woman so soon after attending Holy Mass?'' she bantered.

In a heartbeat. His desire quickened. He took her fingers and kissed each one in turn, then pressed a lingering kiss on her palm. She shivered—from the thrill of his touch, he hoped, and not from the cold. "May I have your gracious permission to kiss you once more, *cara mia*?"

She giggled again. "Indeed, for I think you are doing too much talking with those lips." She laid her head on his chest and looked up at him. Expectation and laughter filled the vast pools of her dark eyes. "And not enough of other things." She curled herself against his hip.

Francis needed no further urging. His lips brushed against hers before she had finished speaking. Jessica returned his kiss with a hunger that belied her calm demeanor. Parting her lips, she welcomed his tongue. The caress of her mouth set him aflame. His pulse throbbed in his temples.

Raising his head from her intoxicating fountain, he traced his fingertip across her love-swollen lips. "You are a temptress, *madonna*. You push a man to the brink of good sense."

She gazed up at him, her brown eyes misty with desire. "I fear I have misplaced my good sense somewhere in the *piazza*," she whispered.

Francis ground his teeth. If ever he had wanted to make love with a woman, it was here and now within the narrow confines of the silent skimming gondola. Cold sweat broke out on his forehead. His loins grew tight and hot, straining against his codpiece. Yet he recognized Jessica's innocence at this stage of their love-play. Taking her now, no matter how much she thought she wanted it, would be a selfish act. A rocking boat in the middle of the Grand Canal with a gondolier as a witness was a knavish place for the initiation of such a sweet virgin as Jessica. Francis had called himself a great many names over the years but "brute" would never be one of them.

Before love, there must be a measure of trust. He ran his

finger just under the line of her mask. "Will you remove this, *cara?*" he asked. "I promise that I will not take anything amiss."

Though he had phrased his question in the gentlest manner he knew, he broke the spell. She sat up and turned away from him. "You ask too much," she said in a choked voice.

Cursing his clumsy tongue, he asked, "Are you still afraid of me? Do you think I would be untrue?"

Jessica faced him once more. The sheen of tears filmed her eyes. "You are the truest man that I have ever met. For that reason particularly, I dare not reveal what is hidden. Your eyes would find it hateful," she answered, keeping all emotion out of her voice. "And your heart."

He took her limp hand in his and kissed it with deep reverence. "The truth is never hateful," he replied.

Her lips parted in a stiff smile. "Isn't it?" she retorted. "Isn't the truth that *you* try to hide from yourself also hateful?"

As surely as if she had stabbed him with a dagger, her question shot a bolt of pain through him. He looked down at her hand that he held within his. How could he explain the emptiness inside him? The gnawing need for an identity? An overwhelming desire to find his own place in the world? He could barely understand these things himself. All he knew was loathing for what he was now with no hope for the future. His mother had wrecked his chance for happiness seven years ago when she had told him the name of his true father—a man Francis knew would never accept him as his son. For the sake of harmony within the Cavendish family, Francis kept the shameful truth to himself.

When he did not answer her question, Jessica continued, "You see? You have your secret and I have mine."

He sighed, then gave a resigned shrug. *"Sì, madonna."*

His torment twisted in the pit of his stomach. "Forgive me for breaking our good cheer." He kissed her hand again. "Let us not part with lukewarm words and sour looks. Our time together is too precious."

She stared at him for a breathless moment before she nodded. She kissed his hand in return. "Hold me, Francis, for a great coldness wraps around my heart."

He held out his arms to her and she lay down with him again. They said nothing more for the rest of their journey. Francis wished he knew how to banish all of their cares forever. He tightened his embrace and softly kissed the top of her head. A long sigh escaped her.

The gondolier rapped on the roof of the *felze,* startling his passengers. *"Ponte San Felice, messere,"* the young man announced. "We have arrived at your destination."

"Grazie," Francis called up to him. "Give us one moment more."

The gondolier chuckled. "All the time in the world, my lord."

Francis framed Jessica's masked face between his large hands. "This night will last a lifetime in my memory, *cara mia.* I thank you for it."

"And I," she replied in a fragile voice. "This night is already engraved in gold upon my heart. You have given me much happiness. I can never repay you."

"You can," he whispered, "with one last kiss." Crushing her to him, he pressed his lips to hers, caressing her mouth more than kissing it.

Moaning in the back of her throat, she twined her hands around his neck, giving herself freely to the passion of his kiss. He tasted her, savored her, impressed her in the depths of his heart before he finally released her. He allowed Jessica a moment to pull herself together before he flung open the curtains. Both of them blinked in the brilliant sunlight. The morning fog had burned away.

Francis helped her alight on the quayside but when he started to follow her to her house, she smiled and shook her head. Without a word of explanation, she turned and ran lightly across the little square. Francis watched until he saw her disappear behind her blue door. Then he climbed back into the boat.

"To the sign of the Sturgeon by the Rialto Bridge," he told the gondolier. He yawned as the high silver-capped prow swung away from the landing.

I am truly fortune's bastard.

Sophia was upon Jessica before she had a chance to remove her cloak and mask. "Well?" the little woman asked with sparkling eyes. "Up so early or going abed so late?"

Jessica leaned against the wall and yawned. A smile played on her lips and twinkled in her eyes. "Do not chide me, Sophia. I have been dancing in Paradise."

Sophia chuckled. "Has Lord Bardolph proclaimed his love for you yet?"

Jessica tossed her a frown. "You are wool-gathering, Sophia. I am not such a silly goose to believe that I am anything more to the gentleman than a passing whim."

Sophia narrowed her eyes. "Did he misuse you?" *I'll cut out his heart myself if he has.*

With a smile, Jessica shook her head. "On the contrary, he was as perfect in his manners as any man could be." She giggled and blushed.

Sophia's heart swelled with gladness. How she had longed for Jessica to be merry and to taste of the delights of love! Clearly the girl was smitten. Who wouldn't be if they had spent the entire night in the company of so handsome and so charming a swain as Lord Bardolph?

Jessica yawned again. "Do I have any patients this morning?" she asked, rubbing her eyes.

Sophia thought for a moment. "Only old Gippetto who needs more ointment for his sore knees. I can attend to that myself. You go seek your bed. By my soul, you are no good to me or anyone else when you are almost asleep standing up. Away with you!"

For once, Jessica did not protest. Still yawning, she stumbled toward the narrow staircase.

Sophia hesitated for a moment before she asked, "Did you take off your mask?"

Jessica paused at the foot of the stairs. "He asked, but I...I could not. Let him think well of me for a little longer."

Sophia came up behind her. "Child, he should know the truth. If he is an honest gentleman, he will not think less of you."

Jessica shook her head. "This has all been a dream. A sudden pleasurable moment in the night. I do not want to wake up just yet." She leaned over and kissed Sophia on her apple cheek. "Let me store up a lifetime of sweet memories now. I know he will soon be gone." With a little sigh, she climbed the stairs.

Sophia stared after her and whispered a prayer to any saint that might give a kind glance to sweet Jessica. The child was ripe for marriage and she needed a gentle but strong man who would love and protect her from the hurtful outside world. The Good Lord knew that Sophia and Gobbo were not getting any younger. Once they were gone who would care for Jessica? Certainly not that cold fish of a father!

Thinking of Doctor Leonardo reminded Sophia of the chest under Jessica's bed, but she hated to disturb her now. Let the child sleep wrapped in sweet dreams of her handsome gentleman. There would be plenty of time later to tell

Jessica about her father's visit. In the meanwhile the chest and its mysterious contents were quite safe where they were.

Jessica lay on a cloak of rose damask—naked. Her raven hair fanned out on a scarlet pillow and her rosy lips parted with anticipation as she held out her arms to Francis. Though her features were still covered with her mask, the shapely beauty of her body and the low, bell tones of her voice tantalized him. The gondola rocked on the placid lagoon when he dropped down beside her and took her in his arms. The rising sun sent streaks of orange and pinks dancing along the ripples in the water and bathing the lovers with blessings of the new morn.

Her ivory skin felt like silk under his wandering fingertips. She purred with pleasure as he slipped his hand down the curve of her hips. She gasped with delight when he cupped her firm rounded bottom.

Francis dipped his head and suckled first one dusky nipple then the other, teasing them into taut buds. Jessica arched her back, begging him for more. He laved the hardened peaks with the tip of his tongue, savoring her taste as he would a sugar cone. Moaning, she gripped his shoulders, pulling him to her. Her soft breasts flattened against his bare chest sending him into an upward spiral of pleasure. As he roused her passion, his own grew stronger.

Kissing her, he whispered his love for her. She answered with sweet words of her love for him. At first, his kiss was as tender and as gentle as a summer's light breeze. His lips feather-touched hers with gentle persuasion. Parting her lips, she enticed him to a deeper intimacy. He could not resist but took her mouth with a savage intensity. She responded in kind, pressing herself against him.

Francis skimmed his hands down both sides of her body

to her thighs. She shuddered with her delight and moaned when he touched her most intimate core. She was moist and ready for him. Jessica whimpered and writhed as he coaxed her into the ascending heights of passion. With her head thrown back and her eyes closed, she clasped him and cried out for release. When he brought her to the zenith of fulfillment, she gasped and shattered into a million golden stars.

"Oh, Lord Bardolph!" she cried.

"Call me Francis," he commanded, his throat raw with his need for her.

She shook his shoulder. "Lord Bardolph," she repeated, this time more insistent.

He eased himself between her golden thighs. "Francis," he entreated. He poised himself to plunge within her honey depths….

"Lord Bardolph, *messere,* awake!" Someone shook his shoulder more roughly.

Francis bolted upright amid the shambles of his bedding. His heart thudded against his sweating chest. "What the devil?" he shouted.

The inn's tapboy jumped back as if he had touched a firebrand. "Your pardon, my lord, but there is a lady downstairs come to see you."

Francis scrubbed the sleep from his face and cursed the boy for waking him in the middle of a most pleasurable dream. "What lady?" he growled, swinging his long legs over the bed frame.

The tapboy shrugged. "I know not. She is masked and did not give her name."

His foul mood lightened. "A pretty lady?" he asked, pulling on his hose.

The child nodded. "To be sure, my lord."

Jessica! his heart sang. His senses tingled with the memory of his erotic dream. She had come to him—and in broad daylight. He hurriedly donned his shirt and doublet. No need to tie up his laces when he had every hope of discarding his clothing within the coming hour. He ran his fingers through his limp hair and prayed that Jessica would not take it too amiss that he had not yet shaved.

"What is the time?" he asked. He rinsed out his mouth with some water from the pitcher. He wished he had some mint leaves to chew.

"Past noon," replied the boy. "Nearer to one, I think."

"Hoy day!" Francis muttered as he hunted for his felt mules.

Just then the door opened, revealing the lady in question.

Chapter Twelve

Everything about Francis deflated—his good spirits, his ardor, his manhood. Even before she removed her mask, he recognized Cosma. His heart sank to the soles of his feet.

The tapboy looked from Francis to Cosma then back to Francis. "Shall I bring up some refreshment, my lord?"

Before Cosma could open her rouged mouth, Francis shook his head. "No need, lad. Thank you. Now be gone and shut the door."

The young messenger nodded then scurried out, banging the door behind him.

Once they were alone, Cosma bestowed one of her sultry, catlike smiles upon him. Then she dropped her cloak and pirouetted for his inspection. Her high-waisted dress of gold tissue fell in soft folds around her ripe body. Her low neckline with its tiny white ruffle barely concealed her jutting nipples. Gold fringe edged her hemline that rose to knee level, revealing a scandalous expanse of her legs encased in sheer white stockings. Gold satin roses decorated her garters and shoe tops. Her auburn hair was piled high in fashionable ringlets with strings of pearls twined through her locks. Her heavy perfume of damask roses filled the room. Cosma had used every art at her command to enhance her endowments. Every revealing inch of her proclaimed that she had invaded his sanctuary with seduction in mind.

Cosma's wanton display turned Francis even colder. How completely artificial she looked compared to Jessica's natural beauty! "Forgive me," he said through tight lips. "I was asleep when you arrived."

Cosma's feline smile widened. "Then let us return to your sheets," she purred, "and I will give you dreams of paradise." She moved toward his rumpled bed.

Francis stepped in front of her. He would not allow her to carry out her obvious plan. Instead he pointed to the stool, the only seat in his sparse room. She ignored it.

"I am not in a sporting mood." He tied his neck bandstrings, then buttoned up his doublet to emphasize his lack of desire. "What do you want?"

Cosma licked her lips as if she savored honey. "You," she murmured in a husky tone. She reached for him. "I burn for you."

Francis stepped away from her. "Then I fear you must seek solace from another source. I have grown weary of you."

She pouted her lips in the most provocative manner she knew. "Then let me spark your interest again." She withdrew a lacy handkerchief from the reticule that hung from her girdle and dabbed her dry eyes. "You were not always so cruel to me. How can you treat me so shamefully when we are such good friends?" She tried to wrap herself around him.

Her touch made his flesh crawl. Grasping her hands by the wrists, he pulled them off his neck. "We were never friends, Cosma. It was merely a business arrangement that pleased us both for a time. Now that time has run its course."

True enough. Cosma had been delighted to introduce her new lover to her wide circle of acquaintants: merchants, councillors, sons of the nobility—in short everyone Francis needed to know for his work. He released her, then made a point of washing his hands at his basin as if touching her had defiled him. The ploy was cruel but Cosma would get the message. "You have done well enough by me," he continued, drying his fingers one by one. "I have heaped ducats by the handful in your lap."

Under her layer of cosmetics, Cosma paled with wrath. She glared at him with wide reproachful eyes. Fury choked her voice, turning her purr to a yowl. "Fie upon you! You have played false with me!"

Francis gave her a sardonic smile. "Sheath your claws, *gatta*. I was always true to you—as your, uh…client. In fact, I paid you double for your time and favors. It is *you* who has been false—to yourself." He stepped closer to her. "Look inside your heart. That is where you will find the lie."

Clenching her teeth, she ripped open her bodice. Several decorative pearls fell to the floor and bounced under the bed. Her nipples, hardened by her emotions, were heavily rouged in a color that nature had never intended. "Tell me, Francis, does your manroot play false with you when you behold these paps? Once you fell on your knees and worshiped them."

Francis winced at the memory. He had degraded himself for King Edward, England's merchant fleet and the glory of Saint George—not out of rapture for Cosma. Her breasts looked ridiculous in their artificial coloring. Barely moving his lips, he replied, "False idolatry."

She waggled her shoulders. Her breasts swayed ponderously. "Tell me, does that black-haired slut have such a

handsome pair of *tette* as these? Or are they as deformed
as her face?''

He glanced at her sharply, his eyes burning with his ire.

Cosma jutted out her chin. ''Not lain with her yet?'' she
sneered. ''Such virtue is commendable in Venice. Have you
even *seen* her face?'' she spat out with contempt.

Francis gritted his teeth. If he were less than a gentleman
he would toss this baggage out the window into the Grand
Canal. What a pleasing splash she would make!

She spread her mouth into a thin-lipped smile. ''I do not
blame Signorina Jessica for keeping you at a distance.'' Her
tone dropped to a more menacing note. ''Trust me, Francis,
to see her unmasked is to look upon the face of hell itself.''

At this attack on Jessica, Francis's careful control over
his emotions snapped. He exploded with anger. ''Get out!''

Cosma backed away from his towering wrath. She
snatched up her cloak from the floor and clutched it in front
of her like a shield. Her voice shook. ''You…will…
rue…those…words, Englishman,'' she spat. She dashed
hot tears real ones—from her eyes. ''I have many friends
in this city—more than you can imagine—who owe me a
favor or two. Jessica Leonardo is a piece of trash that needs
to be swept clean from Venice.''

Francis knotted his hands into fists behind his back. He
could not remember ever being so furious at a woman—
not even his feckless mother. ''Out!'' he bellowed.

Her sharp voice clawed him like talons. ''Jessica's very
presence fouls the air of our good city.''

Grabbing Cosma by her upper arms, Francis lifted her
off her feet. ''I give you fair warning, strumpet. Do nothing
to Donna Jessica. She is honest and pure—a state of grace
you will never enjoy.'' To keep himself from shaking her
like a rag poppet, he dropped her back to her feet and then
turned away.

"Is she so innocent?" Cosma snarled with contempt. "You have much to learn, my Lord Bardolph."

Startled by the menace in her voice, Francis whirled around to face her but Cosma had already slipped out the door, slamming it behind her.

Glad to be rid of her, Francis sank down on his bed. Absently, he rubbed his right shoulder. The old wound ached. As the red haze of his temper drained away, he considered Cosma's parting shot and he shuddered at her open threat against Jessica. Was this the danger that Jobe had foreseen? Francis glanced at the empty bed across the room.

Where the devil was Jobe, anyway?

By the time Cosma returned to her house, she had already formulated her plans. Francis was obviously snared in the wicked thrall of that black-haired witch. The sooner Jessica Leonardo met her just fate, the safer everyone in Venice would be—especially Francis. Once freed from his unholy infatuation of the sorceress, he would revert to his right senses and seek Cosma's favor again. Nothing was going to thwart Cosma's ambition—not even black magic. Feed Jessica to the flames or drown her in the lagoon; her ending made no difference to Cosma. Signorina Leonardo would be only a dim memory by the time Cosma embarked for England as the new Lady Bardolph.

"Nerissa!" Cosma shouted. She flung her cloak into a corner.

When the little maid appeared, she stared aghast at Cosma's torn gown and angry expression. "*¡Madonna!* What happened?"

Cosma sat down at her table. "Shut that prattling mouth, fool!" she snapped. "Fetch my writing portfolio and a bot-

tle of ink. Quit gaping at me! Have I turned green as old
brass?''

''*Sì*...no,'' the flustered girl replied. She dashed into
Cosma's antechamber to get the writing materials.

Cosma drummed her nails on the green velvet that covered the marble tabletop. She stared through her window
at the pink-and-white *palazzo* across the wide canal, though
she was blind to the delicate beauty of its Moorish archi-
tecture. Instead she pondered the words she would write to
the Council of Ten, Venice's feared governing body that
was responsible for the safety of the Republic. Several of
her former lovers were members of that most powerful
group. Once they learned Jessica's little secret and the danger that the woman posed to the welfare of the city, the
Council would waste no time in dispatching Cosma's rival.

When Nerissa returned with the ink and the leather portfolio that held Cosma's writing paper, pens and sealing
wax, her mistress sent her to the kitchen for wine and sugar
wafers.

Once alone Cosma dipped her quill into the ink, then
wrote, ''Most Honorable Lords of the Council of Ten....''

The words, fueled by her poison as well as by the ink,
spewed across the page. Cosma suggested that Jessica Leonardo, the daughter of a known *marrano,* Doctor Leonardo, had relapsed to the Jewish faith of her forebears—
a charge Cosma knew would spark the interest of the Holy
Office. Furthermore, she continued, Signorina Leonardo
bore an unsightly port-wine stain on one side of her face,
a sure sign of her relationship with the devil. Jessica possessed unusual powers to heal the body yet corrupt the
mind. She had already bewitched a visiting English lord.
Venice was not safe with such a powerful and evil witch
in its midst. The city must be purged before this godless

woman led any more souls down the pathway of perdition, she wrote.

Cosma reread her letter, mumbling the damning sentences under her breath. She smiled with satisfaction. *I will set down the words "treason" and "heresy" on this paper, as well. They should be enough to send the Council into a full cry for Jessica Leonardo's blood.*

The work completed, Cosma leaned back in her armchair and sipped the wine that Nerissa had brought. When the ink had dried, she folded the letter into quarters then dabbed a blob of glossy red wax to seal it. No name graced the bottom of the missive; no impression from a signet ring would denote the author. In Venice, this omission did not matter. It was up to Jessica to prove her innocence to the Council—if she could. Within a week, she would be dead. Cosma drained her glass and rang her silver bell to summon her maid.

"*Sì, madonna?*" Nerissa asked a moment later.

Cosma fanned herself with the folded letter. "Tell me, is Jacopo within the house?"

Nerissa dimpled. "He is in the garden, *madonna*, with the monkey."

Cosma curled her lip at the mere mention of the dratted furry beast. "Send Jacopo to me at once—without the monkey. Be quick!"

The maid whirled away toward the staircase. Cosma glanced down at the torn bodice she had not bothered to change. Should she cover herself before the boy arrived? She chuckled. No, the youth had become too swaggering of late. Time to bring him to heel, and what better way than by using her ample arsenal of charms? Sex always worked for her.

When Jacopo caught sight of her bare breasts, he nearly

fell over his large feet. Cosma pretended not to notice the lust in his eyes.

"Do you grow tried of my employment?" she asked.

Turning red as a radish, he stammered, "N-no, *madonna*, never!"

She stretched, arching her back to display her bust to its fullest advantage. "I am so glad to hear that, Jacopo. I had wondered. No matter, your task will soon be completed to our mutual satisfaction."

He inched closer to her. He practically salivated. "You will satisfy me, *madonna*?" He quivered with expectation.

Hiding her grin, Cosma sat up straighter. "Of course, if you prove your worth."

Jacopo licked his lips. "Try me, *madonna*."

She narrowed her eyes. "In due time, not before. Meanwhile, I want you to stay very close to Lord Bardolph—"

"I have been doing that for a fortnight," he complained.

Hating to be interrupted, Cosma glared at him. "Be even more vigilant. Danger stalks the alleyways of Venice."

The youth shrugged. "There is always danger in Venice. A misplaced step on a slippery quayside, a stiletto at midnight, a crack on the head—"

"*¡Basta!*" she said through her teeth. Jacopo was such a dolt. "Enough! You will make my head ache."

He threw himself to his knees. "Never, *madonna!*" He still could not wrench his gaze from her nipples.

Cosma cast a stern look at him. "Pay attention to *me*, you pantaloon, not to my paps."

He blinked but remained silent.

Cosma ran her finger around the blob of sealing wax on her letter. "Good. Listen to me very carefully, Jacopo. I speak of the Council of Ten."

The young *bravo* paled at the name. "Jesu!" he moaned.

Cosma nodded. "Exactly. You must insure that Lord

Bardolph stays out of any action taken by our officers of the law. Is that clear, Jacopo?"

He swallowed. "Do you anticipate that there will be trouble?"

She smiled at the letter in her hand. "I do indeed and it could happen very soon, perhaps even tonight."

"*¡Dio mio!*" he mumbled.

Cosma hurried on, eager to be rid of this groveling insect. "I do not care a fig for what may happen to Lord Bardolph's companions, including Jessica Leonardo or the African giant. But the Englishman is to remain safe from any fracas—even if you have to lock him up somewhere. Do you understand me, Jacopo?"

He pulled himself to his feet. "*Sì, madonna.*" He looked thoroughly unhappy.

Cosma realized that the boy needed some incentive. After all, Francis outweighed Jacopo by a good deal. The English lord could turn the slim *bravo* into a battered pulp if given cause. She rose, crossed the distance between them and kissed Jacopo full on the lips. For good measure she delved her tongue deep within his mouth. Before he could gather his paltry wits and press his presumed advantage, she pulled away from him and moved to the window. "Be gone, Jacopo, and pray, do not fail me."

"Never, *madonna!*" Panting heavily, he rushed from the room.

The winter's early twilight gathered outside her casement. Without calling for Nerissa's help, Cosma quickly shed her tattered golden gown and changed into a plain black one. Then she wrapped herself in her black velvet cloak. Once dressed and masked, she picked up the incriminating letter from her table. Taking pains to make no noise or to attract the attention of her servants, she slipped down the back stairs and exited her house through the tiny garden.

Cosma's heart beat with anticipation as her feet raced through the labyrinth of Venice's back streets. Already revelers emerged from their doorways eager for another evening of riotous celebration. Cosma joined a group until she had crossed the Rialto Bridge, then she fell behind the noisy crowd and continued alone toward her destination. Turning the corner into the Campo San Moise, she saw it—a *bocca di leone*, one of the stone lion's mouths that were scattered about the city. Looking like an ornamental bas-relief on the side of a building, the fanciful lion's head was in fact a post box for Venice's secret police. Sensitive information and denunciations like Cosma's could be dropped through its open mouth into a locked box. She knew that the boxes were emptied several times daily and that the letters were given immediate attention by the authorities. The *bocca di leone* had trapped many a transgressor in its jaws.

Cosma slowed to a walk. She ambled across the *campo* toward the letter drop. Just before reaching it, she paused and looked over her shoulder. No one was in sight. Her hands trembled. Cosma had never before used the *bocca*. She knew that once she dropped her letter, there was no turning back from the events she set into motion. Thinking of the future she craved, she summoned up her courage. The Cavendish fortune and family title were worth a hundred Jessicas.

With a quick flick of her wrist, she shoved the paper inside the lion's mouth. For a fleeting instant she had the uncomfortable feeling that its stone jaws would clamp down on her fingers. The letter rattled through the metal tube of the beast's throat then dropped into the hidden box. Cosma melted into the shadows of the nearby church.

Mischief, you are afoot. Take whatever course you will.

Chapter Thirteen

Shortly after Cosma left Francis, Jobe returned from his night-long revel, looking none the worse for wear. The African's cheerful expression darkened when Francis described his encounter with his former mistress.

Jobe made a sign against the evil eye that he had learned on his travels throughout England. "Madam di Luna is very bad juju," he warned.

Francis shook his head. "Cosma? She's an expensive whore, but dangerous? Nay, she is more of a danger to herself than to me."

Jobe shook his head. "Mark me, my friend. I see evil when I see her."

Francis chuckled. "Aye, she is a nasty piece of work but I can survive her claws."

Jobe shoved him backward onto the bed. "What do you know of women, scholar? Aye, you can swive them like the best of men, but what do you know of the species? Pah! Nothing!"

Francis narrowed his eyes. If he hadn't respected Jobe's opinion so much and if he didn't count him as his best friend, Francis would have challenged him for his ill treatment. "How now?" he asked.

Jobe lowered himself onto the stool. "What do you know of women?" he repeated, this time in a softer tone.

Francis rubbed his chin. "My mother, for one. She had not a brain in her head. She lived for her own pleasure, never caring whom she hurt like my stepfather, myself and my poor little half sisters."

Where were his Bardolph siblings now? A few had died in the sweating sickness epidemic of 1528; the rest were married and scattered among England's lesser nobility. When the Bardolph heir had come into the estate, he had made it plain to Francis that he never wanted to hear from his bastard brother again. No huge loss. Since the age of seven, when Francis had been fostered with the Cavendishes, he had rarely returned to Cloverdale. While he grew to manhood at Wolf Hall, Belle Cavendish was first his playmate, sometimes his nemesis, but always his most beloved sister.

He smiled when he thought of her. "Then there is Belle. You know what she is like."

Jobe rolled his eyes and grinned. "A wildcat, though she has softened since her marriage. Motherhood becomes her."

Francis winced inwardly when he thought of Belle's younger son, Tom. As an uncle and the boy's godfather, Francis had been sorely remiss. He shook away his guilty feelings. He would make it up to Tom in the future. "Belle has wit and cunning, I agree, but she does not have the stomach to plot serious harm. Neither does Lady Kat nor Lady Celeste nor even Lady Alicia, though all of them are highly intelligent women."

Jobe leaned closer so that his broad ebony face was inches away from Francis's. "If danger threatened the children of any of those sweet ladies, I warrant that you would be most surprised at the awesome fury those three could unleash. Listen to me well. While you spent your youth inside great universities, I traveled over much of the world and I have known the women of many countries. Each was different in character but one thing was common to them all. When their anger is aroused, women become more dangerous than men."

Francis laughed aloud. "You jest!"

Jobe did not blink. "Women have no sense of honor nor do they believe in a fair fight. They can turn an innocent toothpick into a deadly weapon. They are devious and have fine-tuned subterfuge into an art. Men with a quarrel will face each other in broad daylight. Women will poison you in the middle of the night. Aye, even good Lady Alicia would do so if her cubs were threatened. Trust me when I tell you that Cosma di Luna is your deadliest enemy."

By the set of Jobe's jaw, Francis realized that he spoke in earnest. "And Jessica?"

Jobe's black eyes glittered. "She is a dove in the thrall of a great snake. *That* much I am sure of."

Francis's stomach knotted with cold fear—not for himself but for sweet Jessica's sake. "Methinks tis time that I quit this fantastical city, Jobe. Let Secretary Cecil send someone else to ferret out its dark secrets."

The black giant grinned. "Your thoughts and mine are twins. In fact, I have been on my ship since early morn getting it provisioned for a long sea voyage. The victualing will take another day or two. Then we can sail away for England."

Francis stood and stretched. "Aye, the sooner the better, and we will take Donna Jessica with us."

Jobe nodded. "Methought we would."

Francis rubbed his bristly chin. He hunted for his razor and leather strop amid the clutter on the table. "In the meantime, I will settle my affairs here in the leisurely manner that befits an idle gentleman.''

Jobe grunted. ''Do not linger in your leave-taking. I sense that danger is much closer than you think.''

Francis lathered up his face. ''Aye, good friend, but I doubt that it will arrive while I am shaving.''

Jobe did not share his good humor.

Francis shaved in silence while his mind hummed with myriad plans for his departure. As soon as he completed his ablutions and changed into fresh hose and a clean shirt, he clapped the brooding giant on the shoulder.

''Let us be off to the Rialto for food. Both my stomach and my mind are famished. And,'' he added with a rueful smile, ''if I am going to return to England, I had best arrive at Wolf Hall laden with gifts.''

Jobe grinned. Shopping always cheered him up. Francis shelved his friend's ominous warnings. Let danger come when it will. For the time being he had other things to do.

After crossing the bridge, his first stop was at a confectioner's stall. With the help of a silver scudo, Francis quickly dispatched a willing urchin to Jessica's house. The boy carried a paper cone filled with sugared almonds and the message that Francis would come at eight in that evening.

''Tell Signorina Jessica that tonight is *Giovedi Grosso,* Fat Thursday, and she cannot miss the Flight of the Turk,'' he instructed his young messenger. ''I hear that is an awesome sight.''

The child gave him a gap-toothed grin. ''*Sì, messere.* I myself have seen it. Truly it is a wonder.''

Francis smiled. The boy didn't look much older than his godson Tom. Now that Francis had made up his mind to leave Venice, he found that thoughts of England had sharpened his desire to return to Wolf Hall, the home he had not visited for over seven years.

After the boy dashed away on his Cupid's errand, Francis sauntered around the marketplace, exchanging greetings with acquaintants. At the goldsmith's he drew on his letter of credit for more ducats. Since he planned to leave Venice in the near future he did not have to worry any longer about husbanding Lord Cecil's funds. Heeding the grumbling of his stomach, he and Jobe sought temporary escape from the chill wind that blew off the Adriatic Sea beyond Venice's lagoon. In a dingy wine shop located on a small side street, they consumed large portions of fried sardines and onions marinated in vinegar followed by a dish of tripe stew served with slabs of fried *polenta*. When Francis caught sight of Jacopo lurking in a dark corner of the shop, he sent him a dish of the sardines with his compliments. Francis had taken a liking to his young shadow.

Fortified by their repast and with money in their pouches, Jobe and Francis continued their leisurely excursion amid the vendors in the Campo San Giacomo di Rialto. They bought lengths of colorful silks for the Cavendish ladies as well as for Jobe's wives. Francis grinned when he spied the beggar that huddled on the church's porch against the bite of the wind. He fished out a coin from his pouch.

"Buon giorno, Giulio," he greeted the ragged man.

Giulio, the blind beggar of the Rialto, had the eyesight of a fox and the keen hearing of a bat. His tatters and filth cloaked his true identity. Though he pretended to be Venetian-born, Giulio was in fact a Genoan of indeterminate age and background who had lived in London during most of his youth and now served as an agent of the English crown. Giulio was the only other person in Venice besides Jobe who knew Francis's secret mission. The beggar was both a repository of information and Francis's one slim link to England.

Giulio did not look at Francis but smiled nevertheless. "You are abroad late today, my lord."

Jobe grunted. "He was carousing until the roosters crowed."

The beggar cocked his head. "You have brought a friend, *messere?*" he asked in an offhand manner. "Does he, too, have a generous heart?" He shook his wooden bowl that held a few copper soldi.

As he had often done before, Francis admired Giulio's acting ability. Without directly looking at the giant, the shrewd beggar probably knew almost as much about Jobe as Francis did.

"This is my boon companion, Jobe the African," Francis replied.

"I am master of the *Jinn,*" Jobe added with a note of pride in his voice. "The finest vessel afloat in the lagoon."

Giulio grinned. "I am honored, *capitano.* Your formidable reputation precedes you. I understand that your most recent voyage netted you a great profit from your Egyptian cotton and sugar as well as the olive oil, wines and sweet honey from Greece."

Jobe chuckled. "It appears that you know my manifest better than my quartermaster."

Giulio's smile grew wider. "And the peppercorns, cloves and ginger root that you, uh… Shall we say you *relieved* those items from a wayward Turkish merchant?"

Jobe laughed. "*Sì,* enlightened one, you could say that. By the beard of my father," he added to Francis in English, "this fellow is a fortune-teller."

Understanding him perfectly, Giulio chuckled.

Francis leaned against one of the church pillars and

crossed his ankles. "What's the news on the Rialto?" he asked casually.

The beggar wet his lips. "One of the ships belonging to the merchant Antonio Solanio limped into the lagoon early this morning. She had been attacked by the Barbary pirates and the captain had to ransom their lives with the cargo. Signor Solanio has suffered a great loss, I hear, and he is in a raging temper."

Francis whistled through his teeth. He had met the wealthy merchant at several social occasions. "Those Turkish rogues are a plague," he agreed.

Giulio held up his finger. "They grow bolder daily. The wind carries a rumor," he added.

Francis pricked his ears. Giulio had just uttered the code for divulging information that would interest England's Secretary of State. "The wind carries much trash," Francis replied, acknowledging the beggar's signal.

"They say that certain factions in the Republic *pay* the Turkish pirates to raid the vessels belonging to the Dutch, the Portuguese—and the English." Giulio named Venice's three strongest competitors for trade in the Mediterranean and the New World.

"The Turks do not care whom they pillage as long as it is a rich prize," Jobe rumbled under his breath.

Giulio nodded. "True, great one, but the prize becomes even more desirable when it is sweetened by the coffers of Venice."

Francis pretended to study the sky. "Is this wind a strong one?" he asked.

Giulio shrugged. "So I have heard it from the lips of a gentleman who should not speak of such things outside the Doge's palace."

Francis digested this nugget. He would add it to his

report. "I find that my time grows stale in this city," he remarked over his shoulder.

Giulio chuckled. "You are wise, my lord. Venice is very dull during the season of Lent." He spat onto the paving stones. "Forty days of *radicchio*, bread crusts and rainwater."

Francis pursed his lips. "My thoughts exactly, ragged friend. How fare your pigeons these days?" he inquired.

Giulio tended a flock of swift carrier birds that were supplied to him periodically by English ship captains in the pay of Lord Cecil. These marvelous pigeons carried tiny messages in canisters strapped to their legs while they flew across the Alps to their home dovecote somewhere near the port of Marseilles in the south of France. From there the information was given to a loyal postboy who rode a series of swift horses through the French countryside to Calais on the Channel. There the missive was passed to the captain of a certain English packet boat who sailed with it to Dover. A message sent today from Venice could arrive on Cecil's desk in London within a fortnight—God willing and if the weather was good.

Giulio considered the question. "I hear the snow still falls in the Dolomites. My children hate winter storms."

Francis dropped a ducat into the beggar's bowl. "Fatten up your best," he told his confederate. "Tell the wind that I plan to seek other climes that are more conducive to my health."

Giulio felt for the coin. When he found it, he made a show of biting it to test its worth, though he knew perfectly well what Francis had given him. "You are wise and generous as always, my lord. In faith, I will starve after you are gone."

With a laugh, Francis pushed himself off the pillar. "I doubt that, my friend. *Arrivederci*."

To Giulio's surprise, Jobe added a scudo to Francis's alms. "Henceforth, I will be your patron. Remember me."

Giulio chuckled. "How could I not? You are already unforgettable."

Francis spent the remainder of the day's waning light visiting more shops. At the printers, he purchased a cheap copy of a Latin grammar book. Tomorrow he would write out his full report to Cecil between the lines of the text using an invisible ink made from citrus juice. He stopped at the bookbinders where he paid for the beautiful book he had ordered for Sir Thomas. *I will keep this myself in remembrance of him.*

At a shop that sold the exquisite glass goods made by the incomparable artisans of Murano, Francis bought a lavish array of ornaments, mirrors, and jewelry for the bevy of Cavendish women whom he loved deeply but had not seen in years. He also purchased a beautiful but deadly glass stiletto. Lord Cecil would be interested to study this unusual weapon that the Venetian *bravi* used primarily for stealthy assassinations. Once the glass dagger had penetrated the body of its victim, the attacker broke off the handle, leaving the rest of the dagger to work its lethal way to the victim's heart. If poison filled the hollow blade, death was almost instantaneous or agonizingly prolonged, depending upon the nature of the vile substance used.

The last stop was Titian's studio where Bassanio had promised that his portrait would be ready. Glowing with pride, the young painter conducted Francis and Jobe to a covered easel.

Bassanio rubbed his hands together with anticipation. "My master is most pleased with the work, *messere*. It is my pleasure to present you to yourself." With a flourish he pulled away the muslin, then stepped back.

Francis went rigid at the sight. His blood pounded in his

ears. His breath caught in his throat while his hands grew cold as ice.

Noting his change of color, Bassanio chewed his fingernail. "*Per favore,* my lord? You do not like it?"

Francis did not trust himself to speak. The artist had exactly caught the posture and the expression of Sir Guy Cavendish as a younger man. The likeness was perfect in every detail.

Oh, Mother! You did not lie—for once.

Jobe hung his arm around Francis's shoulder. To the trembling Bassanio, he said, "Forgive my friend. As you can see, he is struck dumb with delight for indeed you have not only painted his face but his very soul, as well."

Bassanio looked from Jobe to Francis. "This is true, Lord Bardolph? You are pleased?"

Jobe dug his thumb into Francis's shoulder and whispered in English, "Tell the lad how much you like his work before he expires from anxiety."

"God's teeth!" Francis muttered under his breath, also in English. "Do I really look like…like him?"

Jobe stared into his eyes. "Aye, *meo amigo,* you are Sir Guy's mirror image."

Francis shook off Jobe's arm and advanced to take a closer look at the picture. He resisted the urge to tear it to shreds. Later, when he was alone, he would do it. "How long have I looked like this?" he asked Jobe.

The African sighed. "As long as I have known you, though the likeness is more pronounced since you came to manhood."

Francis studied the face that seemed to study his own in return as if the painted visage were equally as surprised to see its reflection in Francis.

"Why did no one tell me?" he asked Jobe. "Surely the Cavendish family must have seen the truth. Lady Alicia, for one. She has the eye of an eagle and the wit to match two and two.''

Jobe lifted a brow. "When was the last time you visited Wolf Hall?''

Too long ago—years. Ever since the day that his mother had told him the name of his natural father. After that, Francis did not dare to look into the blue eyes of that beloved family. He could not bear to be the cause of hurt or dissension among the people who had made their home his home. He especially wanted to avoid Guy's wife, Lady Celeste. She had been kindness itself to him when he was a lonesome child. Only Belle had seen Francis during his brief periodic visits to Lord Cecil in London. Why hadn't she told him?

When Francis did not answer, Jobe nodded. "As I suspected.'' He nudged him. "Come, say something nice to the artist. I swear he will begin to weep buckets at any moment if you do not.''

Francis blinked, then pulled himself together and resumed his dandified role. "Forgive me, Bassanio. You have created a masterpiece. I am quite undone by it.'' *That* was God's own truth! He kissed the tips of his fingers in an expression of highest approval. *"¡Magnifico! ¡Splendido!''* he rhapsodized. "I cannot *wait* to hang it in my hall.''

The young artist exploded with relief and rapture. He leaped at Francis, hugged him and kissed him on both cheeks. He repeated his effusive display of gratitude to Jobe. The other artists in the large studio joined Bassanio. They applauded him, slapped him on the back and called for wine.

All Francis wanted to do was bundle up the thing and flee with it. He pasted on a cheerful expression. "Alas, I cannot stay. We have an engagement—most pressing.

But—'' He opened up his nearly empty pouch. ''Allow me to pay for your celebration. Here!''

He tossed a few ducats to the nearest apprentice who looked as if he might faint. Francis had paid enough for several caskets of excellent wine. To the beaming Bassanio, he counted out the portrait fee plus a generous tip. The artist kissed him again.

While Francis watched with concealed disgust, the painting was carefully wrapped in many layers of sacking, then a wooden case was nailed around it. As soon as this tedious chore was completed, Jobe hefted the painting onto his broad shoulder.

''Trust me, young painter, I will take good care of this.''

With more slobbering compliments, Bassanio showed his patrons out the door. Once back in the street, Francis set off at a quick pace. ''Pitch that horror into the nearest canal,'' he told Jobe.

The African shook his head. ''Nay, it would float too well. The good Bassanio would be devastated if he found out—and you know that he would sooner or later. Besides I gave my promise to take care of it.''

Francis ground his teeth. ''Very well. Just keep the thing out of my sight. It offends my eyes.''

Jobe chuckled. ''It will be aboard my ship before suppertime. But you speak falsely when you say it offends.''

Francis glared at him. ''How now?''

''In truth, it frightens the very devil out of you,'' Jobe observed.

Chapter Fourteen

Sophia rapped on Jessica's bedroom door, then peered around it. "He's here," she announced with a wide grin.

Jessica put her hairbrush down on the table. "I know. I saw them come across the square from my window." Her hands felt very cold. "How does he seem?" Was he still angry at her rebuff when he had asked her to remove her mask? She touched the unsightly stain on her face. "Is he in a gladsome mood?"

Sophia came into the room and stood behind Jessica. She took up the brush and added a few more firm strokes through Jessica's glossy black locks. "As merry as a schoolboy released from his books," she replied. "And impatient to see you."

Jessica relaxed her shoulders. "I feared that he might not call again."

Sophia giggled. "Have you forgotten his gift of sweet nuts? Mmm! Delicious!" She smacked her lips at the remembrance.

Jessica smiled up at her cherished friend. "No, Sophia, I did not, but still…" She creased her forehead into a small frown. "I did displease him."

Sophia dropped a light kiss on the top of her head. "How

could he fail to be pleased with you? You are one of God's own angels come to earth. Now hand me that red ribbon—and the yellow one, as well.''

Jessica toyed with her fingers while Sophia wove the colorful strips of satin through her hair. A fluttering sensation rose in the pit of her stomach when she thought of being with Francis again. She tried to throttle the dizzy current of excitement that raced through her, but to no avail. She couldn't wait to see him—and yet, what if he tried to unmask her when they were alone?

Sophia stepped back to admire her handiwork. "Perfect! You look like a Gypsy in your red and green skirt. The little golden bells on your sleeves are a stroke of genius.''

Jessica jingled her wristlets. "Perhaps we will dance the *moresca* again,'' she mused.

Sophia gave her a prod. "You will do no dancing at all if you continue to sit on that stool. Up, up, child! Time does not wait while maidens dream.''

Jessica rose, tied on her mask, double knotting it under her hair. Then she draped her long cloak over her shoulders and took up the pair of doeskin gloves that Francis had given to her earlier in the week. The evening was already chilly and promised to grow colder. Smiling at Sophia, she swept out of the door and descended the narrow stairs.

"*Buona sera,* my lords,'' she greeted Francis and Jobe in her antechamber.

Sophia followed behind her, clucking like a mother hen. "Good evening, my lords. Now I pray that you do not keep my young mistress out so late tonight. Why, she could barely open her eyes all day.''

Jessica blushed under her mask. "Hush, Sophia!''

Francis swept a truncated bow, being somewhat constrained by the small size of the room. "A thousand pardons, Madam Sophia,'' he apologized, though he had eyes only for Jessica. "It will not happen tonight, I promise you."

Jessica's cheeks grew even hotter under the heat of his devouring gaze. Dressed entirely in white satin and gold lace, he looked even more stunningly handsome than she had remembered. It was as if the Archangel Gabriel had come to call. Her heart hammered against her ribs.

"It is good to see you again, my lord...I mean, Francis," she babbled.

His smile lit up the room. "And I to see you, *madonna*," he murmured to her alone. Then he looked over her shoulder to Sophia. "You should come with us—you and Gobbo. I understand that this Flight of the Turk is a most unusual spectacle."

For a moment Jessica feared that Sophia would accept Francis's generous invitation, then she chided herself for wanting to deny her friends a little pleasure. Relief flooded her when Sophia giggled and declined the offer.

"*Grazie, messere,* but we will find our own amusements." She flapped her little hands at Jessica and her two giant escorts. "Now, go! Away with you! Enjoy, enjoy!"

Jobe grinned down at her. "You are indeed the very mistress of the revels, Madam Sophia. We will obey your command." He slipped on a white half mask over his dark face. Then he flung open the door and signaled their torch-bearers.

Francis took Jessica's hand in his. "Fear not," he said to Sophia over his shoulder. "I will return her early—right after the fireworks at midnight."

"Good!" replied Sophia with mock indignation. "Jessica has several patients to see in the morning. Now go! Go! You waste the torchlight!"

Jessica waved her farewell to Sophia, then with steps lightened by the love she felt for the tall man at her side, she skipped across the *campo* while their torchbearers serenaded them.

This time they did not amble up and down Venice's maze of winding streets. Instead the party hurried directly toward the Piazza San Marco to be in time to witness one of Venice's more unusual pre-Lenten traditions. Francis held Jessica close against him while Jobe kept pace on her other side. The feel of Francis's body heat, the scent of his clove musk, the low timbre of his singing voice lulled Jessica into a state bordering on euphoria—as if she had drunk an elixir of poppy seed. Every time she looked up at Francis, she saw that he was gazing at her tenderly. What a goose she had been to fear his motives! She could tell that he would never seek to harm her. A strange exhalation filled her to the brim. She trembled with happiness.

I shall remember this night all my life—no matter what happens.

They heard the roar of the crowds in the huge square long before they entered it. It seemed as if all Venice had gathered in this one spot. Francis put his arm around her, pulling her even closer to him. She reveled in his nearness and in the magic of the night.

A thin silver crescent of the moon hung over the Moorish domes of the basilica. The *piazza* blazed with firelight. Wordlessly, Jobe pointed to the top of the tall bell tower that stood opposite the Doge's pink confection of a palace. Jessica stood on her tiptoes. She could just make out the figure of a thin little man dressed in a pair of gaudy tights.

Francis whispered in her ear. "Hold my hands tight, *cara mia.*"

Before she had time to wonder what he meant, he lifted Jessica above the heads of the people and set her on his good shoulder. A cry of surprise and delight trilled from her lips. Clinging to his strong hands, she surveyed the scene around her. From her perch, she saw that a narrow wire was strung between the top of the campanile and the Doge's balcony. Just then a fanfare of silver trumpets announced the arrival of Venice's most important citizen, His Most Serene Highness, Doge Francesco Donato.

Jessica easily spied him amid a flock of red-robed councillors that clustered on the palace's loggia. The Doge's purple gown was covered with a magnificent golden cape and a pure white stole. More gold embroidery decorated his cap of office, the *corno,* and the precious jewels set in his headband flashed in the light of a thousand torches. Jessica had never before set eyes on this awesome personage and the sight of him now both thrilled and frightened her. The Doge *was* Venice, representing the great Republic's power and wealth. She gasped under her breath.

Jobe again pointed to the little man in the bell tower. "Watch now," he told her, "and you will see the most marvelous *Volo del Turco*—the Flight of the Turk."

Even as Jobe spoke, the little man saluted the huge crowd over three hundred feet below him, then he climbed to the rail of the tower's balcony. Jessica squeezed Francis's hands even tighter when the acrobat stepped onto the thin wire. An assistant handed him a nosegay of bright-colored flowers. The noise in the *piazza* suddenly ceased. All eyes watched the little man. The spectators seemed to breathe as one.

Holding out his arms for balance, the fearless acrobat steadied himself. Slowly at first, then gaining speed, the man slid down the long wire. As he neared the palace balcony, the crowd began to roar its approval. With cool aplomb, the wire-walker stepped onto the palace railing and, with a flourish seen in the farthest corners of the *piazza,* he presented the nosegay to the Doge. This extraordinary feat had taken less than two minutes to complete.

Jessica joined in the tumultuous cheers. Never had she seen anything so daring in her life! When Francis set her back on her feet she impulsively threw her arms around him.

"I am amazed and know not what to say!" she exclaimed.

Francis returned her smile. "Then say nothing, *cara.* I will stop up your mouth with this."

Lowering his head, his last words were smothered on her lips; his kiss achingly gentle. Spirals of ecstasy whirled through her. She rose on tiptoe and wound her arms around his neck. His moist, firm mouth demanded a response and she happily surrendered herself to the pleasure of the moment, drinking in the sweetness of his kiss. The bedlam in the *piazza* receded from her hearing; the jostling crowds melted into shadows. Shivers of pure delight accompanied his touch. She felt transported high above the noisy square.

Someone bumped against them, breaking their embrace. When they parted, Jessica's lips burned with his passion. She raised her eyes to find Francis watching her. His scorching gaze probed her very soul. A new, deeper emotion awoke within her breast. Her breath came in short gasps.

"Your pardons, *Sior Maschera*," mumbled a drunken youth costumed as Apollo in a golden mask and expensive satins. "The young lady looks delicious," he added with a slur in his voice.

Francis draped his cloak around Jessica, effectively shielding her from the wine-soaked intruder. "*Sì, Sior Maschera*," he returned the nobleman's traditional carnival salutation. "She is and she is mine."

Jessica's heart swelled with pride. No one had ever desired to possess her. She bit the inside of her cheek. Its pain reminded her that Francis did not yet know her shameful secret. He wouldn't lay a claim on her so quickly if he thought she was the devil's spawn. Enjoy the moment, she advised herself. Do not think of tomorrow for it will come soon enough.

Jobe stepped between the two men. "Hark, my friends! The music begins again! This is not the time for idle chatter, but for dancing. Go to!" With that he spun the drunk around a few times, then headed him in the opposite direction.

"Poor man," murmured Jessica watching him lurch through the crowd. "He will have his punishment in due time."

Francis drew closer to her. "How so, *cara mia?*"

She laughed. "He who gets mad drunk offends himself in three ways. He harms his body, he harms his soul and—" She gave a little shrug. "He loses all the wine that he spent his money to consume."

Francis brushed his lips across her forehead. "So wise and yet so fair," he whispered in her ear. His breath was hot on her cheek.

Then he cleared his throat. "Let us not waste the beauty of your bells, lovely Jessica," he said, touching her sleeve. He pulled her cape back over her shoulders and did the same with his, revealing their festival attire to the admiring eyes of the nearby revelers. "Let us dance until our feet grow numb."

Jessica gave him both her hands. "An excellent idea, Francis. Then tomorrow, I can soothe your blistered toes with my ointments," she teased.

His eyes blazed with indigo fire. "My body will be yours to command."

His thinly veiled suggestion weakened her knees. Jessica was thankful that he held her so tightly or she knew she would have collapsed. With an exuberant shout to the cold starry sky, Francis set her twirling in time with the music. The hours of the night flew by as if they, too, danced with the same wild abandon that Jessica felt in her heart.

At midnight, showers of fireworks rose up from the Grand Canal. The people of Venice greeted each display of gold and silver stars with gasps of delight and cheers of approval. Jessica joined in their applause.

Where have I been all my life while wonderful things like this were happening? What a fool I have been to hide behind my little blue door and let life walk by me.

Taking Francis's hand in hers, she kissed it. "Thank you for opening my shell," she whispered.

He leaned over her. "You spoke, *cara?*"

She swallowed the bubble of happiness that knotted in the back of her throat. "Thank you for bringing me here tonight," she said in a louder voice.

Francis threw back his head and laughed. "It is I who should be thanking you, *madonna*. You have saved me from myself."

His words and the look in his eyes filled her with inexpressible joy.

Jobe tapped Francis on the shoulder. "The witching hour has come. Remember your promise to Madam Sophia. I, for one, do not wish to incite the dragon that lurks within that plump pigeon's breast."

Francis nodded. "*Sì*, my friend. I am glad that one of us is still thinking clearly." He lifted Jessica's hand to his lips and kissed it softly. "Come, *madonna* of my heart. I will take you home."

"And we will sing a lullaby under your window," Jobe added.

Jessica joined in their merriment. "My neighbors will be delighted to hear your voice again, Francis. Indeed, they have asked me why you have not sung recently."

"Did you tell them that I have been too busy dancing instead?" he bantered.

Jobe carved a pathway for them through the dense crowd. Laughing, they stepped between the arches below the elaborate clock tower that chimed a quarter past midnight. Just as they turned into a narrow street that led toward the Rialto, a dozen men dressed in dark clothing surrounded them. Jobe drew two of his knives from his bandoleer.

"*Bravi!*" he shouted.

Francis drew his sword. "Keep close behind me, Jessica."

With swift professional dispatch, two of the men disarmed Jobe while a third held a dagger's point to his throat. The leader of the group advanced toward Francis. He held out his hands to show that he was unarmed. The spill of light from a nearby upstairs window revealed the badge of office that hung about his neck. Jessica whispered a prayer under her breath. This man was one of the dreaded Lords of the Night, Venice's secret police.

"Put down your weapon, my Lord Bardolph," he said in a pleasant voice. "I see that you recognize me."

"I do, my Lord Gratiano," Francis replied, though he did not relax his defensive stance.

The man smiled. "I fear I must relieve you of your companion, *messere.*"

"Jobe has done nothing against the city of Venice," Francis replied.

Still smiling, the dark lord shook his head. "Alas, you misunderstand me, my lord. It is the woman cowering behind you that I seek."

Jessica clutched Francis's cloak. Her stomach ached as if the breath had been knocked out of her. Her vision clouded and the street spun around her. *Mother of God, save me!*

"Jessica Leonardo," the man continued. "I arrest you in the name of the Council of Ten for high treason against the state. Seize her!"

"No!" Jessica screamed as two of the guards grabbed her from behind. Her cry echoed off the walls of the shuttered houses. Windows rattled open and curious heads popped out to see the disturbance.

"There has been a mistake," Francis protested. Another guard relieved him of his sword.

The Lord of the Night shook his head. "The Council does not take treason lightly, Englishman. There is no mistake."

Jessica clung to Francis's cloak but the guards painfully pried off her fingers. "I am no traitor!" she shouted to their leader. "Who dares to say that I am?"

Lord Gratiano shrugged. "Who am I to know the details? My orders are to deliver you to the Council, not to ask questions."

Jessica struggled against her captors. "Francis, I beseech you!"

He knotted his fists. Jobe, still pinioned against a wall by the guards, shouted to him in English. Francis snapped a reply. Jobe said something else. Jessica recognized her name. Francis dropped his head to his chest and muttered a word that Jessica thought was an oath—or a prayer?

He stepped to one side, then turned to her. He looked ashen under his white mask. "Jessica, I am sorry," he croaked.

White-hot rage overrode her terror. "Vile betrayer!" She shot him a withering glare. "You have played me for a fool and I, that willing fool, believed you!" She pelted him with harsh words, wishing they were stones. "Why pretend to be sorry? You have kept your appointment with this man marvelously well.''

How right she had been in the first place! This so-called nobleman was indeed one of those scheming Jesuits. All the time he sent her gifts and called her endearing names, he sought to trap her. Did her kisses make him gag? How had he guessed about the mark on her face? Or had they discovered her father's lapse in his religion? Either way, she was doomed. No one that went before the Council of Ten emerged to freedom.

Jessica shook with her impotent rage—and her fear. ''You are as false as sand!'' Her growing fury rendered her practically speechless. Hot tears welled up in her eyes.

Francis stood stock-still as if he were chiseled in marble. ''Forgive me, Jessica,'' he finally said.

She curled her lips with disdain. ''Must all men kill the things that they do not understand or love?'' Her low voice filled with accusation, stabbed the cold night air.

His great shoulders shook—with mirth? ''Jobe reminds me that I am a stranger in your city. I cannot meddle in the affairs of Venice.''

Lord Gratiano nodded. ''The Ethiope is wise for an infidel; he gives you good advice. Quit this place, my Lord Bardolph. Return to your room at the Sturgeon and think no more of this strumpet. She is nothing but chaff in the wind and you are well rid of her.''

Francis clenched his hands at his sides. He did not look at Jessica. When he spoke, he broke her heart. ''You are right, my lord. I have had my pleasure with her, but that is over now.''

Jessica's breath burned in her throat. She thought she would gag on her bile. A loud roaring swelled in her ears. The Lord of the Night snapped his fingers. His guards dragged Jessica back through the clock tower arch.

She screamed over her shoulder, "May you rot in hell for this, Francis Bardolph!"

The still figures of Jobe and Francis receded from her sight. Jessica was only vaguely aware of the jeers of the carnival crowds as she was pulled through them. The Doge's palace, obscene in its pastel beauty, loomed ahead.

Jessica's anger drained away from her, leaving her weak with despair. Betrayed! Abandoned! Alone! Heartsick, the anguish of her plight almost overwhelmed her self-control. Hysteria bubbled up inside her and threatened to erupt in a mad frenzy. Jessica bit her lower lip until it throbbed with pain. She tasted the salt of her blood.

Her feet refused to move of their own accord as the guards pulled her up the wide marble staircase that led into the palace. She did not notice the magnificence of the gilded, frescoed chambers that they dragged her through. Nothing mattered to her now but her survival.

Chapter Fifteen

Jacopo had followed the Englishman out of the *piazza* so closely that he nearly stumbled into one of the hidden men-at-arms that accompanied the Lord of the Night. Thanking his guardian saint for protecting him in time, the youth slipped into deep shadows between two houses. Cosma had warned him that there was danger afoot—but this? The young *bravo* shivered. He had no wish to attract the attention of the minions who worked for the Council of Ten. Yet he must protect Lord Bardolph. Jacopo quaked inside his thin cloak. Madonna Cosma had asked the impossible.

The confrontation between the nightwatch and the English lord lasted only a few minutes, but to Jacopo it seemed like an hour. For an uncomfortable moment, he thought that Lord Bardolph would attack the men who held Donna Jessica in their grip. The aspiring *bravo* drew his stiletto and waited. He had no idea how he could protect Cosma's lover when even the mighty African had been so easily disarmed. The youth tasted his raw fear in the back of his throat.

Fortunately Jobe said something in English that held Lord Bardolph in check. Jacopo sagged with relief against the clammy stone of the building behind him. Then the men-at-arms dragged away that poor girl. The youth knew that she would be imprisoned in the depths of the *prigione*—a vile dungeon that Jacopo prayed to never see for himself.

Once the Lord of the Night and his prisoner had departed the scene, Jobe and the nobleman conversed in low voices, then they turned and headed down the street toward the Rialto Bridge. Jacopo followed as closely as he dared. He had no wish to walk into another ambush amid the winding streets. The pair did not halt their fast pace until they entered the Sturgeon Inn on the far side of the bridge.

Skulking on the bank of the Grand Canal, Jacopo pondered his next move. Should he linger here until the dawn or could he presume that Lord Bardolph had had enough excitement for one night? The image of Doctor Leonardo's treasure chest danced in his head. Surely the news of Jessica's arrest would soon reach the ears of both her father and those dwarves with whom she lived. Judging Jessica's father to be prudent as well as greedy, Jacopo knew that the doctor would no doubt hurry to her house to retrieve his treasure.

The youth turned away from the canal. Lord Bardolph did not need the boy's vigilant watch while he tossed on his bed. The time had come for Jacopo to take his future into his own hands.

He slipped away through the dark streets like one of Venice's alley cats. Within fifteen minutes he stood outside Jessica's house. The lantern by her door was lit in expectation of its owner's return. The rest of the house was dark.

Jacopo cast a furtive look around the square. All was quiet, even the dogs. He lifted the latch and grinned when he discovered it was unlocked. How foolish were those servants of hers! Casting another glance over his shoulder, Jacopo slipped inside the silent dwelling.

* * *

A heavy pounding on his door interrupted Doctor Leonardo's slumbers. When he opened the window and thrust out his head to investigate the source of the disturbance, a young boy shouted up to him.

"Come quick, doctor!" the child babbled in a loud voice made more shrill by his excitement. "Your daughter has been arrested by the Lords of the Night. They have taken her to the palace."

The doctor's neighbors on both sides opened their windows. Without giving the messenger a reply, Stefano ducked back inside his bedroom and slammed the shutters against each other. Lucia, his timid wife, clutched her blanket closer to her sagging bosom.

"What did he say?" she asked.

Stefano groped for his dark gray robe and his street shoes. "Something about Jessica," he replied in a brusque manner.

Lucia would learn of their daughter's arrest soon enough. The doctor had no time to deal with his wife's wailing now. His only thought was the casket that was hidden under Jessica's bed. It was only a matter of time before the authorities would search her house for incriminating evidence. What would she tell them about the chest—and its damning contents? Stefano's hands trembled as he pulled on his hose.

"Is Jessica ill?" Lucia asked in a thin voice.

Her husband ignored her. Speed was of the essence, not idle prattle.

Lucia asked again, "What is the matter with her?"

"I don't know," Stefano snapped over his shoulder. "But I am going to find out." He jammed his cap over his disheveled hair, then he glared at his wife. "Under no circumstances will you admit anyone to this house. Do you understand me, Lucia? No matter which neighbor is outside, keep the door barred.''

She stifled a cry. "Is Jessica in trouble?"

"Jessica has always been trouble," he growled. "She was marked with misfortune from the moment of her birth. I should have drowned her."

Leaving his wife to weep into her pillow, the doctor dashed downstairs and out the door. He ignored the neighbors' questions. Busybodies all of them! His mind concentrated on the contents of the chest. His wife's precious gold-and-turquoise ring lay beside his silver kaddish cup and menorah. That cup, candlestick and Tubal's Hebrew books would leave no doubt of the doctor's lapsed faith in the minds of the Council of Ten. In his imagination, Doctor Leonardo saw all the profits of his hard work evaporate. He could almost feel the flames of a heretic's bonfire licking his shins. All because of his cursed daughter and her wanton disregard for his rules! Stefano swore under his breath.

When he reached her *campo,* his heart plummeted. A half dozen torchbearers lit up the square. Jessica's house blazed with lights in every window. In the street, Sophia and Gobbo were held in custody by men dressed in the somber uniforms of the nightwatch. Sophia wept loudly on her diminutive husband's shoulder while Gobbo stared straight ahead, his face like flint.

"We know nothing!" she wailed. "Oh, my poor lamb! What have you done with our mistress?"

The guard grunted something that caused Sophia to weep afresh.

The doctor pressed himself against the nearest wall and prayed that he had not been seen. Just then two more watchmen emerged from the house. One held a struggling, nondescript youth in his tight grip; the other carried the damning chest under his arm. A droplet of cold sweat rolled down the doctor's spine. The dwarf was sure to tell whose property it was. How much time did Stefano have to flee Venice before the Inquisition issued a warrant for his arrest? A few hours at most. Would Jessica betray him outright or would they have to torture the information from her lips? Torture would buy him more time.

Be true to me, daughter!

Stefano did not linger at the scene. Pulling his dark cloak tightly around him, he sped from the square. Sophia's shrieks echoed behind him. A mask! As much as he had eschewed such Christian frivolities in the past, the carnival revels would be his salvation. He would melt into the crowd of merrymakers then hire a gondola to take him to the mainland. From there, he could work his way to sympathetic friends in Padua.

He gave no second thought to the possible fates of his wife and daughter.

Francis drove his dagger into the tabletop. The dry wood splintered on impact. "What a slinking, craven maggot I am!" he raged at Jobe who sat cross-legged on the bed opposite Francis. "I should never have listened to your words of caution. I am nothing better than a puling milksop! The fairest flower in all of Venice now lies in some foul cell while I—" He could not go on. Hot tears stung his eyes. His cowardice gnawed at his gut.

Jobe regarded his friend through hooded lids. "Had I not stopped you in time, you, too, would be in that same prison for murdering an officer of the Republic. The councillors here take a very dim view of foreigners meddling in their affairs."

Francis gnashed his teeth. "Jessica Leonardo is my affair!"

The African raised a dark brow. "Is she worth more than England?"

Francis narrowed his eyes. "How now?"

"If it were discovered that Lord Bardolph was not a foppish nobleman but instead a spy that is well paid by the English government, your life would not be worth an English farthing," Jobe replied.

Francis knotted his fist. "I care not a whit!"

The ebony giant shook his head. "You Cavendishes," he muttered under his breath. "You are all mad. In the name of love, your family flies into the teeth of danger at every opportunity. Think with your head, scholar, and not just with your heart."

Staring at his friend, Francis saw a gleam dance in the black man's eyes. He stopped his pacing and sat down on the foot of Jobe's bed. "Speak to me. Have you a plan?"

Jobe gave him a wicked grin. "Not yet, but with two of us now thinking clearly, we will form one. Mark me well, Francis, you cannot storm the walls of the Doge's palace as the Crusaders of old attacked the walls of Jerusalem. Though the palace may look like a confection, it is made of marble, not spun sugar. You would be a dead man before you crossed the courtyard. What good would you be then to Donna Jessica?"

Francis moistened his dry lips. "Tell me. Does your second sight reveal anything?" he asked in a low voice.

Jobe lifted his chin and stared into the middle space over Francis's shoulder. "Darkness," he replied in a deep, hollow voice. "Fog and cold dank walls. Great danger, yet I *do* see a light in the far distance, but there are many hazards in between."

Francis gripped his friend's muscled forearm. "To free Jessica, I will give and hazard all I have."

Jobe nodded. "You may have to do just that."

* * *

Jessica curled herself into a tight ball at one end of the wooden plank that served as her bed in the low, arched prison cell. She heard the slap of the canal water against the wall beside her. Through the tiny grilled window high above her she watched the stars wink out one by one like snuffed candles and the sky change from blue-black to dove gray. Though she had not slept a wink this whole terrible night, she did not feel tired. Every nerve jangled.

At least, she had not been molested by her jailers as she had feared. On the contrary, the minute the Night Lord had pulled off her mask and seen her disfigurement, not one of them dared to touch her except at sword point. They made the sign of the cross and murmured invocations against the evil eye. Those strong hulking men had blanched at the sight of her face and called her a witch.

From far beyond her window, Jessica heard the bells of Saint Mark's Basilica calling to early worshipers. I will miss Mass, she thought. She closed her eyes and murmured prayers for her salvation, though her hope dwindled. Behind her eyelids, memories welled up to torment her.

Sweet memories of Francis—that smiling villain! She should have known from the very first moment that the perfidious wretch was too good to be true. Hadn't her instincts warned her? She gnawed her lower lip to keep from crying. How that handsome snake had lulled her, wooed her, pretended that he cared for her! How gullible she had been! For a few sweetmeats, a ribbon or two, a sweet-singing canary and a handful of kisses she had tossed away every shred of her common sense. Her lips burned at the memory of those kisses—a lie, every one of them.

As she recalled Francis's gentle touch, she heard again the blandishments he had whispered into her ear. She felt again his breath warming her cheek. She vividly remembered with agonizing detail his sudden magnificent smile like the sun after a rainstorm; his gentle finger on her chin; his lips nibbling on her earlobe. The sound of his voice, singing a lullaby under her window, echoed with a mocking croak in the black stillness of her mind.

Then at last, when he gave her into the hands of the nightwatch, he had stepped away from her as if she were nothing but a discarded nutshell. *That* memory hurt her most of all. He had said, "I'm sorry." Hollow words from a hollow man. She should hate him; she did. And yet she knew that if Francis Bardolph appeared this very moment at her side with more of his sweet kisses and beguiling words, she would melt into his embrace. She squeezed her eyelids tighter. What a fool she was! She should have minded her father's restrictions.

Doctor Leonardo's face replaced that of Francis in her half dream. Did her parents know that she had been arrested? She shivered. There would be no help from that quarter. While she had stood steadfast in her Catholic beliefs, Lucia and Stefano had secretly returned to Judaism. They would not jeopardize their own lives for the sake of their disfigured daughter. Yet Jessica knew she would never denounce them—not even to save her own life. Her ties to them were too strong.

And what of Sophia and Gobbo, the two people who had given Jessica the only real love she had ever known? How strange fate was! Gobbo, the reformed pickpocket, was now a gifted musician, and Sophia, sometime fortune-teller and cony artist, had turned into a respectable housewife all because these two unfortunates had taken pity on another younger outcast. Looking beyond Jessica's damning mark, they had recognized her healing gifts. They had taught her all they knew of herbs and medicines gleaned from their wandering across Europe. Now, after years of living within the law, would Sophia and Gobbo suffer for their good deeds instead of for their past crimes? Jessica beseeched heaven to protect her protectors.

The sky turned to a pale blue wash and the bird-like cries of the gondoliers sang through her window. By the light of day she could read the graffiti carved into the walls by former inhabitants of her cell. *Disce pati,* wrote one Lachinur de Cremona on the 31st of January 1458. Learn to endure. What had been his crime? His fate?

Her empty stomach rumbled. How soon would the guards come for her? She doubted they would feed her before they drowned her. Images of that silent death terrified her: her mouth opening in a scream and the green water of the lagoon rushing in to fill the void. Jessica gulped several deep draughts of the dungeon's fetid air.

Surely they wouldn't condemn her without a trial first. As a citizen of Venice it was her right to have a hearing before learned judges. She prayed that they would be reasonable men. And yet, what defense could she give when the devil's own mark branded her face for all to see?

¡Dio mio! Please send me wisdom and the wit to use it. I will endure!

"What's the news on the Rialto?" Francis stepped out of the shadows cast by the bulk of San Giacomo church.

Not looking at him, the beggar replied, "All abuzz, *messere,* and your name mentioned—among others."

Francis nodded. In a city such as Venice, gossip ran on the heels of events. "Tongues love to wag," he observed, assuming a languid stance with his back to the *campo.*

Giulio cocked his head as if he listened to the silent rumors in the morning breeze. "They say that Jessica Leonardo is a witch," he began.

Even though Francis had steeled himself to hear this very

lie, it made his blood burn within him. "Indeed? I thought witches were old and gnarled. Donna Jessica is quite the opposite."

The beggar sniffed. "Your heart is showing on your sleeve, my lord. Hide it away."

Francis yawned. He needed no pretense for that. He had not slept since the nightwatch had arrested Jessica. "What else does the wind say about this accused witch?"

Giulio smiled, displaying badly stained teeth. "There is to be a trial. Everyone wants to attend if they can gain admittance."

Francis tensed. Sweet Jessica on display before a jeering mob? And yet this may be just the opportunity that he and Jobe needed to free her. "When? At what hour?"

"On Tuesday next at three in the afternoon. The Doge himself will sit in judgment in the Hall of the Great Council on the second floor of the palace. But, *messere,* it would be very dangerous for *you* to attend. Your life hangs by a thread as it is."

The back of Francis's neck prickled at this news. He slowly pivoted so that his back was now against a pillar. "How so? I am merely a gentleman traveler in your fair city."

"Sì," his informant agreed, "but your mask has slipped a bit. There are whispers of a spy among the foreigners."

Though every nerve quivered, Francis pretended to yawn again. "How fare your feathered children?" he inquired in a mild tone. He prayed that several of Giulio's marvelous pigeons were even now winging their way to France with the message that he was leaving Venice.

The beggar grinned. "A few have gone to visit their cousins."

Then nothing holds me here but Jessica's fate. I vow I will not leave Venice without her. Aloud he said, "I am glad to hear of that. I think I shall attend this trial. It may amuse me.''

Giulio muttered a curse against madcap Englishmen. "Then I bid you farewell, my lord, for I doubt we shall meet again in this life."

Francis maintained a smile on his face though the beggar's words sank in his soul like a dagger. "If so, I hope that you will remember me in your daily prayers and that you will inform my father of my misfortune."

Giulio curled his lip. "Your father will not weep long, I suspect, but will send another one of his sons on his fool's errands."

Francis wondered what the illustrious Sir William Cecil would think if he knew he had suddenly become a father to many two-faced children. After giving the bustling square another visual sweep, he drew a small book wrapped in a filthy rag from his doublet. He had spent the past few hours transcribing his notes on Venice in invisible ink between the lines of the Latin text. Squatting down, he slipped the package under Giulio's loose gown. "Then I leave a book for him as a remembrance of me."

Giulio nodded indicating that he understood the importance of the book. "A rich gift," he remarked.

"From a dutiful son," Francis answered. He plucked twenty gold ducats from his pouch and dropped them into Giulio's bowl.

The beggar grinned. "You are more generous than usual, my lord. With this fortune, I can feed my children for a year."

"Good! Where I am going I will not need much coin. Come success or failure, it will be by my own hand, not bought with gold. And you, Giulio, watch out for yourself."

For the first time in their acquaintance, Giulio's eyes

focused directly on Francis. "May Saint Michael the warrior angel ride upon your shoulders, my friend."

Francis flashed him a quick smile. "I hope he hangs on tightly for I intend to leap into the lion's mouth of Venice."

Chapter Sixteen

The next three days crept by on leaden feet. Jobe spent the time provisioning his ship and making it ready for a quick departure. He sent his sailors all over Venice visiting many wine shops and brothels in hopes of gleaning more information about the impending witch trial. The whole city throbbed with tales, most of them false. Many people had been questioned by the Council of Ten. The agents of the Holy Office were also very active. The population of the large Jewish Ghetto stayed closer to their homes over the Sabbath lest they attract unwanted attention from the Inquisition. The most interesting news to Francis was the disappearance of Giulio, the blind beggar of San Giacomo. Francis hoped that his confederate had taken his own advice and removed himself to safer climes. For once he turned a deaf ear to Jobe's dark prophecies. He had set his own course and he was prepared to see it through. If nothing else, he vowed that Jessica would not die alone.

Gaining admittance to the Hall of the Great Council was much easier than Francis had expected. In his guise as the jaded traveler, he sought out Niccolo Dandelli, one of the pleasure-seeking young bloods of the Venetian nobility that Francis had cultivated. Niccolo looked forward to attending

the trial of a witch and he welcomed the company of his
English friend. Like the majority of the spectators inside
the hall, Francis and Niccolo were masked. The anonymity
of painted visages protected the reputations of the thousand
people that packed the Council chamber.

Wedging his large frame next to Niccolo on one end of
a hard wooden bench, Francis surveyed the excited throng
around him. Bickering among themselves for the best seats,
the spectators crowded on the makeshift rows of long
benches that ran along three sides of the vast chamber. The
late and the unlucky had to content themselves with standing in the doorways or perched on the sills of the wide-
arched windows that overlooked the Grand Canal. On the
vast ceiling high above the crowd, a massive fresco depicted the Last Judgment. The majestic figure of Christ on
His throne appropriately hung over the raised dais where
the Doge and the Council of Ten would sit. The huge chamber soon warmed with the body heat of the people. A thousand cloying perfumes that cloaked earthier odors rose and
mingled in the air. The babble from a thousand throats
made conversation almost impossible. Francis did not
mind; his own thoughts were company enough.

While waiting for the arrival of the councillors, Francis's
gaze roved slowly over the spectators on the opposite side
of the room. A clutch of gaudily dressed women quickly
attracted the appreciative attention of every male in the hall.
Venice's celebrated courtesans had turned out *en masse* to
gloat at the misfortune of a woman not one of their own.
Cosma di Luna sat in the center of the colorful coterie.
Though she, too, was masked like the rest, Francis recognized her instantly. She apparently had not seen him. Attended by Nerissa, she fanned herself, gossiped with her
friends and ate sweetmeats from a small inlaid box in her
lap. Francis swore under his breath in disgust.

"Grown tired of our Cosma?" Niccolo asked in a cheerful voice.

"*Sì,*" Francis replied with a casual shrug. "I seek fresher faces, merrier company."

Niccolo jabbed him in his ribs with his elbow. "Come sup with me this evening. I have discovered the most delectable little Venus, new to the city— Ah! It begins!"

A richly garbed herald strode to the open center of the room. With his thick staff of office he rapped on the polished floor three times to signal the start of the proceedings. The hall instantly fell silent. The door nearest the dais opened and the prisoner was led in by four guards. Everyone craned their necks to get a better view of the accused witch. Some stood on the rear benches. Being taller than most, Francis could see all too well. The sight of Jessica stabbed him to the core of his heart.

After four days' imprisonment, her pretty little gypsy costume was filthy. Her unbound hair hung over her shoulders and cascaded down her back giving her a certain wild beauty.

"*¡Che bella!*" Niccolo remarked in Francis's ear. "But I wonder why she is masked?"

Francis did not bother to give him an answer. For Jessica's sweet sake he was glad that her mysterious disfigurement would not be put on display for the titillation of this rabble. Though she moved slowly toward the chair in the center of the floor, she held her head up proudly. Before seating herself she looked around the chamber. She froze when she spied Francis.

Though a wide gulf separated them, he felt the fire that he saw in her eyes. Her silent accusation scorched him, though why she had called him her betrayer he still did not understand. At this moment of extreme jeopardy, she made it plain to Francis that she hated him. He touched two fingers to his lips, kissed them, and pointed them to her. He did not care who else witnessed his demonstration of loyalty and love.

Jessica shivered when she saw his winged kiss. Her lips softened a fraction, then she turned away. Before she could take her seat, the herald rapped his staff again.

"All rise and give honor to His Most Serene Highness, Doge Francesco Donato, and to the Council of Ten."

Processing into the hall in a single file, the ten most powerful men in the Republic of Venice mounted the dais. They were dressed identically in long black robes with wide red sashes of silk that hung over their left shoulders. Small round black hats adorned their heads, each topped with an incongruous red fluffy pom-pom. All concealed their faces behind black leather masks.

Solemnly, they took their places on either side of the Doge's gilded throne. The Doge came last, robed in his gold-and-white gown with his ornate *corno* on his head. He was one of the few people in the chamber who dared to reveal his face.

On closer inspection, Francis curled his lip. *The Doge looks as if he, too, did not sleep well last night. He has the expression of a dried prune.*

The Doge lowered himself onto his throne, carefully arranged the fall of his garments, then gestured for everyone else to be seated. He nodded to the herald who stepped forward to read the charge from a black-bound ledger.

"This court is convened this day in extra-ordinary session to try the accused, Jessica Leonardo, here present, for the grave crimes of heresy, witchcraft and treason." He cleared his throat. "Heresy, in that the accused, being baptized in the Catholic faith as an infant, has relapsed in her beliefs and has returned to the Jewish practices of her family."

Jessica gripped the arms of her chair but said nothing. She lifted her chin higher.

Francis silently applauded her courage. *Oh, most cherished Jessica! You are the only innocent soul in this pesthouse.*

The herald continued in a rush with his lengthy charge. "Secondly, witchcraft in that the accused is known to practice certain strange arts and she manufactures mysterious potions, elixirs and ointments that contain demonic powers. Furthermore, the accused bears the mark of the devil upon her face."

Jessica shook her head though she remained silent.

The herald turned a page of his book. "Finally, the accused has committed the heinous act of treason against the Republic by seeking private information of a political nature from well-placed men who had sought her services as a healer of pain. Furthermore, she revealed this information and conspired with several Englishmen who are suspected to be spies."

The spectators gasped in outrage. Witchcraft was one thing—a church matter—but betraying the secrets of their beloved city was something that hurt the general populace. At the words "Englishmen" and "spies," Jessica jerked in her chair as if she had been struck. Across the room, Cosma turned pale and choked on a sugared nut. Francis shivered and held his breath. If Jessica glanced at him now, she would doom both of them before he could carry out his plan. One look from her would confirm a conspiracy. Both Giulio and Jobe had been right. Somehow he had overtipped his hand. His skin grew icy cold. He fought back his instinctive urge to flee the room.

Staring at the herald, Jessica straightened herself again. "Never!" she protested. Her clear musical voice carried to the farthest corner of the packed chamber.

A lawyer, clad in a dark gray gown and white mantle, rose from the table just below the dais. "The prisoner will remain silent until spoken to. How do you answer to these charges?" he continued in a booming voice.

Jessica shot a haughty look at the man. "I am innocent. There is not one grain of truth in any of those accusations."

The lawyer lifted an eyebrow. "Indeed?" he sneered. "Let us examine the first charge. On your oath before God Almighty to speak the truth, are you a Jew?"

Jessica looked directly at the Doge. "Before the Lord God, I swear I am not. I have always been a faithful daughter of Holy Mother Church."

The lawyer waved his hand dismissively. "If this is true then please explain to the Council about the casket found under your bed."

For the first time Jessica appeared uncertain. "What casket?"

With a flourish made for the benefit of the spectators, the lawyer turned to his table and lifted a burgundy napkin that had concealed a cedar casket the size of a large Bible. "Do you recognize this, Jessica Leonardo?"

Jessica dug her fingernails into the palms of her hands to keep them from shaking visibly. Under no circumstances would she betray her terror to the mob in the chamber. For the past few days she had thought through her defense against the charges of witchcraft and heresy but the sight of the strange chest unnerved her. She had no earthly idea whose it was nor how it had gotten under her bed.

She cleared her throat. "I have never seen that box before in my life."

The lawyer narrowed his eyes. "And you swear that you know nothing of these?" He opened the chest and took out a number of items, one by one. "Your Highness and my lords, here is a sack of money containing five hundred ducats.''

A murmur of wonderment ran around the room. Jessica gasped under her breath. She had never possessed that much coin. *Had Gobbo reverted to his former criminal occupation? Pray God, no!*

The lawyer opened a smaller pouch. "Here is a fine turquoise set in a golden ring valued at fourscore ducats.'' He held up the costly jewel.

Jessica sucked in her breath. She recognized the ring as her mother's bride gift from her father. Lucia had only worn it for special occasions. One day it was supposed to belong to Jessica. The money pouch must also belong to her father, she concluded, but why did he hide his treasure in her house and why didn't he tell her about it?

Aloud she remarked, "I did not know it was a crime in Venice to own money or jewelry. If that is true, my lord, perhaps you should arrest everyone in this room.''

The lawyer held up his hand to silence the wave of laughter. A catlike smirk played on his lips. "I agree that such a display of wealth while most interesting is hardly incriminating.'' He picked up two books and waved them over his head. "But what of these, *signorina?*''

She stared at them. "What are they?''

He opened one and thrust it under her nose. "Read the title,'' he commanded.

Jessica shook her head. "Alas, my lord, I cannot,'' she replied in a stronger voice than she felt. "I never learned to read.''

Inwardly, she quaked for she recognized the characters as Hebrew. Now she understood Doctor Leonardo's reason for secreting this casket away from his own home. He feared that his religious relapse had been discovered. She pressed her lips together as the shock of her father's perfidy seeped through her. *Is there no mercy in heaven—or on earth—because I am my father's child?*

"And these?" The lawyer held up a golden menorah candle holder and a silver cup that Jessica also recognized as her father's. "Do you know anything of these pieces of idolatry?"

I must chose my words with care lest I doom my parents. Though her father had banished her from his home twelve years ago, she could not bring herself to hate him or her mother.

Aloud, Jessica replied, "I believe they are things that the Jews use but I have never used them." She stared directly into the lawyer's muddy-brown eyes. "Forgive me for my ignorance of the law, my lord, but I thought that the Jews of Venice were free to worship in their own manner as long as they obeyed the rules of the Council."

He glared at her. "Ah, I perceive that you show the whole wealth of your wit in an instant. Do not play your weak words on me, *signorina.* I am better at this game than you will ever hope to be. Tell the Council—are these things yours and are you a Jewess?"

Jessica's temper flared. "No, my lord, I swear that they are not mine, nor have I ever used such items. I am not a Jew now nor have I ever been one. I attend Mass daily. I pray to God every night for His blessings. Furthermore, I am not a witch."

"Oh?" The lawyer laid the menorah and kaddish cup back on the table, then he advanced toward her. "Very well, let us examine the second charge. Many witnesses say that you have healed their aches and pains with your secret potions. In fact, you are renowned in this city for your wondrous healing powers. You have already professed that you are uneducated. How did you come by this skill if not by witchcraft?"

Jessica tossed her hair from her face. Now she was on firmer ground. She had prepared herself for this question. "It is a gift from God, not the devil. I do only good not harm. How can the devil perform good works when he is evil?"

One of the anonymous councillors leaned down from his chair. "Remove your mask, girl," he barked. "Let us see your face."

A shiver of panic ran through her. The moment she had most feared had come. "I beg your pardon, my lord, but my face is much disfigured. The sight of it would sicken you."

The councillor sat back in his chair, said nothing, but nodded to one of the guards that stood behind Jessica. Before she realized what had happened, the man reached over her shoulder and yanked the mask from her face. At the sight of the damning mark on her left cheek, the reaction among the Council of Ten was instantaneous. They drew back in their ornate chairs and crossed themselves. The spectators on the left side of the room that could also see her shame voiced their dismay and revulsion. Even the smug lawyer retreated before her.

Now that her nightmare had come to pass, Jessica lifted her head higher. Very well, let everyone take a good look. She was tired of cowering in the shadows. From the corner of her eye, she glanced in Francis's direction. Was he also horrified by her face?

Though taken by surprise, Francis sent her a smile that melted her heart. Filled with a surge of conflicting emotions, she trembled then looked quickly away from him. His smile had been unmistakably one of love, not of gloating. If he had not denounced her, then who had done it?

The lawyer recovered himself. "Not a witch?" he cried

out. "Yet you carry the mark of Satan himself. Observe, my lords, where his infernal kiss has burned her skin!"

Jessica touched her cheek. "Not so, my lord. I have never lain with anyone and certainly not with the devil. This is only a discoloration that I have carried since my birth. Ask my parents if you do not believe me."

The lawyer looked down his nose at her. "Doctor and Madam Leonardo have taken the wise decision to depart the city rather than befoul themselves with you. I doubt they will ever return. You have no witnesses to this claim."

Though I am glad of their escape, I am now truly alone in this world. Tears rose behind her eyelids. "I am a good Catholic, my lords," she repeated in a soft voice. "I have led a chaste and simple life. I swear to you upon my soul that I have never lain with the devil, nor with any man."

A sudden movement from the rear benches made her look up. Dressed in the most garish crimson clothing and standing taller than everyone else around him, Francis Bardolph raised his voice over the murmuring of the crowd.

"I will be her witness. Your Most Serene Highness and worthy members of the Council, will you give me leave to speak?"

Jessica's body went rigid with tension. *No, Francis, sit down! Live and compose an epitaph for me.* Her eyes begged him to be silent. Instead the gaudy Englishman made his way through the press of people.

The Doge, taken aback by these startling events, conferred with the councillors that sat on both sides of him. Then he nodded to the herald to rap his staff for silence.

When the Great Hall grew quiet, the Doge crooked a languid finger at the masked gentleman. "Draw hither."

Jessica clasped her hands together as Francis strode to her side. He flashed her a quick smile before he began. "Donna Jessica speaks the truth when she says that she is a good Catholic. I have seen her often at prayer in Saint Mark's. This sweet girl is not a witch but as wise, virtuous and gentle a Christian soul as can be found in all of Venice. Ask anyone who has enjoyed her healing touch. Believe me, I know whereof I speak, my lords."

Turning, he stared directly at the gaggle of courtesans and at Cosma di Luna in particular. "For the past five months I have sampled a great many favors offered by Venice's famous beauties. I am a man of the world and I know the difference between a dove and a well-used polecat."

One of the courtesans gasped, then turned a mottled crimson under her mask.

Francis chuckled and pointed toward the fuming Cosma. "See, my lords? I am followed even into this august hall of justice by their odor."

The crowd erupted in hearty laughter. Jessica leaned toward Francis and whispered out of the side of her mouth, "You should not be here."

He bowed his head closer to hers. "Where else could I be but at your side?" He lifted her chin and stroked the pad of his thumb over the hated mark on her face. "I did not betray you, *cara mia.*"

"I realize that—now," she murmured.

The herald rapped again and again for order. Once the people had settled down, the Doge beckoned Francis to the foot of the dais.

"Reveal yourself."

Francis untied the black ribbons that held his mask in place. Then he tossed it among the nearest group of spectators. Sweeping off his plumed hat, he gave the Doge a deep courtly bow.

The Doge sniffed. "Who are you?"

"Francis Bardolph, a holiday-maker visiting your fair city."

The Doge stroked his chin with his forefinger. "And what is the precise nature of your business with this woman?"

Jessica held her breath. Turning his back on the entire Council of Ten, Francis crossed to her side once more. As he took one of her cold hands in his warm one and kissed it, Jessica's toes curled inside her shoes.

"Jessica Leonardo is my betrothed," he replied in a loud ringing voice. "We had hoped to be married before the season of Lent began."

Jessica gripped his hand tighter as the room whirled about her. Didn't Francis realize that he had just signed his own death warrant?

Chapter Seventeen

"He's bewitched!" someone shouted.

The Hall of the Great Council erupted in a babel of confusion. The thousand spectators all spoke at once. The ten black-robed men on the dais muttered among themselves. The herald's call for order could barely be heard. The Doge pursed his lips as if he had bitten into a lemon.

At the center of the storm, Jessica whispered to her would-be protector. "Francis, you are moonstruck! Your offer will come to nothing. I am a commoner."

He gave her the most enchanting, infuriating grin. "And I, sweetheart, am a bastard."

Wishing she could pound some sense into that handsome head, Jessica gripped his hand tighter. "*Sì*, you are a rogue, indeed, but this is no laughing matter, Francis."

"I do not jest," he murmured, kissing her hand again.

Jessica shook her head. "It is the law in Venice that if a nobleman marries a commoner, he will be stripped of his title and property."

Francis lightly stroked her cheek—her ugly cheek. "Have you forgotten that I am an Englishman? Besides, there is no title to strip away." He leaned closer and brushed her lips with his. "Be brave, *cara*."

Her emotions whirled for a moment and then skidded back to reality. "You are not only a rogue but a fool, Francis Bardolph," she whispered with a fierce intensity. "By such a public demonstration of your affections—" Her tongue savored the place where he had kissed her. "You have put yourself in grave danger. Look around us. See how the people regard me with revulsion? How can *you* bear the sight of my face?"

Francis caressed the despised birthmark with a touch as gentle as an angel's breath. "You have a pleasing face, beloved. One that I cherish."

His words rippled through her. "Do not speak to me of love. I pray you, do not mock me. I could not bear your scorn heaped upon all the others."

He raised her from her chair and enfolded her in his arms. "Do I look scornful, sweet Jessica?" A teasing smile played across his mouth.

Despite her harrowing predicament, she returned his smile. "No, Francis, you look like you were dressed by a cross-eyed, color-blind tailor."

He chuckled. "I agree."

Drawing her against his broad chest, he dipped his head once again to recapture her mouth. His tongue parted her lips in a soul-reaching message of love. Casting her caution to the four cardinal points, Jessica returned his kiss with abandon, savoring every exquisite moment. She knew this would be their last kiss and she did not care if she shocked the Doge and the entire Council of Ten into seizures. Francis's lips were warm and sweet as spiced wine. She drank him in with a frenzy close to madness.

The rough hands of the guards pried them apart. When she opened her eyes, Jessica realized that the hall had become deathly still. Their shameless display had accomplished what the red-faced herald could not. Tossing her hair out of her eyes, Jessica resumed her seat. Francis stood close by her side. Jessica closed her eyes until her heartbeat settled back to its regular pace.

The young lawyer, pale with either anger or outrage, cleared his throat. "Your Highness and my lords, let us return to the question of this casket." He picked up one of the Hebrew books, but before he could begin his harangue the dark figure of the Lord of the Night stepped to the center of the floor.

"Most Serene Highness, I beg a word."

Jessica opened her eyes. Though this officer of the law had treated her sternly at the time of her arrest, he had not been cruel. For that, she respected him.

With a small sigh of resignation, the Doge nodded. "Be brief, my lord," he instructed. "The hour grows late."

Lord Gratiano nodded then said, "Regarding the casket, Your Highness, there is a young man in my custody who might shed some light upon this matter. I apprehended him in the act of stealing this chest."

A spark of interest flickered in the Doge's eyes. "Indeed? Bring forth this thief."

Two more guards dragged the quaking form of a terrified youth into the chamber. The crowd murmured among themselves.

"Poor Jacopo," muttered Francis out of the side of his mouth.

The lawyer stared first at the boy then at Jessica. "Aha! I see it plainly. This *ruffiano* is one of Signorina Leonardo's minions whom she ordered to spirit away this piece of incriminating evidence from her house. Is that not so?" he asked her.

Jessica shook her head. "No, my lords," she replied in a clear, steady voice. "I swear that I have never seen this boy in my life." She regarded him with a perplexed look.

The thief, viewing her birthmark, made a fluttering sign of the cross and stumbled backward as if he sought to put more distance between them. He dropped to his knees before the dais.

"I have never had dealings with this witch. Believe me, my lords," he babbled. "In truth, I am in the employment Donna Cosma di Luna. It was *she* who ordered me to steal the chest."

The box of sweetmeats slipped off Cosma's lap, clattering to the floor. She bolted from her bench. "No," she shrieked. "He lies to save his skin. I know nothing of this chest. How could I?"

A sudden inspiration flashed into Jessica's mind. This unexpected opportunity might be her salvation. She rose. "Your Highness, Signorina di Luna came to my house a few days ago. She was consumed with jealousy and she ordered me not to see Lord Bardolph again. Furthermore, she threatened me with dire consequences if I did not heed her."

Turning around, Jessica faced down her rival. "Perhaps Donna Cosma herself hid the chest while she was in my home in order to convict me of heresy. Indeed, I have every suspicion that it was the hand of Signorina di Luna that wrote to the Council of my so-called crimes."

Again, the chamber buzzed with excitement. The city would savor this afternoon's events for the entire forty days of Lent. Having said her piece, Jessica sat down and smoothed her filthy skirts. *I will endure.*

Jacopo, bug-eyed with fear, bobbed his head in assent. "*Sì, sì,* Your Highness. In fact, I accompanied my mistress when she visited Signorina Leonardo. Indeed, I carried the chest." He licked his lips.

Caught off balance by this twist in the trial, the Council conferred among themselves. Jacopo groveled on the polished floor while several guards took the protesting Cosma into their custody.

"This is news to me," Francis whispered to Jessica. "Jacopo has been my second shadow for over a fortnight. He must hope to save his miserable hide by casting the blame on Cosma."

The Council returned to their seats. The Doge stood under his scarlet canopy of state. The Great Hall dropped into profound silence. The Doge began, "We, the Council of Venice, sentence this thief to three years as a galley slave aboard the military ships of our Republic. It is hoped that the time spent in the service of his city will allow him to repent of his poor choice of employers."

Jacopo swooned, whether from shock or relief, Jessica could not tell. The guards lifted him like a sack of grain and dragged him from the chamber.

The Doge then motioned for Cosma to be brought forward. When she came before the dais, she dropped a deep curtsy to the Doge and his Council. "I am, as always, your most humble servant, Your Highness," she murmured in honeyed tones.

The Doge was not moved by either her voice or the generous display of her bosom. He frowned down at her. "Mistress, your part in this sad affair is confusing at best and may never be fully understood." He held up one pallid hand before Cosma could protest her innocence. "But for the sake of the young gentlemen of Venice who might chance to fall within your snares, the Council has decided that you will enter the convent immediately. There you may pray for God's forgiveness at your leisure."

"*What?*" Cosma exploded, all simpering guile fled. "How can you do this to me? Many of you have enjoyed my company and my favors. Is this your gratitude?"

Francis chuckled. "I have heard it said that it is easier

to get something out of the mouth of a lion than out of the pocket of a prince,'' he observed in an undertone.

The Doge curled his thin lips with distaste. "You grow tedious, my dear." He motioned to her guards. "Take her to the Convent of the Maddalena on Giudecca at once. There you may pray for me," he added as Cosma was pulled away.

"Rot in hell," she snarled. Turning to Francis, she spat on him before the guards controlled her.

Francis wiped his face with his lace handkerchief. "An alley cat to the end, *gatta mia.*"

The Doge fastened his steely gaze on the pair before him. "My Lord Bardolph, it seems we have nothing against you save the fact that you are English and are obviously under the spell of this woman." He pointed his index finger. "On the other hand, we cannot help but suspect that you might be the English spy that has been mentioned in our reports."

Jessica quivered. Could Francis really be a spy? And yet she had known from the first he was not the idle gentleman that he pretended to be.

The Doge coughed, then continued. "Since we prefer not to waste our time or yours, Lord Bardolph, we hereby banish you from Venice forever. You have twenty-four hours from this moment to quit our city or your life will be forfeit."

Like every other Venetian in the room, Jessica was aghast at the sharp penalty. She could not imagine living— or dying anywhere else but in her beloved city.

On the other hand, Francis merely shrugged. "Very well, Your Highness, I will obey your edict. In truth, I have grown tired of the gaudy face of this city that hides so much corruption behind it. I will take my dearest betrothed and we will be gone."

The Doge narrowed his eyes. "Venice will be well rid

of you, *messere,* but you will sail away alone. Jessica Leonardo, by the demonic brand upon your face and by the strange arts we know you to possess, we find you guilty of witchcraft.''

Jessica clutched the arms of her chair for support. What a fool she had been to think that she might possibly slip through the Council's net! Francis put his hands on her shoulders while he addressed the court.

''Your Serene Highness, noble lords! By what proof do you condemn her other than a most unfortunate accident of birth? Call more witnesses. There must be many—even in this very room—who will testify of the good works and holiness of this most maligned woman.''

The Doge glared at him, then looked out at the avid spectators. ''*Is* there anyone here who dares to speak on behalf of this witch?''

No one stirred. The people shrank back against each other. Looking at the masked assembly, Jessica thought she recognized a few of her former patients. How craven and ungrateful they were now! Francis squeezed her shoulders.

''Courage,'' he whispered.

The Doge flicked away a piece of fluff from his mantle. ''Very well, justice has been served.'' He returned his attention to Jessica. ''But we will not be guilty of shedding your blood. Instead you will be executed at night either by strangulation or by drowning, as it pleases the Council.''

Though she felt sick to her stomach, Jessica pulled herself to her feet and faced her judges. ''May I speak, Your Highness? It is my right as a citizen of Venice.'' *I will endure.*

The Doge rolled his eyes, then returned to his throne. ''Very well. Say your piece and be done with it. My time grows short.''

Jessica seized upon his words. She stared at the old man

in his massive golden chair. "Indeed it does, Your Highness, and soon you, too, will stand before a judge seated upon a throne." Looking up to the ceiling, she pointed to the painting of Christ at the Last Judgment. "And when that day comes for you and for all of you that condemn me here, you will remember this moment because I will be standing there, too—at the right hand of the Lord God."

People gasped and many crossed themselves. The Doge's skin took on a decidedly greenish tint. Many of the councillors shifted in their chairs.

Jessica plunged ahead, no longer caring about her fate. She knew her words would live in the memory of every Venetian who heard them. "For I am wholly innocent of these weak and ill-proved charges and well you know it, my lords. Never let it be said that Venice is not diligent in uprooting heretics. I will go to my death to appease the hounds of the Inquisition who snap at your precious heels."

"Hold your tongue!" shouted one of the councillors.

Francis attempted to take her hand. "Sweet Jessica!"

She stepped away from him. This was her last speech and she would make it unforgettable. "I have done nothing wrong and you, in your dark and devious hearts, know it. How can you hope for mercy when you give none? Yes, my honorable lords and judges, remember me well for we shall meet again, and I promise you, you will rue what you do this day. God Almighty will be my defender then."

"B-blasphemy!" cried one of the councillors. "Take her away!"

Before the guards could prick her with their pikes, Jessica spun on the balls of her feet and stared at Francis. His expression was one of dire calamity. His blue eyes brimmed with unshed tears. He reached for her.

"Remember me, as well, Francis," she said more softly.

"Jessica!" He lunged for her but several guards held him

at bay while Jessica was forced from the chamber. "Jessica, I love you!"

When she glanced back at him over her shoulder, he blew her another kiss. She opened her mouth to shout her love for him but the heavy door slammed behind her. Lifting her chin higher, she refused to give the men-at-arms surrounding her the pleasure of seeing her weep.

I will hold you close to my heart, my love, and pretend that you really would have married me.

When the chamber door shut behind Jessica, Francis felt as if the sun had been extinguished. His mind reeled. A red haze clouded his vision. Had he been allowed to keep his sword on his belt, he knew he would have leaped to the dais and slit the gizzard of that sanctimonious weathercock in the purple and gold robes. Everything that Jessica had said was true. Francis knew it—and he realized that everyone else in that huge chamber knew it, as well. Jessica was completely innocent but would be sacrificed so that the great men of the city would not look like the fools they were. Indeed, the Doge would have much to answer for not only in the next world, but in this one, as well, Francis thought with grim satisfaction.

One of the guards gave him a rough shove toward the exit. "Away with you, dog of an Englishman."

Pulling his shattered wits together, Francis smiled at the burly fellow who reeked of garlic. Then he executed a courtly bow full of sarcastic flourishes. "Since you have called me a dog, beware my fangs," he snapped. He whipped his cape over his left shoulder and walked away.

People parted before him as if he were a leper. In their eyes, he was as infected as one. Niccolo brushed past him on the stairs and averted his face when Francis looked at him.

"Excuse my haste, Bardolph. The honor of my family's name, you understand," the shallow gentleman mumbled as he ran down the wide marble staircase.

When Francis found himself outside in the *piazza,* he noted with surprise that the twilight of this infamous day had crept over the city. Overhead, the campanile struck the evening hour of five. Masked revelers, bent on enjoying the last moments of pleasure before midnight signaled the beginning of Lent, again filled the great square.

Jobe stepped out from behind one of the white pillars of the palace's portico. "How goes it?" he asked, falling into step beside Francis.

Francis headed for the Molo. "All the way to hell," he snarled.

Turning sharply to the left, he strode toward the *prigione* where he knew Jessica was imprisoned. He wanted to examine the outside of this forbidding building before the daylight faded completely. Since his first plan had gone badly awry, the time had now come to take more desperate measures. He would free Jessica or die in the attempt. Now that he had set his mind on this certain course, a feeling of peace settled over him. More surprising, he felt buoyant, almost elated.

Jobe and Francis halted opposite the prison. Francis studied the building for several minutes, paying special attention to the enclosed bridge arching over the Rio di Palazzo that linked the Doge's palace with the *prigione.* "The Bridge of Sighs," he murmured. Had his beloved Jessica wept when she was led across it to her cell? "For every tear she has shed, I will exact a price in Venetian blood."

Jobe whistled through his teeth. "Thus speaks the scholar who exchanged combat of arms for combat of wits? You much amaze me, *meo amigo.* I have never known you to be so bloodthirsty."

Francis bared his teeth. "I have learned a new lesson this day." He pointed to the stout building. "Oh, coffin of base lead," he said, referring to the heavy roof that concealed the poor wretches under its eaves. "You hide so rich a prize!"

Jobe grunted. "And you seek to win this game?" He narrowed his black eyes as he studied the thick walls.

"I will not leave Venice without Jessica," Francis replied in a deceptively soft voice.

"I know," Jobe agreed without protesting the insanity of such an undertaking. "And I will not leave without you."

Francis stared into the African's face, seeking the answers to questions not yet formed in his own mind. "Tell me true, does your second sight see my future linked with Jessica's?" He held his breath as Jobe summoned up the rare gift that had fascinated the entire Cavendish family ever since they had first known Jobe.

The black giant finally nodded. "Aye, but I cannot tell if you will be together in this world or the next."

Francis clapped him on his shoulder. "That is enough for me! Let us quit this doleful place and repair to the Sturgeon. We have not a moment to lose."

Jobe pointed to his sleek English corsair that rocked at anchor in the middle of the lagoon. "My ship is ready and the crew are aboard. We will sail at your command."

"You are a piece of work, Jobe!"

As they pushed their way through the holiday crowds, Francis quickly outlined what he required. "Send some of your men to Jessica's house. We must see to the safety of her two servants."

Jobe agreed. "They will be on my ship within an hour's time."

They hurried over the Rialto Bridge. "I need the robes of a friar—a Dominican if possible."

The African furrowed his brow. "I know not the types of priests by name. What color robes?"

"Black," Francis answered as they entered their inn's common room. "Also I will need the costumes of Arlecchino and Columbina, as well."

Jobe rolled his eyes. "Next you will tell me that you will want the moon in a lantern."

Barely greeting their gaping landlord, the conspirators took the stairs two at a time. Once inside their chamber, Francis continued, "Also I require a corpse—a fresh one."

Jobe fingered his daggers with a smirk. "How recent?"

Francis shook him. "Banish that bloody thought! I do not mean one that is even now walking about the city."

Jobe frowned. "Your tender conscience is most inconvenient."

Francis peeled off his bright-colored doublet and hose. "Find me a body that is already dead—one that is slim of build, with long dark hair." He changed into black tights and a brown leather jerkin. He kicked the heap of gaudy clothing under the nearest bed. He had shed the skin of pretense once and for all. For the first time in his life, Francis Bardolph was his own man.

Jobe grinned at him. "Your plan sounds like most excellent sport."

Francis slipped a thin stiletto down his boot. "You can count on it."

Chapter Eighteen

While Jobe prowled the backwaters of Venice in search of a suitable body, Francis packed the belongings and gifts he wanted to take with him or to be sent back to England to his diverse relations. Hesitating in front of the huge crate that contained his portrait, he considered what he should do with the thing. Though the likeness unsettled him, he realized that the work was well done and did not deserve a bonfire as its final fate. Taking a piece of scrap parchment, he wrote ''To Lady La Belle Hayward, Bodiam Castle, East Sussex, England,'' then tacked the address to the crate's frame.

Each time the nearby church bells chimed the quarter hour, Francis's skin prickled. How long did it take to find a body? Every morning, the canals were filled with them; poor people that could not afford the cost of a decent burial. Now, when he needed a corpse, the population of Venice seemed uncommonly healthy. Two sailors from the *Jinn* arrived, gathered up Francis's bags, boxes and the painting and then departed without a word. Francis wondered if he would ever see his books again, then put that depressing thought out of his mind. He needed to concentrate on the hours ahead of him—and to pray that Jessica's execution was not to take place until after midnight.

Outside Francis's window, the merry noise of *Carnevale*'s last night filled the streets and canals. The Doge and all the nobility would be busy celebrating the traditions of *Martedì Grasso*—Shrove Tuesday—until the great bells of the campanile ended the festivities at twelve o'clock.

Where in God's good name was Jobe?

Just as the church bells struck the half hour past eight, a handful of pebbles pattered against Francis's shutter. At last! Jobe's prearranged signal. His heart pounding with a surge of excitement, Francis lifted his lighted candle and traced the sign of the cross in front of the window before he extinguished the flame. Jobe would know that he had heard him.

Francis pounded down the stairs and filled a wineskin from the small cask on the counter in the common room. He thrust a full pouch of ducats into the landlord's hands. "For your many services," Francis muttered. Then he dashed out the door before the man had a chance to count the coin. No matter. Francis had paid his reckoning twice over. Where he was bound, he had no need of money.

Francis joined Jobe and a number of the crewmen in a narrow side street. All the houses were shuttered against the cold and thieves. "Were you successful?" he asked.

Jobe rumbled a chuckle in the back of his throat. "Did you know that tis harder to find a holy man's robe than a corpse in this city?" He handed a bundle to Francis. "I located the laundry of a monastery. No time to choose the correct size."

Francis shook out a Dominican's hooded robe and nodded his approval. It would fall a bit short on him but in the darkness of the *prigione* who could tell? "And the other item?"

Jobe pointed to a long bundle that lay against the wall. "Twas a pretty Greek boy by the look of him. Fifteen years or so with lovely long black hair. He died of a fever—or so I was told." He wrinkled his nose. "He does not stink too much as yet, but his joints are stiff as pokers."

Francis eyed the dead boy. "Fever?" he echoed.

Jobe clapped him on the shoulder. "Not the plague. Too early in the year." He pointed to one of his men. "And David, my first mate, persuaded a pleasant company of actors to part with these." He held up costumes from the Commedia dell'Arte.

Francis smiled grimly. "You have done very well, my friend."

Jobe pulled the robe of the doctor character over his head, then he adjusted the long-nosed mask. "Spare me your thanks until a later time. We must hurry. The tide will turn against us soon after midnight."

Without another word, Francis donned the Arlecchino's cheerful red-and-yellow-diamond motley. He stuffed the friar's robe into a pack and wedged it under his shirt in the guise of a hump. Together, Jobe and Francis dressed the corpse as Columbina. As a final touch Francis uncorked his wineskin and doused the body with the sour vintage so that the boy reeked more of cheap wine than of death. Then he hoisted the body over his shoulder. The youth had been ill-nourished and weighed less than Francis had expected.

"Heigh ho, Jobe! Let us join the festivities."

Despite the press of people, the band of conspirators arrived at the edge of the *piazza* within a short time. None of their fellow revelers noticed that a member of the comedy troupe had passed out from too much drink. Many people in the great square were in similar states of intoxication. Laughing good-naturedly and pretending to be tipsy, Jobe,

Francis and the costumed sailors wove their way across the great square until they reached the comparative quiet under the arches of the palace portico. Here and there amid the shadows, couples engaged in vigorous lovemaking and took no notice of the ragged pack of actors.

Jobe pointed to the clock tower. "We have come just in time." The great statues of the Moors began to strike their bell, signaling ten.

Just then, trumpets blared overhead, alerting all within earshot that the Doge and his court were about to make their appearance. Francis hunched inside his cloak and hoped he looked shorter. He watched the colorful procession pass close by them. The throng cheered as the Doge and the noble senators marched to the base of the campanile. The annual carnival ritual of the Twelve Pigs was about to begin.

"Twill take those old men some time to mount the stairs to the top and more time to throw down the pigs," Francis whispered to the others. He hoped that the condemned porkers would put up a fight before they were tossed from the top of the bell tower. He needed every precious minute those piglets could buy him.

Eyeing the crates that held the squealing guests of honor, Jobe snorted. "And they call *me* a barbarian!"

As soon as the last of the scarlet-gowned men and their ceremonial guards had disappeared into the campanile, Francis and Jobe each hooked one of "Columbina's" arms over their shoulders, supporting the corpse between them. The Greek boy's head fell forward; his long hair and the cheerful mask covered his ashen face.

Francis winked at Jobe. "Let us charge into the lion's den."

Jobe gave his men the signal and they tottered their way

through the palace's open gate and into the courtyard. At the base of the wide staircase, a lone guard stopped them.

"Ho, there, my friends," the man said with a grin on his face. "You've come the wrong way. The *piazza* is through there." He pointed to the tall archway.

One of the sailors, a native-born Venetian, pushed himself to the front of the group. Francis and Jobe hung back beyond the circle of light cast by the watchman's torch.

The sailor, dressed as Pantalone, returned the guard's grin. "No, worthy officer, we were just commanded to go to the Doge's suite where we will have the honor of entertaining our noble prince and his family as soon as the pig ceremony is done."

The guard's expression turned wary. "Who told you this?"

The sailor merely shrugged. "He did not give me his name. Who are we but motley players? The noble gentleman did not exchange pleasantries with our lot. He was the one who wore a red gown and he stood close to His Serene Highness." The sailor drew closer to the guard. "We are to be a surprise, you see."

Francis tightened his grip on the body. If the guard became difficult, they might have to kill him. Despite the vow he had made in the heat of his anger, Francis hoped to avoid unnecessary bloodshed.

The guard studied the "players" one by one. When he spotted the sagging Columbina in the shadows, he relaxed. "Oh, ho, I see why you look so abashed. You had best sober up your little lady there before the Doge returns."

The sailor and his companions, including Francis and Jobe, bowed and scraped before the guard. "*Sì*, very unfortunate," the Venetian agreed. "Please, my friend, say nothing. We will wake her, I swear on my mother's soul. She will delight, I promise you." He thumped his chest.

"We are the best—the very best actors in all of Venice this night."

Amen to that, thought Francis.

Grinning again, the guard waved them by. "I hope so for your sake. And, Signor Pantalone, if the Doge is generous…" He rubbed his thumb and forefinger together. "I pray that you remember me."

The sailor laughed. "We will indeed, good *signore. Arrivederci!*"

With more words of cheer and bawdy jokes, the masked invaders hurried up the huge staircase into the palace. Jobe and Francis with their ghastly burden kept to the middle of the group until they reached the long gallery on the second floor. As Francis had hoped, the great palace appeared deserted. Everyone had gone to see the grisly highlight of Fat Tuesday's revels.

Jobe posted the Venetian sailor as their lookout at the head of the stairs. Tossing the Greek boy over his shoulder, Francis ran down the gallery to the room he knew led to the Bridge of Sighs. At various intervals along the gallery, Jobe stationed his crew members. Finding the bridge's antechamber deserted, Jobe and Francis slipped inside and closed the door.

Francis laid the body down near the bridge entrance. Then he took the Dominican's robe from his pack and dropped it over his colorful costume. Jobe removed his doctor's costume so that he was once more attired all in black. He held up his red devil's mask to Francis. The Englishman grinned in the darkness. *A most excellent idea in case the next guard is not as stupid as the last one.*

Francis wrapped the body in his dark cloak, then peered across the bridge. Beyond the narrow enclosed passage, he saw the glow of a lantern. Before stepping onto the bridge, Francis added one more touch to his disguise: pox marks made of wax on his forehead and cheeks. For good measure, he added a large wart on the end of his nose.

Jobe came up beside him. "Good hunting and may the spirit of your noble grandfather be with you," he whispered into Francis's ear.

Sir Thomas would have indeed enjoyed this adventure. Francis clasped Jobe's forearm, then he stepped onto the bridge. From now on he could not—would not—turn back from this enterprise. He had never felt so exhilarated nor so alive as he did at this moment.

Once across the bridge Francis cleared his throat and called, "Peace be upon you" to the guard that sat on a stool under the lighted lantern.

Jumping to his feet, the man shielded his eyes with one hand while he gripped his pike with the other. "Who goes there?"

Keeping his black hood well down over his bright hair and face, Francis sketched a quick blessing in the air in front of him. "A friend. Peace be with you," he repeated in a guttural tone.

The guard reacted with an automatic "And with your spirit, good father."

Francis stepped to the left of the guard, forcing him to turn away from the bridge. "Tell me, my son, does the witch still live?" Pray God that Jessica did. Francis held his breath.

The guard spat against the wall. "*Sì*, father, but not for long."

We're in time! Aloud, Francis continued, "I have been sent to shrive her of her sins—if she will listen to me."

Again he took another step to the left. Now the guard had his back to the bridge. Francis saw Jobe's shape, blacker than the night, flit across the divide. He carried the dead boy in his arms. Safely across, he flattened himself against the wall.

The guard swore an oath, then apologized. "The girl is a clever minx, father. Best not get too close to her. I heard tell that she damned His Highness and the whole Council this afternoon."

Francis folded his hands as if in prayer. "Wicked!" he agreed, though he laughed inside. "But perhaps there is still some little spark of hope I can give her."

"Hope for what?" the guard snarled. "A quick death?"

"Hope for her immortal soul," Francis answered. "To save her from the fires of hell. Is she lodged above—under the roof?"

The guard chortled. "No, they put her deep in the Wells." He jerked his thumb in the direction of a downward spiral staircase.

"Below the water. It must be freezing there," Francis remarked more to himself than to the man before him. Poor Jessica! If they had taken away her cloak, her dainty little costume would afford her sparse protection from the cold.

The minute he learned where Jessica was located, Jobe with his bundle snaked under the low arch and down the stairs to the dungeons. Meanwhile the guard regaled his listener with a vivid description of the horrors that awaited the condemned witch when she rejoined her demonic master.

"She'll be warm enough there I'll warrant," he concluded.

Francis gave him a solemn look though he seethed inside. He itched to throttle the unfeeling brute for his cruel thoughts toward Jessica. "Be it as God ordains, my son, but the hour grows late. Lead me to this most unfortunate sinner."

The guard rested his pike against the wall, then unhooked

his lantern. He picked up a candle stub from a nearby table and lit it. Holding it out to Francis, he remarked, "You'll need this, father. It is blacker than the devil's throat down there."

Francis gripped the taper. Jessica—alone and waiting for death in the dark! When they were married, he would light a hundred candles in her honor. The guard brushed past him and began the descent into the lower depths of the *prigione*. Francis followed closely behind him, marveling how Jobe had managed to find his way down these treacherous steps in the pitch black. The African had always sworn that he had the night vision of a hunting owl; now Francis believed his boast.

At the bottom of the stairs a foul stink of urine, stagnant water and raw fear assailed his nostrils. Francis nearly gagged. Jessica had already endured four days of this stench. Squinting against the light of his candle, Francis cast anxious glances on both sides of the passage in search of Jobe, but the giant had melted into the darkness. Snores, an occasional cough and low moaning told Francis that Jessica was not the only prisoner on this level. When the time came, he must move very quietly, as well as quickly lest the other wretches raise a clamor for their own release.

The guard reached the far end of the passage, then turned to the left. He stopped before a stout wooden door pierced by a double-barred window. Though Francis could see nothing inside that black hole, he detected soft breathing. His blood pounded in his temples. Jessica was there. Even though he could not see her, he felt her presence. He wanted to call out to her not to be afraid but he dared not give away his game just yet. He gripped the candle stub tighter.

The guard fumbled for several agonizing minutes trying to find the right key. Down the passage, an unseen prisoner howled and wept. The sound sent chills down Francis's spine. With a grunt of satisfaction, the guard inserted the key into the rusted lock and turned it.

The door swung open on creaking hinges.

Chapter Nineteen

No one had brought Jessica food or water since she had returned to her cell. By that sign, she knew that her execution would take place before the next morning. Standing on tiptoe at her narrow window, she watched her last sunset fade into purple. After dark, a breeze blew through the opening and slopped the canal water down inside her cell.

In the waning twilight, Jessica traced the words carved into the wall with her fingertip. "Learn to endure." I *will* endure, she vowed, even to the very end. The wind carried the sounds of carnival through the bars. How cheerful the flutes and tabors sounded! Remembering her fleeting few hours and the pleasure of dancing in the *piazza* with Francis, her heart ached. She longed to whirl away this nightmare in his strong arms.

I must not be afraid. I am going to a much better place where there is no pain or hunger.

Sinking to her knees beside her hard cot, she buried her face in her arms and prayed for courage and strength. She must face her death bravely so that her executioners would know that she was truly not a witch. But sheer terror closed in around her. Her breasts rose and fell under her labored breathing. Once when the jailer had walked past her door, her throat closed up. She gripped the wooden board of her cot until the man's footsteps receded down the passageway.

Jessica clasped her hands together. "Please, dear God, please let it be over quickly for me. Don't let it be painful. I am so afraid of pain." Her mouth tasted like old parchment, dry and dusty.

Her one crumb of comfort was the memory of Francis's last words to her. How brave and splendid he had looked in the middle of the Hall of the Great Council—like the Archangel Michael! How his eyes had flashed with that special blue fire she had grown to love! How golden his hair gleamed in the late afternoon sunlight like a halo! "I love you," he had shouted; his declaration echocd around the room and in her brain.

No one had ever said "I love you" to her—not even her own mother. She knew that Sophia and Gobbo loved her, but they had never said it in so many words. Her patients had liked her; some of the men had even tried to pursue her with a lusty intent, but none of them had loved her— until Francis came into her life.

She played with the red ribbon she had tied around her wrist—his gift. Four days ago—a lifetime, it seemed—she had worn it in her hair. Now her tresses were tangled and matted with dirt and straw from her bed. Kneeling on the rough wooden floor in the cold darkness, she caressed the smooth piece of satin against her cheek and held her memories of Francis's love close to her heart.

A lantern's feeble light shining through the window of the cell door startled her. The key rattled in the lock. Jessica's pulse throbbed erratically. An iron weight sank into the pit of her stomach. Panic rushed into her mind.

The hour has come! I will be dead very soon. Courage! I must be strong now! She rose to face her fate.

The guard pushed open the door. Jessica squinted against the brightness of the candlelight.

"A priest for you," the man wheezed. "Come to save you, says he."

Her reprieve almost undid her. Her knees trembled. She put her hand on the damp wall for support. "Welcome, father," she rasped, her throat sore with her anxiety. "You come in good time."

A man dressed in dark robes stepped past the jailer and into her cell. "Peace be with you, my child," he growled at her. He held a small candle.

A familiar scent wafted around her—one of cloves that made her instantly think of Francis. She braced herself against the wall. What cruel trickery did her wits play on her taut nerves?

"Withdraw," the priest instructed the other man. "I need some privacy if I am to attempt to do God's work with this sinful soul."

The guard guffawed. "A waste of your time, father."

The priest lifted his candle higher; its golden beams fell across Jessica's face. "It is my duty as a priest from the Holy Office to proffer God's mercy to even the most wicked of sinners."

¡Dio mio! The dreaded Inquisition! Putting her hand over her eyes, Jessica leaned back against the rough wall. Now that they had condemned her, couldn't they leave her alone? Would this man torture her through the night before they killed her? She dug her broken nails into the skin of her palms. *I will endure this. I must show my innocence by my strength. God be with me!*

The jailer shut the door with a thud. "Very well, father, go to. Give a call when you are done with her. I will be at the bend of the passage." He turned the lock and departed.

The priest anchored his candle on the end of her cot then

stepped toward her. "Jessica," he whispered as he drew closer. "Do not be afraid. It is me."

Had her ears deceived her? Was she going mad with hysteria? "Francis?" she croaked. What had happened to his face?

In answer, the priest swept her into his arms, and rained kisses on her forehead, her cheeks, her nose, her mouth. He whispered her name over and over. "My love, my sweet Jessica! Oh, angel mine!"

She blinked back her sudden tears of joy. "Francis! But how—"

When he stopped her mouth with a hard kiss, she knew he was truly with her by the touch of his lips on hers. She threw her arms around his neck and clung to him.

The key rattled in the lock again though there was no light without. Francis sprang away from her.

Once against the door swung open. "There is time enough for wooing later, Francis," said Jobe, stepping inside the cell. "For now, we must make all haste."

Francis clapped his hand over Jessica's mouth to muffle her cry of surprise. Then he closed the door once more. "The guard?" he asked.

The giant, blacker than night, chuckled under his breath. "I tripped him. When he awakes, he will think that he stumbled over his own big feet. But he has a hard head and will not sleep for long." He dropped a long bundle onto the cot.

When Jessica beheld a youth dressed in the garish costume of Columbina, she almost screamed again. Pulling her against his chest, Francis stroked her quaking body. "Hush, *cara*," he crooned. "It is only a poor boy whose death this morning will do you a great service tonight. He is your passport to a new life."

Jessica recoiled. "I will not have someone's blood pay

the price for my freedom. I could not bear to live with myself.''

Francis continued to stroke her, running his warm hands along her spine. ''He died of a fever sent by the Angel of Death, not by my hand.''

From his place by the door, Jobe hissed at them. ''*¡Silenzio!* Be quick!''

Francis gave her a hurried kiss. ''Trust me, my love. Now undress! Do not stand on modesty. We must exchange your clothing with the boy's. Courage!'' he added.

Though she still trembled from the shock of Francis's unexpected appearance with his lifeless companion, Jessica understood exactly what he had in mind. Moving quickly, she unlaced her tattered costume and stepped out of it. Meanwhile Francis undressed the corpse. He handed her the pink-and-white skirt. Wrinkling her nose against its strong odor of wine and decay, she tied it around her waist; then the black bodice and finally the beribboned cap. Francis quickly clothed the dead boy. By the time Jessica had finished tying the mask's ribbons under her hair, the body on the bed looked remarkably like her. She shuddered at the sight.

''Done,'' Francis told Jobe.

''Good, for the jailer stirs.''

Francis led Jessica to the door. ''Now we must fly like the wind on silent feet.'' He reached for his candle. Then he paused over the cot. ''Sleep in peace, young Greek, and may the angels escort you to heaven with joy, for you have well earned your reward.''

''Amen,'' Jessica murmured.

Jobe pushed open the door as quietly as its hinges allowed. Holding her with one hand and the candle stub in the other, Francis drew Jessica behind him along the narrow stone corridor. She glanced over her shoulder in time to see Jobe shut and relock the cell door.

Francis tugged at her, then pointed to where the dazed jailer groaned next to his lantern. Hopping over his prostrate form, the two fled down the long passage to the staircase. Jobe paused long enough to place the ring of keys in the guard's hand, then he dashed after them.

Though Francis held his candle high, Jessica could barely see where to put her feet on the murky stairway. When she stumbled, Jobe scooped her under his arm. She curled herself around him and shut her eyes, opening them only when a cold breeze of fresh air blew against her face. They crossed the far end of the connecting bridge. Once inside the Doge's palace, Jobe set her on her feet again. She almost fell, but Francis caught her. He blew out the candle.

"Now we will transform ourselves once more," he told her as he pulled off his priestly robe.

When Jessica adjusted her eyes to the darkness, she saw Francis stuff the robe under the back of his colorful shirt.

He chuckled to her. "I fear your reputation as a witch will be assured after this night's work. That man will have a hard time explaining to the authorities how you changed into a boy and how you made me disappear."

"We are not out of the bag yet," Jobe mumbled from behind his comic doctor's mask. "Getting in was easy. Now comes the sticky part."

Outside of the palace, a great cheer went up. "They must be throwing down the pigs," Francis muttered. "Time to be on our way."

Another cheer filled the air.

Jobe stuck his head out into the gallery. "My men are still in place. Let us go!"

He slid through the narrow opening like a shadow. Jessica followed, her hand in Francis's. As they raced down the long hall Jobe's crew members fell in behind them. Jessica saw the glint of naked daggers in their hands, but there was no time to think what the men might do for her sake.

At the top of the great staircase Jobe tucked her arm through his. Francis took her other arm. "Look a little dazed," the African told her as they descended. "The guard below thinks you are drunk with wine." Then he said to Francis, "If the need arises, we will run with her to the Molo. One of my skiffs waits there for us. My men will delay any pursuers."

Francis nodded, then he whispered to her. "Ready?"

Jessica gulped then nodded. "*Sì,*" she replied and added, "but don't let go of me."

Freedom danced before her eyes. She drank in the sweet cold air as they crossed the tiled landing to the final flight of stairs. The roars of the crowd grew louder as another pig fell squealing to the pavement of the *piazza*. Jessica had heard of this strange ritual that had its roots in the pagan days of ancient Rome, but she was glad she did not have to witness it. Death had hovered far too close to her for comfort.

Hearing them, the guard turned. He grinned when he saw Jessica. "I see you have managed to revive your Columbina."

One of Jobe's sailors replied, "*Sì,* a lot of water did the trick. Now we are ready for the Doge!" He puffed up his chest.

Ready for what? Jessica wondered. She never wanted to lay eyes on that dreadful old man again.

The guard frowned at the costumed sailor. "But the Doge has not yet returned from the *piazza*. What *is* this?" He punched the sailor in the stomach with the butt end of his pike. "Why have you returned so soon when the Doge has not even seen your performance? He is still with the pigs. Have you stolen anything?''

''Only a witch,'' Francis whispered in Jessica's ear. He tightened his grip on her arm. They sidestepped a few paces nearer to the gateway's arch.

The sailor raised both hands in protest. ''Of course not! I may look like a fool but I assure you I have all my wits.'' He moved closer to the guard and confided in a loud whisper, ''The truth of the matter is that our little Columbina...well, she puked on the floor of the gallery before we could stop her. It did her a world of good.''

The guard's face turned mottled red. ''What?''

''Jesu,'' Francis swore under his breath to Jobe. ''That idiot's mouth will doom all of us. Be ready to run,'' he told Jessica.

She swallowed the knot in her throat. She didn't need to feign sickness now; her stomach lurched. She gripped the sleeves of her two supporters.

With a show of bravado, the sailor hung his arm about the guard's neck. ''Have no fear, my friend. We cleaned it up. We did not want *that* mess to be our surprise for the Doge. We are men of honor.'' He belched in the man's face.

The guard shoved him away. ''Get out of here, you drunken sots!'' He swept his pike in a semicircle, forcing the conspirators to back toward the gate. ''Away with you! If I ever catch any of you near here again, I will skewer you like one of those puling pigs!''

While the Venetian sailor continued to play his sniveling role, Francis and Jobe hustled Jessica through the gate just as the last pig fell from the bell tower. It landed near its brethren with a sickening thunk. Jessica averted her eyes.

''This way!'' Jobe turned toward the Molo where a number of gondolas and other watercraft bobbed at the landing.

Jessica didn't know whether to laugh or cry. Was she really free? Or would the nightwatch suddenly close in upon them? She glanced over her shoulders. The ducal heralds trumpeted again, announcing the end of the Twelve Pigs and the imminent return of the Doge to his palace.

At the edge of the landing, Jobe whistled into the glistening darkness of the Grand Canal. An answering call to the right signaled where the promised skiff lay. Jobe guided Jessica and Francis to the boat. He jumped in, then lifted Jessica and placed her on a seat in the middle of the craft. Francis followed heavily. The boat wobbled while the two oarsmen cursed.

Francis dropped down beside her. "I am no sailor, *cara,* as I fear you will soon discover."

She snuggled against him, savoring his warmth. "Are we safe yet?"

Untying the mooring line, Jobe pushed the boat away from the landing with a mighty shove of his foot. Then he sat in the stern and took the tiller in his hands.

"Soon, little one," he told her in a low tone. "See out there?" He pointed over her shoulder.

Turning in their seats, Jessica and Francis peered down the canal toward the wide entrance of the lagoon. A number of large vessels swung on their anchors.

"The second one from the right," Jobe continued. "That is the *Jinn,* my wife at sea."

The dismaying truth dawned on Jessica. She squeezed Francis's hand. "We are going to sail away from here? L-leave Venice?" she stammered.

He kissed her forehead. "If you stay, you will die," he told her in a gentle voice. "There is no other way."

"Sophia and Gobbo are already on board," Jobe added. "They were more than happy to quit this city."

She twisted her fingers nervously in her lap. "They were

not born in Venice as I was,'' she responded in a low, agonized voice.

Tears of deep regret filmed over her eyes. The torchlights in the *piazza* melded into a blur of color. The sounds of gaiety and music grew fainter. The oars dipped and rose in the water with silent precision, pulling her farther away from her beloved home.

Francis kissed her again. ''Where did you think we would hide you?'' When she gave him no answer, he continued, ''Venice has cast you out, my sweet—and me, as well.''

With a dull inner pain in her breast, she acknowledged, ''You speak the truth, Francis. I am quite literally adrift.''

He held her closer to him. ''You are with me now.''

But for how long?

Jessica remained silent for the rest of the journey to Jobe's ship. Suddenly it loomed out of the darkness above them. Used to seeing only gondolas, the large vessel's bulk startled her. Before she had time to think about it, the skiff bumped along the dark wooden sides of the *Jinn*. One of the oarsmen grabbed onto a rope ladder, then he held out his hand to Jessica.

She stared at the gently rocking ship. ''Up there?''

Jobe chuckled behind her. ''*Sì, madonna,* freedom and peace of mind await you—and so do your friends.'' Reaching around her, he placed her hands on the ropes. ''Now, step up. Don't look down. I will not let you fall.''

She cast a quick glance over her shoulder. ''Francis?''

He gave her a wobbly grin. ''Let Jobe escort you for now, Jessica. It is better that I make my own clumsy way myself.''

''He suffers from seasickness,'' Jobe confided to her as he guided her up. ''Even in this little pond. In an hour when we reach the Adriatic, he will look like walking death. You'll see.''

"Oh,'' said Jessica, wondering if she, too, would fall prey to the same illness.

Many hands helped her over the ship rail onto the deck. With a cry of joy, Sophia ran to her and threw her arms around Jessica's waist. Gobbo took her hand and kissed it. Both their eyes glittered with tears.

"We prayed for you, my child.'' Sophia hugged her. "Oh, how we prayed! And when Jobe said they would spirit you away, well—'' She could not continue but instead gave way to her tears.

Overcome by their love, Jessica wept with them. It was the first time in four days that she had allowed herself that comforting release.

While Jessica and her friends clung to each other in a tight circle, Francis pulled himself onboard.

As soon as his feet touched the bobbing deck, he groaned under his breath. "God's teeth,'' he muttered. He put his hand over his stomach.

Jobe grabbed him by the shoulders and shook him. "What ho, *meo amigo,* we did it!''

Francis staggered to the nearest masthead. "Aye.'' He swallowed back his queasiness. "Is the tide still running with us?''

Jobe chuckled. "Tis, and here comes the rest of my crew.'' Leaning over the rail, he called down, "Is everyone accounted for?''

"Sì,'' answered the Venetian sailor as he clambered over the side. "You owe me a bounty, *capitano,* for my stupendous performance.''

Jobe lifted the man off his feet in a giant bear hug. "You will have your reward—as soon as we catch the next Turkish merchant.'' He put his finger to his lips. "Shush, softly now, my children. We must slip away before the lion of Venice notices that we have bolted from his cage.''

Within minutes men of many nationalities swarmed over the ship. The last crewman was barely out of the second skiff before it was hauled aboard. With a low rumble, the sailors winched up the anchor. A dozen agile men ran barefoot up the spiderweb of ropes to the great crosstrees where the sails were tied. Within minutes they freed yards of ivory-colored canvas that billowed out with the freshening wind from the nearby sea. In silence, Jobe's sleek ship moved slowly away from her sleeping neighbors.

Resting his head against the base of the mast, Francis watched Jessica's reunion with her friends. Now that their bold escapade was completed, a strange weakness overtook his limbs. He gripped one of the ropes that hung down from somewhere aloft. For the first time the full impact of their daring hit him. Not until this moment did he realize that he had fully expected to fail and to die at Jessica's side. He closed his eyes in a silent prayer of thanks to the Cavendish patron, Saint Michael.

Jessica's hand touched his face. "Francis? Are you ill?"

When he opened his eyes, he found himself staring into the unmasked face of the loveliest woman in the world. He gave her a weak smile. "Have I died and gone to heaven for I see an angel before me.''

She laughed—her first laugh since she had been dragged from his side on that dreadful Friday night—then shook her head. ''I do not think that angels have such dirty faces or such ragged clothing.''

He reached for her and she glided into his embrace. ''I have paradise in my arms now,'' he murmured.

She laid her head on his shoulder. Together they watched the glow that was Venice grow smaller. Just then, over the water, the great bell of the campanile tolled. "Twelve," counted Jessica. "Midnight."

Francis gave a little laugh. "In England we call it the witching hour. Have I a witch in my arms?"

She did not return his smile. "I am afraid I cannot join in your mirth. The scars are still too fresh."

He kissed her forehead. "A thousand pardons, my love, but I am in a lighthearted mood. In fact, I feel reborn."

She slipped her hands under his cape and encircled his waist. "So do I," she whispered.

They watched the islands melt into the darkness behind them. "Soon they will discover that I am gone. Do you think we will we be able to get away in time?"

Jobe materialized beside them. He laughed. "First someone will have to be brave enough to approach your cell."

Sophia marched up to him. "How so?" she asked with her hands on her hips.

Jobe regarded her with a grin. "Because, Madam Mouse, I put my devil's mask over the boy's face. In the lantern light, they will swear that Madonna Jessica had turned herself into the devil and that she ate up the poor priest." He laughed again. "By the time those guards have matched their slack wits together and pieced out our device, we will be sailing on the high seas!"

Francis swallowed hard again. "Mother of God," he murmured. He hated ships and sailing!

Gobbo yawned and his little wife led him belowdecks, clucking like a mothering hen.

Jessica sighed. "I have never left my city. It is a strange thing. Even though I lived in fear every day of my life in Venice, I loved her. It is my home."

Francis let go of his rope, braced his feet wide apart on the deck and turned Jessica so that she fully faced him.

"Then it is time for you to live without fear, starting now. Kiss me, sweet Jessica, to toast this happy beginning."

She lifted her lips to his. Her kiss comforted his tired soul. "You are home to me now, my love," he whispered.

Chapter Twenty

"Do you still live?" Jobe asked Francis nearly a week after their flight from Venice. A bright sun streamed into the tiny forecastle cabin where Francis lay wedged in a too narrow bunk.

Rolling over, Francis barked his raw shins against a protruding beam for the hundredth time since this poxy voyage had begun and opened one red-rimmed eye.

"That depends upon your definition of living," he groaned. His joints ached from the confinement of the cramped space. His head ached from bumping it every time he attempted to stand in the low-ceilinged cabin and his stomach lurched with every motion of the ship. "Go away and let me die in peace," he growled.

Jobe did not move from the hatchway. "Tis too bad you are not like your kinsman, young Kitt Cavendish. That boy has saltwater in his blood."

Francis closed his eyes, wishing that Jobe would disappear. "The Cavendishes come from Viking stock," he mumbled, "while my mother's people hugged the land." He pulled the bran sack that served as his pillow over his head.

Jobe chuckled. "You will soon become used to the ship's roll."

Francis gritted his teeth. "You told me that two years ago when you brought me down to Genoa." That short voyage from Marseilles had been a nightmare from start to finish. By the time Francis had arrived in Italy, he was a gaunt man. "Shouldn't you be doing something else instead of plaguing me with your deuced good health?"

Jobe crossed his arms over his chest. "The seas run before us like a skein of silk. The wind blows steady and true. We will pass through the Straits of Messina before this day is out."

Francis merely groaned in reply. Only halfway around Italy with most of the Mediterranean to sail before they even reached the stormy Atlantic? He would not live to see England.

"Madonna Jessica has got her sea legs now," Jobe continued in his blasted cheerful voice. "She even ate a good dish of salt beef this morning."

Francis's stomach heaved at the thought. He swallowed several times in quick succession. "I am glad to hear it," he muttered. He felt under the low bed for his slop bucket—just in case.

"She asked to see you," Jobe continued.

"Hoy day!" Francis rubbed his chin, now covered with a short reddish-blond beard. "I am not fit for a pigsty much less for a fair maid's company. Please give her my compliments and tell her that I am reeky and green-sick."

With a low chuckle Jobe stepped aside. "Tell her yourself."

Like an angel in a dream vision, Jessica took Jobe's place. She removed her mask and smiled at him. *"¡Buon giorno! Francis,"* she said in that low musical voice of hers.

He started to sit up, banged his head on a low shelf above him, and fell back on his pillow, cursing under his breath.

"If you need a whip to tame him, call me," Jobe remarked to her before he vanished from sight.

Francis winced. "Your pardon, *madonna*. I am not myself."

She knelt beside his bunk and put a cool hand on his brow. "Isn't this how we first met?" she asked with a twinkle in the depths of her lustrous brown eyes. "You were lying in pain under my hands."

"My gut did not play the fool with me on that occasion," he reminded her. "My eyes rejoice to see you, Jessica," he added. He tried to sit up again, but she gently pushed him back.

"I am not familiar with this sea infirmity but I know what works for women who are in the early stages of their pregnancy."

He rolled his eyes to the ceiling.

She took his hand in hers, turned it palm up and pressed down hard on a sensitive point between the tendons just above his wrist. She applied that pressure for a few minutes of silence, then released him and vigorously rubbed the area.

Francis snorted to himself. It was his stomach not his arm that plagued him, but he would say nothing to her. If she didn't mind his stink and bedraggled appearance, he rejoiced in her company. She massaged the hollow just behind his ears, then she gently rubbed his temples. He almost purred.

She held up a small covered bowl. "The sea is calm today so the cook was able to light his fires. He made a good beef broth for you."

At the aroma of the soup, Francis's stomach lurched again. "My thanks, but it will not stay with me."

She made a soft sound of disagreement. "You need nourishment. Look at your wrists—all bones, no meat." She lifted the pot cover and stirred the broth with a wooden spoon. "Please, Francis, take some."

He wanted to fling the bowl against the bulkhead, but for her sweet sake, he would try. Though his stomach cramped and protested, he opened his mouth and let her feed him. He could barely swallow the scalding stuff.

"Good," she crooned. "And another."

Francis eyed his slop bucket. "You ask a great deal, *cara*," he muttered. He swallowed down another spoonful. To distract himself from his innards, he seized upon the first subject that came to mind. "Why do you still wear the mask?" he asked, pointing to the thing that lay on the floor beside her. "You are among friends now."

A blush stained her cheeks. "Sailors are a very superstitious lot. The crew knows I was condemned as a witch. I do not want to give them any cause to toss me overboard."

He gripped the low wooden sides of his bunk. "I would run through any man who dares to touch you. I will never again abandon you, Jessica. Forgive me for that lapse."

She smoothed his cheek with her fingers. "There is nothing to forgive, Francis. I understand...now. Jobe told me a great deal about you this past week." She slipped another spoonful between his cracked, dry lips.

Not all the sordid details, I hope. He swallowed then asked, "Did he tell you that I love you?"

Jessica looked down at the broth. "Jobe said something like that, but I knew that he was only being kind." She lifted her head and stared into Francis's eyes. "I will never forget that moment when you proclaimed to all of Venice that we were betrothed. Your sweet words will linger in my heart forever. But..." She lifted one shoulder in a dismissive gesture. "The time of danger is now past. Both of us must think of the future."

A pang of fear added to his discomfort. He cupped her chin with his shaking fingers. "How now? What words hang in the air between us? I meant what I said. I will marry you as soon as I can stand upright."

With a sad smile, she shook her head. "You promised marriage merely to save me. I know that and I am most grateful, but now—"

"You do not love me?" He tried to pull himself up, but she stopped him once again.

"It is not a question of love, but of practicality, Francis. In England, you are a fine lord, a member of a noble family. Look at me. Even if you were mad enough to pursue this idea of marriage between us, your family would never permit it."

He would have laughed if he could muster the strength. Instead he put his hand over hers. "Didn't Jobe tell you about my mother?"

Jessica gave him a steady look. "He repeated what you had once said—that she was light of virtue and that she died in a convent a few years ago."

Francis lay back on his bran sack and stared at the low ceiling. "You think that Lord Richard Bardolph was my father? A lie—like everything else in my life."

She froze, the dripping spoon in midair. "*¡Dio mio!*" she murmured; her dark eyes grew enormous.

Francis turned down the corners of his lips. "Lord Bardolph loved young animals—puppies, kittens, colts, piglets—and children. He fathered all seven of us in a perplexed sort of way. You see, he never really knew whether his increasing offspring were his by blood or by...accident."

She fed him another spoonful of the now cooling soup. "Were *you* an accident?" she asked in a low voice.

He snorted through his nose. "I was the eldest of the cuckoos."

Jessica searched her mind for the meaning of his strange word. "I do not understand. What is a cuckoo?"

He bared his teeth. "It is an English bird that lays its eggs in the nests of other birds. The unsuspecting foster parent hatches the cuckoo chicks and raises them as its own. My stepbrothers—the real sons of Lord Bardolph—turned that word into a name of derision. It went hardest on my younger sisters—half sisters, that is. None of us shared the same father."

Jessica fed him in silence while she considered this shocking revelation. Francis watched her face for signs of anger or revulsion.

When she spoke at last, her voice quivered. "Did you ever learn the name of your natural father?"

He stiffened.

"You need not tell me, if you do not—"

He closed his eyes. "My mother was a clever woman, I'll give her that much," he snapped. "When we were old enough to be fostered in another household—a custom in my country—Lady Olivia sent us cuckoos to the homes of our paternal families. The Cavendishes hid their surprise very well when I appeared at Wolf Hall. I did not realize that I might be one of them until the day I began to shave." He rubbed his bearded chin.

Jessica furrowed her brow. "What has shaving got to do with it?"

Francis gave her a short, mirthless laugh. "I saw my true reflection in a looking glass instead of in the muddy waters of the moat. The Cavendish family possess the most singular looks—and they all look alike. If you see one, you have seen them all—even a stray cuckoo.''

"Oh!" Jessica gasped. "So you are also a Cavendish?"

He grimaced. "My grandfather, Sir Thomas Cavendish, was the late Earl of Thornbury. He had two sons, Brandon and Guy." Brandon, so worldly wise, fearless and good-natured, and Guy, the quiet intellectual that once sought his destiny in a monastery. Feeling uncommonly sleepy, Francis yawned.

"Do you know which one is your father?" Jessica prodded.

"*Sì*, I do," he replied, his eyelids growing heavier. "But my father does not know he has a son." He yawned again.

Jessica sat back on her heels. "Sleep well, Francis, it will do you a world of good for your body—and your spirits."

He could not keep his eyes open. "Did you put something in that soup?"

She nodded. "A little juice of the poppy. If you sleep, you will not lose this food too soon for it to help you."

"Great Jove!" he muttered in English. "You are a minx."

Her laughter tickled his ear. "When you are yourself again, Francis, you must teach me how to speak your language."

He started to reply that he would teach her English and a good many other pleasant things, but instead sleep overcame him. He had no idea when Jessica left his side.

When Francis awoke after dark, he felt a little better in body, though his mind tumbled with disquieting thoughts. He reviewed his conversation with Jessica and wondered how she had reacted to his disclosures. He cursed his seasickness. If he had not felt so weak, he would never have divulged so much of his sordid history to her. Now what did she think of the great English *messere* who had proved himself to be a coward, a liar *and* a bastard? He vowed to ask her the next time she visited him.

But when Jessica returned, Sophia accompanied her. As much as Francis liked the little woman, he could not speak his private thoughts to his beloved with Sophia in attendance. The next day Gobbo came with Jessica and played his lute while she massaged Francis's temples, coaxed more food into him and fed him an infusion of powdered ginger root to settle the humors of his stomach.

During the following days this same frustrating pattern repeated itself time and again. Once or twice Francis had ventured to speak of their future together when they reached England, but she always changed the subject.

One morning Jobe paid him a visit. "You look better, but why the frown?"

Francis pointed to the ceiling. "That!" he snapped. On the deck just over his head, Jessica held court with several of Jobe's crew. By the sounds of her laughter mixed with theirs, Francis deduced that the girl had utterly charmed the rough sailors.

Jobe grinned. "The men worship her and she keeps them happy. I shall be sorry when she leaves us."

Francis glared at him. "Leaves? What jest is this? She is going to England with me."

Jobe pretended to be surprised. "Indeed? Then why does she plan to join Sophia and Gobbo when we dock at Genoa this afternoon?"

Francis gaped at him. "Is this her gratitude for saving her from death?"

Jobe cocked an eyebrow. "Have you made your intentions known to the lady?"

Francis growled, "Aye, in the middle of the Doge's

Great Hall! By my every look and thought! How could she doubt me, unless…'' Unless Jessica was no better than the grasping, greedy Cosma. "I told her the truth of my birth. She knows now that I have neither title nor estate to my name. Mayhap, she is no longer interested in me."

Jobe shook his head. "Is that what you think, *meo amigo?* Then you must speak to her—and quickly. We will enter Genoa's harbor within the hour."

Balling his hand into a fist, Francis pounded the bulkhead. "God's teeth, I have tried, Jobe!"

Jobe's dark eyes warmed with his merriment. "Then I suggest that you take matters into your own hands. Do not wait for moonlight and mandolins, strike now! But first you will have to get out of that bed."

Francis gnashed his teeth. "Very well, I will."

Ducking his head to avoid the shelf, Francis pulled himself upright. Then he swung his long legs to the floor. Jobe gave him a hand and helped him to his feet. Francis shook his head to clear his giddiness.

Jobe pushed him through the hatchway. "Go to! Most excellent hunting!"

Francis climbed the stairs, inhaled the fresh tang of salty air, then looked to where a knot of admirers surrounded his masked beauty. With her black hair billowing about her face like a sea nymph's, Jessica kneaded the shoulders of a particularly husky Frenchman. Compressing his lips with his jealous anger, Francis crossed the deck in three long strides. Without bothering to apologize for his intrusion, he closed his hand around Jessica's slim wrist, catching her in the middle of a sentence.

She stared up at him with her mouth agape. "How now, Francis? You are up! It is good to see you looking so, um…well." A scarlet stain spread over her cheeks, making her even more beautiful than before.

Francis pulled her to her feet. "Signorina Leonardo and I have some unfinished business," he informed the surprised men. He all but dragged her toward the steps that led to Jobe's large cabin in the ship's stern.

Jessica tried to wriggle out of his grasp. "Francis, what is the matter? Please, you are hurting me."

He turned a deaf ear to her entreaties until they reached the cabin that Jobe had given to her and her friends for the voyage around Italy's boot. Inside, Sophia and Gobbo paused in their packing when they saw them. Francis tossed a polite smile to the dumbfounded couple.

"*Per favore,* may we have some privacy?" he asked them. He did not loosen his grip on Jessica.

She tore off her mask with her free hand. "These are my friends—my family. You may speak to me freely in their hearing."

Francis ignored her. To Gobbo he said, "You know how it is with women. Sometimes a firm hand is needed. I beg your understanding."

Sophia swelled up. "Now see here, my lord! What cause do you have to barge in and order us about as if we were nothing but dogs beneath your feet?"

Before Francis could muster a reply, Gobbo pulled his sputtering wife out of the cabin. "*Sì,* it is better that they talk without our ears flapping in the breeze." He closed the door behind them.

Francis released Jessica, but blocked her reach for the latch. Catching her in his arms, he held her tightly. It had been too long since she had last been in his embrace. "Is this what you really want to do? Leave me and live in Genoa? Cower behind that damnable mask for the rest of your life?"

Jessica's lower lip quivered though she did not look

away. "I will be better off with my friends. I can do what I did in Venice—be a healer."

Francis stroked her hair. "You have not healed me yet," he murmured. Indeed, the dampness of the ship had aggravated his shoulder though he spoke of the emptiness in his heart.

Jessica blinked then said, "I thank you for your many kindnesses, Francis, but I—"

His self-control snapped. "Kindness?" he thundered. He gave her a little shake. "Is saving your life a kindness? Why shouldn't I do that for the woman I love?"

She pressed her hand over his mouth. "I pray you, do not misuse such a precious word. I cannot bear to be mocked."

Francis knotted his brows together, perplexed by her words. Hadn't he shown her how much he loved her? "How have I mocked you?"

After thinking for a moment, Jessica explained, "You confuse love with pity."

"I risked my life for you out of *pity?*" he bellowed. In the back of his mind he suddenly realized that he sounded exactly like his grandfather, Thomas Cavendish. The thought gave him courage. "Do you take me for a complete fool? Do you think that I do not know my own heart?"

Jessica placed her hand over his. "No, you do not," she replied in a gentle voice. "You wage a fearful war within yourself. I understand that now. Until you can face the truth of your birth, you will never be fully healed." She raised one of her raven-winged brows. "Or do you hope that I will fight your battle for you? With this face?" She touched her birthmark.

Uttering a low sound in the back of his throat that was more like a sob than a growl, Francis crushed her against his chest. He couldn't let her go—ever! "I need you so much, *cara mia*," he whispered.

He is trembling, Jessica thought as she held him tightly. She cleared her throat. "You will find another woman who will soothe your hurts," she murmured, though she did not pull away from him. "There will be many English ladies who will be happy to give you comfort." She laid her cheek against his breast. The pounding of his heartbeat startled her.

His lips grazed her earlobe. "It is not my body that needs you as much as my soul."

Her pulse quickened. "Then seek out a confessor who—"

He stopped her further advice with a bruising kiss. The touch of his lips sent thrilling waves of shock cascading through her. Ignited by the intensity of his passion, she arched against him. The hardness of his thighs and the harder place between them made her body long for his. All her cold logic melted in his heat.

His kiss softened like a murmured prayer. He withdrew slowly, leaving her mouth yearning for more.

"Jessica," he whispered into her hair. "There is no other help for me but you—your love."

He dropped to one knee before her and took her hand in his. "Can you find it in your heart to love me even though I have no noble title, no great wealth? I cannot shower you with costly jewels or velvet gowns as you deserve. I earn my daily bread in the service of King Edward of England. Though my birth was not an honorable one, I have always striven to live an honorable life. Will you share it with me?"

Jessica's ears burned. Her knees trembled. She could not believe his ardor nor the truth of his words. It must be a dream or a hideous jest. She took his hand to steady herself.

He kissed her fingers, making it impossible for her to think clearly.

"I do not crave jewels or beautiful clothes," she replied. She must not lose her head. "Does this home you offer to me have love residing in it or will I be just the latest one of your mistresses?" She thought of Cosma and all that creature represented.

Francis grinned at her. "Is *that* what troubles you? On my honor, I swear that I have never had as many mistresses as I claimed to the Doge. That boast was only part of my disguise. In good truth, *cara,* I am not the vain fop that I portrayed. Surely you can see that by now?"

Jessica refused to accept his protestations. No man in his right mind would want to marry her. There must be some other reason that she had not yet considered. "Then you want me to be your housekeeper—until you can marry a fine lady of a nobler station?"

He closed his eyes for a moment and muttered something that sounded like an English oath. "You are driving my patience to the very brink, sweetheart. Listen to me well. There is no other lady on the face of God's green earth— not in all of Italy, nor in France, nor in Spain." He rose and circled his arms around her. "Nor in Portugal, Scotland, Ireland, the kingdoms of Flanders and Germany, nor even in England itself—none are more noble than you."

He kissed her moist eyes, first one than the other. "If I traveled to Egypt or Cathay or India or even to the wilds of the New World, I know I would not find a woman to match you." He kissed the tip of her nose. "Only *you* do I want. Only *you* will I have. Do you understand me now? I speak of the honorable state of matrimony—with me and very soon. Be my wife."

Jessica's throat closed up. "I thought you only said that at the trial to free me."

He framed her face in his hands. "I said it because I meant it. I still mean it, now more than ever."

She wanted to believe him with all her soul. "I have no dowry—"

Francis's face turned red. "Damn the dowry! Will you sail with me to England? Will you marry me now—today?"

Jessica knew she would marry him that moment if a priest were at hand, but she also knew that there were still those demons of his that sat on his shoulders and threatened their future happiness. "*Sì*, Francis, I will marry you, but there are several conditions."

His face brightened in astonishment. "Did you just say you would marry me?" He lifted her off her feet.

She gripped his jerkin and ducked her head before she hit it against the cabin's low ceiling. "Francis, listen to me." He set her back on her feet but did not release her. "First, you must teach me English."

"A pleasure. Let us start with a kiss." He leaned down.

She stopped him though her heart ached. "Second, since it is now Lent we cannot wed until we reach England, but only after your family has met me. They must approve the match."

She knew that once those noble Cavendishes saw the devil's mark on her cheek, they would forbid the marriage, but she could not bear to abandon Francis now.

He snapped his fingers. "Done! Wolf Hall has a fine chapel just made for our wedding. But until then, we can practice what it is to be man and wife." He leaned down toward her again.

Again, though with less resolve, she stopped him. "Third, that you honor my maiden state until our wedding night." She held her breath.

He puffed out his cheeks. "Whew! You drive a hard bargain."

She gave him a crooked little smile while her blood surged with desire. "I am a Venetian. We are born to bargain."

He snorted. "Very well, I agree though I do not understand why. I have already plighted my troth to you. All Venice witnessed my promise."

She couldn't help but smile at that memory, then she grew more serious. "I do not want you forced into marriage with me against your family's wishes because I am pregnant."

He chuckled. "No one forces me into anything. I am my own man now. Ah, Jessica, you have set a hard trial upon me, but I will endure it for your sweet sake." He kissed her. "And do not worry about the Cavendishes. They are a romantic clan and will never believe the priceless pearl that I have found."

Jessica swallowed. "You speak the truth, Francis. They will never believe what you have found."

Not a pearl but a mangy stray cat.

Chapter Twenty-One

Northumberland, England
April 1550—Easter Monday

Francis rose in the worn stirrups of his rented horse. He waved his cap over his head. "There it is!" he shouted, his breath puffing white in the cold air. "Wolf Hall!"

Clutching the fox fur robe tighter around her shoulders, Jessica poked her head out of the carriage window and scanned the frosty landscape that Francis's noble family called home. Since the carriage paused just below a small rise, she could see nothing except her beloved mounted on his sturdy chestnut gelding. Despite the trepidation in her heart, she smiled to see him so happy. Pure joy had turned his handsome features into those of one of Bellini's angels. All Francis needed was a thin golden halo over his wind-blown hair.

He rode back to her. "The castle lies less than a mile from here," he told her. "You will be able to see it when we cross over that hillock." He beamed like a schoolboy on holiday.

As casually as she could manage, she asked, "Perhaps your family are in London. After all, it is the Eastertide."

He tapped her cold nose with his gloved fingertip. "Fret not, sweetheart. The Cavendishes rarely go to court and only when it is absolutely necessary. I know they are at home and that they await us. Flags fly from every battlement of the castle. You will see it anon."

Jessica gripped her warm robe. "Do they know about me?" She touched her birthmark. "About this?"

Still grinning, he leaned over in his saddle and kissed her forehead. *"Sì, cara,"* he replied. "I sent them letters at every port stop we made on that blasted journey. One or two of them are bound to have arrived by now."

"Oh," she muttered, her uneasiness growing by the minute. Francis swore that his father's family were good and kind. Jessica prayed that he spoke the truth. Maybe they would let her have her own little cottage in one of the villages that dotted the Cavendishes' large estate, instead of tossing her out on the road like a Gypsy.

Jobe, mounted on a large black horse, drew up beside the couple. "Banish the fear from your eyes, little one," he told her with a wide smile on his face. "The Cavendishes accepted me at first sight and I am *all* black. You have only one little brown spot. Nothing!" He dismissed her shameful stain with a snap of his fingers.

Jessica shivered though not with the chill damp wind that blew through her open window. Francis saw her trembling and smiled at her. "We burn daylight and you are cold. Sit back inside and we will be off. Driver," he shouted in English to the man he had hired in Newcastle where the *Jinn* had docked a few days ago, "Let us go on at a smart pace and make a brave show. Yonder is my home!"

Francis wheeled his horse and raced to the crest of the rise, then disappeared over it with Jobe in hot pursuit. Both men shouted at the tops of their voices. Jessica pulled down the leather window cover and buckled it against the frigid air that cut through her like a knife blade. Then she buried herself deep inside the fur robe that Francis had bought for her on her first morning in this freezing country. With a sharp crack of the whip, the team of horses leaped forward. The leather springs rocked the carriage so violently that Jessica clung to one of the straps that hung beside her. *¡Dio mio! Let me arrive in one piece!*

The rollicking ride lasted a scant five minutes but to Jessica it seemed an eternity. She hoped that their luggage had not tumbled off onto the muddy road behind them. Her stomach felt queasy though whether it was the jolting ride or her nerves, she could not tell. She sighed with relief when the driver pulled his team to a stop. Someone rapped on the window cover.

"Look, Jessica," Francis said when she raised the shade. "It makes a grand sight!"

Jessica gaped at the huge forbidding stone fortress before them. Its tan-colored stone walls glistened with a sheen of ice. Her slim thread of optimism snapped asunder. *This* rockpile was the ancestral home of a noble family? How unlike the beautiful gilded, pastel-colored *palazzos* of faraway Venice! Just then a number of unseen heralds on the battlements blew a fanfare on unseen trumpets. The martial notes hung in the crystal-cold air. A dozen or more flags of bright-colored silk snapped at their poles over the tooth-like crenels that lined the tops of the high walls. Over all the banners flew a blood-red one with the image of a silver wolf's head. Jessica knew from her long shipboard conversations with Francis that she gazed upon the personal badge of the powerful Cavendish family.

Before she could gather her scattered wits, Francis dismounted and swung open the carriage door. "Come, my love," he said with warm encouragement. "It is not as grim as it looks once you are inside, I promise." He helped her down to the cobblestones. "The original keep was built four hundred years ago to protect the countryside from the Vikings." His deep blue Viking eyes danced with merriment. "Sometimes it didn't work," he added with a grin.

A pack of the largest dogs Jessica had ever seen tumbled out of the massive double doors at the top of a low flight of stairs. She gripped Francis's hand tighter and wondered if she would be eaten alive before she ever met the family.

He chuckled in her ear. "The hall is always full of dogs—savage on the hunt but lambs in front of the hearth. Let them sniff you."

A dozen cold wet noses pushed through her fur robe and investigated her hands. One even licked her stiff fingers. Unused to dogs in general and such large ones in particular, Jessica gritted her teeth. A number of children in many ages and stages of dress followed the dogs.

"Uncle Frank!" shouted a lusty boy of five or six years. He launched himself at Francis from the second to the bottom step.

Francis dropped Jessica's hand in time to catch the child. With a whoop, he swung the squealing boy high over his head. "Nay! Tis not young Tom, is it?" he asked. "Methought you were still in leading strings."

Young Tom flailed his fists and feet in the air. "Put me down, Uncle Frank. I am not a baby anymore!"

A slightly older boy made a face. "Aye, but he still sucks his thumb."

"Heigh ho, Johnny!" Tucking the squirming Tom under one arm, Francis swept the second boy under his other. Turning, he presented the wriggling pair to Jessica. "My esteemed nephews," he told her, speaking slowly in English so that she could understand his words. "The one on the left is John Hayward and this piglet on the right is Thomas Hayward, my godson.''

Johnny pushed a hank of medium-brown hair out of his blue eyes and asked, ''Did you bring us presents?''

Jobe came up behind the boy and lifted him out of Francis's grasp. ''Oh, ho, young master, do you think your good uncle would not? I was there to make sure that he did.''

Both children chortled with glee while other little ones clamored for attention. ''For all of us?'' asked one of the young serving maids.

Jobe grinned at her. ''Indeed, little miss, for every last one of you.''

His announcement incited more joyful cries. The giant African appeared to be a particular favorite among the castle's younger set, servants and family alike. Jessica adjusted her veil so that it would cover the half of her face that might frighten these adorable poppets. After six weeks in the company of sailors and Francis, she was cheered to see the children—and to see how comfortable Francis was in their company. *He will make an excellent father one day.* Jessica did not dare to think who would be the lucky mother of Francis's future offspring.

Hard on the heels of the children came a foursome of young adults dressed in rich velvets and damasks. The three girls with hair almost as dark as Jessica's looked like triplets—a phenomenon that she had seen only once in Venice. The young man in their midst was as fair as they were dark. His cap of golden hair shone in the early afternoon sun and his eyes mirrored Francis's own color. He bolted past the trio and grabbed Francis by his arms.

''Tis high time you've come! We have been awaiting your arrival for over a week!''

Francis laughed. ''Hoy day, Kitt! When did you grow to be a man?''

The tallest of the girls arched one dark brow. "Aye, Francis, we have been wondering the same thing—will Kitt *ever* grow up."

"And wondering when it will happen," the middle girl added.

The three broke into giggles among themselves.

Francis chuckled. "Jessica Leonardo, my betrothed and my saving grace," he said to the young man. To Jessica, he continued, "Christopher Cavendish, son of my lord...that is to say...of the new Earl of Thornbury." A hint of sadness swept across his features for a moment. The heir! Aware that many eyes watched her every move, Jessica bowed her head and dropped Kitt a deep curtsy. "I am very honored to meet you, my lord," she pronounced carefully.

With a laugh, Kitt raised her up and held her cold hand within his. He cleared his throat. *"Benvenuto a casa, Signorina Jessica,"* he said slowly; his ravishing smile forgiving his rough accent. "You are most welcome to Wolf Hall." He kissed her hand, then winked at her. "Did I say that well enough?" he asked.

Touched by the thoughtfulness of his greeting in her own tongue, Jessica expressed her thanks in a quick rush of Italian, but Kitt shook his head.

"Hold, good mistress," he pleaded with a most charming grin. "You have heard the entire sum of my Italian vocabulary. I have been practicing for weeks ever since we got Francis's letters."

Jessica returned the young man's smile. "I am honored," she repeated, meaning it this time. "You speak very well," she added.

"Your English puts my Italian in the shade," he replied. He stepped closer to her. Before she realized what was his intention, he took her face between his hands and kissed her cold cheeks, first on her good side, then directly on her birthmark.

Francis growled in the back of his throat. "Go find your own lady to woo, Kitt. Jessica is already spoken for."

"We will be friends, *sì?*" Kitt whispered before he stepped aside.

"Aye," she answered. At least she now had one ally in this cold country—besides Francis.

Out of the corner of her eye she saw that more people crowded on the landing. The Cavendish family stood tall, golden and proud in their splendid clothing. Jessica marveled at the resemblance among them; even the dark-haired girls possessed the family's looks. A young matron, her bright blond hair gleaming under her headdress, flew down the steps. With the cry, "Francis! You maggot!" she hurled herself into his arms.

His face lighting up with brilliant joy, Francis hugged her, murmuring, "Belle, Belle" over and over.

A little worm of jealousy gnawed at Jessica's heart. So this stunning lady was Francis's beloved sister...or cousin as the case may be. Whichever, Belle was the one woman who had held the keys to his heart for most of his life— and the one whom Jessica most hoped would accept her. Adjusting her veil over her bad side, Jessica waited for Francis to make the introductions.

After what seemed like an eternity, Francis set Belle back on her feet. "You must greet Jessica as warmly as a sister," he told her. "She is very frightened," he added in an undertone.

Jessica overheard him. She squared her shoulders under her furs and attempted to look more confident than she felt. *I will not be presented as a sniveling weakling.* She executed another deep curtsy. "I am very honored to meet you, Lady Belle."

Jessica wished she had a better command of English to tell Francis's sister how beautiful she was. They are all beautiful, Jessica realized with a pang of dismay. What was she doing here among this flock of golden angels? Why hadn't Francis explained more fully what he had meant when he told her that all the Cavendishes looked alike? It was as if the frescoes on the walls of Venice's many churches had come to life and had moved to the north of England. Jessica was not in the company of mere mortals but among the saints and angels in heaven—albeit a frosty heaven.

Belle pressed her cheek against Jessica's good one. "You are freezing to death," she noted. "Francis, you clodpole! Jessica is not used to our weather. She will turn into a piece of ice if we linger out here."

Belle put her arm around Jessica and escorted her up the steps. Francis trailed behind them, leaving Jobe to cope with the children and the baggage. Jessica wanted to look over her shoulder to seek Francis's reassurance but she didn't dare to move her head for fear of revealing the hideous stain. Perhaps it will be dark and gloomy inside and no one will see it too quickly, she hoped. Yet Kitt had seen it and he had not shrunk away from her.

"You are very kind," she murmured to Belle.

Belle tossed her beautiful head. "Nonsense! I am practical, which is more than can be said about my woolly-headed brother. Venice is a warm city, isn't it?"

Jessica nodded. "Much warmer than here," she said with a trace of homesickness.

Belle gave her a little squeeze. "Then we shall heap high the logs on the fire and fill you full of hot spiced wine." She dropped her voice. "But first you must meet my papa who guards the door like one of our mastiffs."

A tall man in the prime of his middle years smiled at

them; his striking wife by his side. Taking Jessica's hand in his, Francis led her to the landing. "My lord, my lady," he said to the imposing couple before them. "May I present my betrothed, Jessica Leonardo? We crave your welcome and your blessing."

Doffing his hat, Francis swept a courtly bow. Jessica followed suit with her best curtsy. Her knees trembled beneath her layers of plain woolen skirts. She did not dare to look into the probing eyes of the Earl and Countess of Thornbury.

Sir Brandon Cavendish rumbled a deep laugh. "He asks our welcome, Kat?" He turned to the auburn-haired beauty at his side. "And our blessing? Aye, Francis, you have them both in full measure. By the rood, tis long past due time for you to return home."

Francis rose, bringing Jessica with him. "Tis good to see you again, my lord," he answered with the reverence of a retainer, not a son.

The earl enveloped him in a bear hug that threatened to knock both the men off their feet. The countess took Jessica by the arm.

"Welcome to our home, Jessica," she said with a sincere smile on her lips and in her green eyes. Leaning forward, she kissed the shivering girl on both cheeks as her son Kitt had done. Straightening up, the countess cast a fond glance at her husband and his former squire. "You must forgive Brandon, my dear. He has sorely missed Francis. It has been seven long years since the boy was last at Wolf Hall."

Far too long to hide from himself.

Merry laughter rippled behind Jessica. "Heigh ho, Kat!" teased a lady in a lilting French accent. "Do you mean to keep Francis's jewel all to yourself? Ha! I think not!"

With an answering laugh, Lady Kat turned Jessica to face the raven-haired speaker. "A thousand pardons! Jessica, this is my sister-in-law Celeste Cavendish and that gentle-man over there who looks like our holy patron Saint Michael is her husband, Guy Cavendish.''

Jessica again curtsied. ''I am very honored to meet you, my lady,'' she intoned, wishing she knew something else appropriate to say. Francis had not taught her any other English greeting. Jessica had not expected to meet his family one-by-one.

Like the other members of the Cavendish clan, Celeste kissed her on both cheeks. Were they all blind? Jessica wondered. Surely they could see the damning mark in the bright sunlight. Why didn't they say something as the spectators at her trial had done?

When she saw Guy at closer range, she gasped aloud. The man was an older version of Francis!

He tilted his head and smiled in the same way that Francis smiled with one corner of his mouth turned up higher than the other. ''Welcome to Wolf Hall, Signorina Jessica. Thank you for bringing the prodigal son home to us.''

You do not realize the truth of your own words, messere. Couldn't anyone else besides Jessica notice the uncanny resemblance? She looked around at the milling family and servants, but everyone seemed oblivious to the truth. Perhaps they saw Francis as they remembered him when he was younger and not fully developed. A man changed much in seven years. Glancing at Jobe, she saw that he intently observed Guy through hooded eyelids. Then he noticed Jessica. He nodded once.

The countess flung open the heavy oaken door and pulled Jessica through its portals. ''We would stand outside all day if we waited until those two men regained their senses. Francis is like a son to Brandon,'' she explained as she led Jessica into the castle.

Though the interior of Wolf Hall was not as colorful as

a Venetian palace, it was cheerful and inviting. Sunlight streamed through the diamond panes of glass in the great arched windows. The northern light illuminated the colorful tapestries that hung on the paneled walls. Turkish carpets covered much of the polished wooden floor, reminding Jessica of the rugs she had seen in the homes of some of her wealthy patients. Crimson banners, each one displaying the Cavendish wolf head, hung down from the dark rafters. Cupboards gleamed with a plethora of polished silver and gold plates. Dogs of all sizes, colors and descriptions lounged everywhere.

In the center of the great hall a large fire crackled in a massive stone hearth. Standing in front of the blaze was a tall woman. The silver amid her golden hair revealed her great age far more than the lines in her face, or the ebony and ivory cane that she held. This must be Lady Alicia Cavendish, Jessica thought, the Dowager Countess of Thornbury. The woman's plain dark gown and black headdress proclaimed her widowed state. She held out her hand to Jessica. Unlike her bejeweled daughters-in-law and her granddaughters, Lady Alicia wore only a single ring—a broad golden wedding band.

"Draw near, child," she invited in a warm voice that was still firm in its gentle authority. "My eyes are not what they used to be."

This will be my undoing, Jessica thought as she crossed the floor. Half in anticipation, half in dread, she stopped in front of Lady Alicia and nearly fell into her curtsy.

"I am very honored to meet you, *contessa bella*," she said, her panic making her forget the rest of her English.

Keeping her head bowed, Jessica clenched her teeth. *Now she will see it. This great noble lady has the eyes of a hawk. She will not allow her grandson to marry the mistress of the devil.*

Glad that Francis was not here to witness her downfall, Jessica raised her face to Lady Alicia. She pushed back her veil and turned her bad side toward the light cast by the fire so that the old countess and the younger one standing beside her could not miss seeing her shame. Now, Jessica thought in the lingering silence, now they will scream and cross themselves, then toss me outside their thick doors. Jessica swallowed the lump in her throat. Her lower lip trembled.

Lady Alicia smoothed her fingers across Jessica's cheeks. With the pad of her thumb, she circled the strawberry-shaped birthmark that had given Jessica such a life-time of misery.

Tears welled up behind Jessica's eyelids. Farewell, Francis my love! "Forgive me, *contessa*," she whispered to Lady Alicia. "Forgive my shame and my...my...." She groped for the English word for boldness but could not think of it. "*Arditezza mia.* I tell Francis not to bring me here, but his heart..." She floundered with her emotions as well as her vocabulary. "My heart...it is *impossibile*. I will go away."

The new countess looked to her mother-in-law. Lady Alicia's expression filled with warmth and understanding. "I perceive that Francis has chosen a pearl of great price, Kat," she remarked while she still stroked Jessica's face. "He wrote to us of your courage and your strength as well as your intelligence. I see now that he underestimated you."

Jessica blinked. "But this?" She pointed to her disfigurement.

Lady Alicia raised her up. "An accident of birth, nothing more, my child. Ah! Your eyes tell me that your mind tosses on an ocean of doubt. Robe yourself with your courage, Jessica. You are most welcome to Wolf Hall—and to our family."

Jessica's confidence spiraled upward. "And Francis? Is he, too, welcomed to your family?"

"How now?" murmured Lady Kat. "This is his home."

Lady Alicia nodded. "Ah," she murmured to herself.

Having opened this Pandora's box, Jessica plunged ahead. "Your pardon, my lady. You welcome me into your family and I am most grateful, but have you ever welcomed Francis?"

Lady Kat frowned. "Mamma?" she asked her mother-in-law.

Lady Alicia twined Jessica's fingers through hers. "You are as wise as you are beautiful, my dear. Indeed, Francis chose well."

When Brandon released Francis from his friendly tussle at the top of the steps, Francis turned to speak to Jessica and found her gone.

"Oh-la-la," Celeste said with a broad smile. "Kat took her to meet Mamma."

"Jesu!" Francis muttered under his breath. He had meant to be at Jessica's side when she faced the Cavendish matriarch for the first time. Not that his grandmother was unkind by nature, but Francis knew from past experience that Lady Alicia could be formidable if she chose.

Without further ado, he pushed open the door and raced down the passageway to the great hall where he suspected Kat had taken Jessica. The rest of the family as well as the servants followed behind him, anxious to not miss a thing.

He found the three women chatting before the cheerful hearth in the hall; his grandmother seated in a high-backed chair, Jessica on the footstool beside her and Kat in the armchair opposite. The three sipped wine from silver goblets and nibbled on sugared wafers that were in a silver dish upon a spindle-legged table beside Kat.

Alicia smiled at Francis. "Come here, you wicked boy! Tis a sin to have stayed away so long."

Francis knelt beside her chair and kissed her hand. Under his lips, her skin felt as fragile as thin vellum. "I have missed you, my lady," he replied in a voice grown husky with tenderness. "The sad news of Sir Thomas's death..." He swallowed.

Alicia tucked a bit of his wavy blond hair behind his ear. Her touch was a caress of comfort. "He loved you very much, Francis," she told him. "And he would have rejoiced as I do to meet this most excellent woman who has snared your heart." She smiled at Jessica.

Francis gave her fingers a little squeeze. "Then we have your blessing to marry?"

Alicia took Jessica's hand and placed it in Francis's. "Aye, with all my heart and soul." She chuckled. "Mayhap she will keep you in England."

Francis gazed into Jessica's brimming eyes. "I have already promised her that."

The gentle scene was broken by the arrival of the children—the young and middling ones. Jobe followed behind them with the look of a cream-filled cat on his face.

Tom Hayward skidded to a noisy stop before the adults. He held up a small linen sack of sweetmeats in an already-sticky fist. "Look, grand ladies!" he entreated, not knowing to which grandmother or grandaunt he should direct his announcement. "Uncle Frank has brought all the wealth of Venice back to us!"

Francis kissed Jessica's hand. "The boy speaks the golden truth," he whispered to her.

Jessica blushed and dipped her head with a grin.

Johnny joined his brother. He produced a small dagger,

its scabbard embellished with silver filigree. He planted his short legs wide apart in front of his great-grandmother. "Mama says I am too young to have this!" he all but shouted.

Belle, a bit breathless, materialized behind her son. "'Tis not a plaything! Francis, what *were* you thinking when you got him such a weapon? The boy is barely seven."

Johnny opened his mouth to protest, but Lady Alicia held up her hand for silence. "Belle, my dear, you were much younger when you sliced up the hunting tapestry in the west gallery," she remarked with a twinkle in her eyes. The hall filled with good-natured laughter at Belle's expense.

"*¡Madre del Dio!*" Jessica whispered in Italian to Francis. "You told me your sister was high-spirited but you forgot to elaborate."

Francis lifted his brow. "I feared that you would jump overboard if I told you the infamous details."

Twenty-year-old Tonia, Guy's eldest daughter, touched the shimmering glass beads at her throat. "Look, *Maman,*" she crowed to Celeste. "Francis got these for everyone! Your taste has improved with age," she added to him.

"So has yours," he shot back with a grin.

"Look! Look!" chorused Tonia's younger twin sisters who brought up the rear of the giggling mob. "See what Francis has brought for Belle! Open it, coz!"

Between them, they half carried, half dragged the wooden crate containing Francis's portrait. In his excitement to be back at Wolf Hall, he had completely forgotten about it. But Jobe should have known! He shot the African a frown. Jobe returned his look with a slight smile and the lift of an eyebrow.

God's teeth! He put the girls up to this!

"I am undone," he muttered in Italian.

Jessica caressed his hand. "Why, Francis? What ails you?"

Belle, her eyes wide with surprise and excitement, clapped her hands. "For me? Stars! Open it, someone! Quickly! Oh, Francis!"

Fighting to keep his composure, he rose. "Tis nothing, I assure you."

"Tis his portrait," rumbled Jobe from the back of the gathering. "Painted by an apprentice of the renowned Titian."

Francis knotted his fist behind his back. *Why are you doing this to me?* Aloud he said, "Tis a knavish piece of work. I thought Belle could use it on her archery range as a target."

Jobe laughed. "Francis protests too much. The likeness is most excellent."

Francis glared at the traitor. Didn't Jobe realize that once the family saw this painting, they would know without a shadow of doubt who his father was? What would Brandon say? Or Guy? For seven long years, Francis had fled from just this moment.

Two of the menservants worked to pry open the protesting wood. Belle danced around them, urging their labors and dismissing their splinters. The seated women, Jessica included, looked on with interest. Brandon, Guy and Belle's husband, Mark Hayward, moved closer. A buzzing noise grew inside Francis's head. Silently he damned the portrait, damned the artist and damned himself for not pitching the thing into the Mediterranean Sea when he had the chance.

Francis wiped his dry lips. "Do not look upon it. Tis trash."

Everyone laughed at him and they encouraged the servants to greater speed. Francis glanced at Jessica. Only she looked at him while all the rest were riveted by the emerging mystery. He read uncertainty in her eyes.

"What is it?" she asked him in Italian.

He tightened his jaw as the men sliced the canvas wrappings. "The end of my happiness."

"I thought I was your happiness," she replied with a note of sadness in her voice.

Before he could explain what he meant, the twins pulled away the last covering. With a collective "Oh!" everyone stepped back to admire the work. A silence filled the hall. Clenching his hands, Francis closed his eyes. *Why, Jobe? Why?*

Almost in answer, the African's strange prophecy "You will die, be reborn and new baptized" echoed in the recesses of Francis's mind. He looked again at Jobe and the latter nodded several times. A sick feeling swooped through Francis's stomach.

Alicia rose from her chair and moved closer to the painting that was held by the twins. The family parted before her. "Get a candle, Brandon," she instructed her elder son.

Jessica moved to Francis's side. She said nothing but slipped her arm around his waist. He did not lean toward her, though he was glad of her comfort. Nothing could heal the breach that was about to happen, not even Jessica's skill.

Brandon lifted a fat taper from the chimney piece and brought it closer to the portrait.

Finally, Alyssa, the elder of the twins, broke the spell. "Tis not Francis at all," she scoffed. "Tis Papa!" She grinned at Guy.

"Tis Papa to the letter—only younger," Gillian, the other twin, concurred. "You jested with us, Francis. Shame on you!"

Francis opened his eyes to find the entire family looking

at him—except for Guy who stared at the work as if he had never before seen paint on a piece of canvas. Surprise and disbelief filled his expression.

Alicia nodded with an enigmatic smile on her lips. "You speak the truth, my chicks. Tis the very image of your father indeed."

The buzzing in Francis's head increased. Breaking away from Jessica, he spun on his heel and fled the hall, wishing he could flee to the ends of the earth.

Chapter Twenty-Two

Jessica finally found him in the old earl's library, thanks to the help of Belle and some of the castle servants. When Francis did not respond to her knock on the closed door, she lifted the latch and entered the tiny book-lined sanctuary. With his head bowed, he stood at the narrow lancet window, staring with vacant eyes across the expanse of moor beyond the castle walls. He did not move until Jessica touched his elbow.

She looked up into his pain-etched face and wished she had some soothing ointment to erase the lines of sorrow there. "Francis, your lady grandmother wishes you to attend her in her solar."

A muscle ticked at his jawline. "With Brandon and... Guy?"

Jessica ached for him. "They accompanied her when she left the hall."

He said nothing but returned to his study of the empty countryside.

Jessica laid her cheek against his arm. His muscles tensed into knots. "Do you intend to keep running away all your life?" she asked.

"That is my business," he snapped, not looking at her.

At his stinging rebuke, she bit her lower lip in dismay. Summoning resources from deep within herself, she shook her head. "No, Francis, if I am to be your wife, then this…this thing is *our* business."

He leaned his forehead against the chill glass of the windowpane. "How can you know what anguish lodges in my soul?"

"Tell me," she whispered. She could feel him slipping away from her like water through her fingers.

He groaned deep within himself. "That rank painting has torn asunder all that I held dear."

Jessica winced at these words. "Not me—not Belle, and certainly not Lady Alicia."

He continued as if he had not heard her. "When I first came to Wolf Hall as a child, Brandon took me as his page. He treated me as a son, making no attempt to mask his affection for me. And I…like a starving dog…lapped it up."

He turned away from the window. "But he never…not once acknowledged me as his natural child, even when my Cavendish looks grew more pronounced." His mouth twisted into a bitter smile. "He always proclaimed Belle as his daughter, though she, too, was born on the wrong side of the family blanket—but me? Never! Yet I always held out a hope that one day…"

Jessica put her arms around his stiff body. "Why did you flee to France, then to the Lowlands and finally to Italy?"

He snorted, though he did drape one arm around her. "My mother sent for me. Fool that I was, I thought that Lady Olivia had finally decided to act maternal now that I was twenty-one and no longer needed my nose wiped or my manners improved."

Jessica drew his arm tighter around her in a vain effort

to shut out the cold that had come between them. "And did your mother tell you that she loved you?"

He barked a rough laugh. "Love? She never knew the meaning of that word. After all those dalliances of hers, the only thing she learned was that she had the French pox."

"*¡Dio mio!*" Jessica shuddered.

"*Sì,*" he replied. "Those were my words exactly when I saw her for the first time in nearly ten years. She made no excuses, merely told me in a matter-of-fact way that she was dying and she wanted to clean her mottled conscience before she locked herself away in a nunnery. Then she told me that Guy was my father. She called their brief affair a delightful amusement that whiled away the time between her seductions of both old King Henry VIII and King Francois of France."

"Your mother bedded kings?" Jessica gasped. The woman must have possessed great charm and beauty. No wonder her son was so appealing!

He drew in a deep breath. "*Sì,* she told me that she named me Francis after the French monarch because she initially thought I was his bastard. Time, of course, proved her wrong."

Jessica could think of nothing to say that would ease the pain in his heart, or hers. Their strained silence hung in the tiny chamber. Only the ticking of the old earl's curious timepiece on the mantel broke the stillness.

Finally Jessica gave herself a little shake. "Your grandmother awaits you," she reminded him. "You must go to her."

He suddenly grabbed her by the shoulders, his eyes wild. "We will take our leave in a twinkling. The coach is still here. We will go to London—"

Jessica drew away from him. "No, Francis," she said

quietly but firmly. "You may continue to run away if you wish, but I will not accompany you. I cannot marry you."

He gaped at her. "What madness is this?"

"I refuse to marry a sponge full of tears of self-pity."

His face turned an alarming shade of red. "Ungrateful cat! I saved your wretched life."

"*Sì*," she replied, though her heart wept. "And for that I will bless your name until my dying day but I cannot marry a man who has only half a heart. I will never be able to make you whole. Only here and now will that happen— and only if you are brave enough to face your demons who have pursued you throughout Europe. Go to your grandmother or go to the devil. There is nothing more I can do for you. You must heal yourself."

Though her knees quaked, Jessica walked away from the only man she knew that she would ever love. A string of oaths rang in her ears as she shut the door behind her. She stumbled to a secluded alcove where she sank down on a stone bench and allowed her tears to flow freely.

Lady Alicia smiled warmly at Francis when he finally made his appearance. Brandon and Guy sat far apart from each other. Brandon's face was the picture of dejection while Guy looked—impassive. Francis kissed Alicia's hand. "My lady, I have come as you bid me."

The countess arched a wry brow. "I hope you came because you also love me."

"Aye, I do," he mumbled, "though you have much to thank Jessica for. She is your advocate."

Alicia glanced at her sulking sons. "Listen to me, you three stubborn mules, tis high time for all of us to shed pretense. It does no one a whit of good and only festers like a canker in our souls."

Still holding Francis's hand, she seated herself on her

favorite cushioned chair and continued. "Francis, your grandfather and I knew you were a Cavendish from the beginning—though whose son you might be was a moot point. It mattered nothing to us. We loved you."

"Aye, my lady, I know."

She gave him a little shake. "Francis! For God's sweet sake, please call me Grandmama as all my other grandchildren do. Tis your right and I have longed to hear it from your lips."

A huge lump rose in his throat. How could anything so painful as this interview also be so joyful? "My lady Gr...Grandmother." He said the words like a prayer. It felt like one.

"Better! You will grow more used to it with practice." She turned to her elder son. "Brandon was never sure if you were his, were you?"

The new earl flushed. "Ah, that is...did your mother ever mention me? That we had—" He broke off with a cough.

Francis swallowed. "Aye, my lord, she mentioned you—among others." He did not dare to look at his grandmother. He didn't want her to think that her beloved sons were a pair of randy cocks.

"Ha!" Brandon actually grinned. "So I was merely a jotting in Olivia's book of memory? I hate to think what a man had to do to earn a full page."

Alicia clicked her tongue with a hint of disapproval though her eyes gazed warmly on Francis. Guy stirred himself from his refuge by the hearth.

"And I?" he asked in a odd, strained voice. "Did Olivia speak of me?"

For the first time, Francis looked his father squarely in the eye. *God's teeth! We are truly mirror images!* "She did. She told me you were my real father." He could not help adding, "Instead of the King of France."

Brandon whistled through his teeth. "I never knew you kept such lofty company at the Field of Cloth of Gold. And only nineteen years old! Well done, little brother."

Before Guy could frame a retort, Alicia rapped the floorboards with her cane. "Brandon! This is not a tavern. Watch your tongue."

The handsome man looked abashed. "Your pardon, Mother," he mumbled.

Alicia now turned her attention to Guy. "I presume you have been shriven for your behavior in France thirty years ago?"

The tall, angelic-looking man stared at his toes. "Aye, Mother, and I did many penances for my lusty life while I was a novice at Saint Hugh's." He gazed at Francis. "I never realized that I had a son," he said softly. "Olivia should have told me."

Alicia pursed her lips. "In my opinion, Olivia Bardolph never knew one end of the alphabet from the other, let alone the family trees of her numerous offspring. Besides," the countess continued, "you had already joined the monastery when Francis was sent here to be fostered. We thought you would be a monk for the rest of your life."

A sheepish grin played across Guy's lips. "So did I. Thank God, Celeste showed me how wrong I was to run away from myself."

Alicia cast a fond glance at Francis. "I perceive that the acorn did not fall far from the tree. Running away appears to be a family trait. Isn't that why it has taken you seven years to come back home, Francis?"

"Aye." They had come to the sticking point. He may as well push the blade in up to the hilt. "After the little chat with my mother, I was afraid to face you—all of you.

I didn't want to hurt Sir Brandon who had always been good to me, nor did I want to upset Sir Guy and his family after it had taken him so long to find his own peace.''

Guy wet his lips. "You are my son—*my* own son." He stared at Francis as if seeing him for the first time. "I always wanted a son but could not tell Celeste. It would hurt her deeply if she thought I had ever been disappointed with her."

"Your daughters are growing into lovely, accomplished and beautiful young women," Alicia pointed out, "but they should have a brother who will look after them." She paused, then added, "Death comes so very quickly and never when we expect its arrival."

Francis knew that she thought of Thomas—they all did. He kissed her hand again. "Do not upset yourself, Grandmother." The word rolled more easily off his tongue.

She shot him a piercing look. "Nay, we need to be shaken up. This family has been slumbering too long."

The three men, each one so like the other two, stared at the Cavendish matriarch in wonderment. Francis hoped that her grief at the loss of her husband had not unhinged her wits.

Alicia gripped his hand. "Help me up, Francis. I have something to show you all—something that has lain in a dark corner for over fifty years."

A sense of déjà vu washed over Francis. "A family secret?"

"Aye," she answered slowly. "One that transcends the secret of your paternity. How did you guess?"

Francis answered slowly. "One of Jobe's weird sayings. You know how vague he can be. He told me once that the Cavendishes harbored a secret that..." He paused to recall the words. "...that was bright-shining like the sun in his splendor but hidden deep among the roots—our roots, methinks.''

Alicia's face took on an odd expression. '''The sun in splendor,''' she repeated. ''Jobe said that?''

''His very words.''

She chuckled to herself. ''I have often thought that Jobe is not a mortal but instead a half angel come down among us unawares.''

Francis laughed aloud. ''He has four wives, Grandmother!''

She cocked her head. ''Indeed? And where in Holy Writ does it say that angels cannot marry?'' When no one answered her, she continued. ''Whether angel or man, Jobe spoke the truth.'' She moved toward a bright tapestry that covered the wall opposite the fireplace.

Brandon exchanged puzzled glances with his brother and nephew but said nothing. Alicia stepped behind the tapestry. The large needlework bounced on its pole while she rummaged out of sight. Presently, she backed out, pulling a large square package. Francis had a sinking feeling in the pit of his stomach. The mysterious thing reminded him of his portrait that was still the object of attention downstairs in the hall. Guy leapt forward to relieve her of the burden.

She pointed to the window seat with her cane. ''Stand it against the wall there for a moment. Now, then.'' She faced them with a very serious expression. ''Only Thomas knew my secret—aye, *mine*—and I promise you it is more startling than Guy's recent discovery.''

Brandon shifted his feet. ''Now, Mother, we know that you were not nobly born. That a goldsmith and his wife adopted you after you were…er, abandoned. There is no need to revive such old news.''

Alicia again rapped the floor with her cane. ''Hush, Brandon, that is the crux of my tale. Now, where was I?

Ah! When Thomas took me for his wife we promised each other that the secret would never pass our lips.'' She gave a little shake of her head. ''How young and foolish we were! We thought that if we did not speak of it, the danger would go away. Alas, it has not.''

Fear prickled the short hairs on the back of Francis's neck. ''What danger? Who threatens you?''

Guy placed his hand over his heart. ''You know we will defend you to the death, Mother.''

She dismissed his pledge with a wave of her hand. ''Tis not only I but now you and your children that share this danger. It runs in your very blood—your *Plantagenet* blood.''

The three men ceased their nervous shuffling. They hardly dared to breathe. Finally, Brandon asked, ''Who has Plantagenet blood? King Richard was the last one and he died in the 1480s.''

Alicia shook her head. ''Have you so soon forgotten the shameful execution of the Countess of Salisbury a scant nine years ago?'' She curled her lips with scorn. ''Poor Margaret Pole was condemned by our late good King Hal under the convenient charge of treason. Her real offense? Margaret's Plantagenet bloodline made the Tudor uneasy. She was closer to the throne than he liked. The countess was seventy years old—nearly my own age—when they dragged her to the block in the Tower of London. She refused to kneel for the headsman. He had to chase her around the scaffold hacking at her until she finally fell.''

The iron taste of bile rose in Francis's throat.

Alicia straightened her shoulders. ''Margaret Pole was the daughter of the Duke of Clarence, the niece of King Edward IV—and my first cousin.''

Guy stumbled against the stone window seat then sat down hard on it. Brandon's complexion paled. A vein in

Francis's temple throbbed a warning of an impending headache.

Only Alicia looked serene. "Surprised?" she asked.

Brandon mopped his brow with his sleeve. "Aye, the world turned upside down in a single moment."

Alicia pointed to the shrouded package. "Uncover the portrait, Guy."

With a reverence akin to awe, her younger son untied the bindings and removed the linen that had covered a painting in a gilded frame. With a sickening start, Francis recognized the likeness of King Edward IV. He had seen a portrait similar to it in the old palace of Westminster. That king had been Henry VIII's grandfather on his mother's side. "Second cousin," he murmured. "You are second cousin to the old king and third cousin to his son who now sits on the throne?"

Alicia smoothed a crease in her sleeve. "You were always quick-witted, Francis. You have hit upon the nut and core of our family problem." She moved closer to the portrait and gazed upon it with a fond look in her eye.

"I was Edward's last living child—quite illegitimate, of course. See the brooch that he wears on his bonnet?" She pointed to a large ruby with an equally large teardrop pearl hanging from its golden setting. "My royal father left it in safekeeping as my dowry. The goldsmith who reared me was in truth one of his loyal courtiers."

A deathly chill crept through Francis's veins. He recognized the fabulous jewel. Alicia had given it to Belle as a wedding gift. Belle wore it on special family occasions. No wonder his grandmother kept this portrait well hidden! Francis's mind spun with the ramifications. Even though old King Henry was dead, England still seethed with political and religious unrest. Young King Edward VI, sickly a good deal of the time, was under the complete domination of his scheming Seymour uncles. The Catholic Church had been forced underground following Henry's break with the pope in Rome. Francis had already warned Jessica that she must practice her faith in secret. In the wilds of Northumberland, she would be safe.

Or so he had thought until this moment. Were all the Cavendishes still in jeopardy? What would happen if King Edward died without an heir, as it looked like he might? The Princess Mary had been declared a bastard; so had the Princess Elizabeth. Would there be another purge of Plantagenets—even remote twigs on the family tree—to satisfy the ambitions of the powerful men that hovered like buzzards around the throne?

"'Tis no wonder you rarely went to court, Mother," Guy said at last. "I see now where our coloring comes from. I had always thought it was the result of a lusty Viking or two."

Alicia smiled at him. "'Tis true that your father had Viking ancestors but this—" She pointed to the portrait once again. "This cuts much closer to the bone."

Guy exchanged looks with Brandon. "What do we do?"

The new earl stroked his chin. His eyes looked older and more tired. "We will continue exactly as Papa did. We will live out our lives quietly here among our own people and retire from the brilliant light around the Tudor court. We will pay our taxes on time, make no show of arms and fade from Tudor memory. That is true for you, as well, Francis."

"I have already submitted my resignation to Lord Cecil. The life of intrigue holds no appeal for me now that I wish to marry." *If Jessica is still speaking to me. God rot my tongue for what I said to her!* He itched to leave the solar with its threatening pall and to seek out the comfort of her arms. He would make a thousand amends to her.

"And the children?" Guy continued. "What do we say to them?"

"Nothing!" said Alicia brusquely. "Belle is tucked away at Bodiam and is under Mark's protection. God save us all if that little spitfire ever discovered the truth. Thank the Lord, her boys inherited their father's looks. Your daughters' black hair will also serve them well and soon they will be married to perfectly fine, unsuspecting gentlemen."

Guy crossed the room to stand beside Francis. "My girls will have both a father and a brother to watch over them in the meantime." He extended his hand to his emotion-racked son. "God shield us, those three minxes will keep our hands full. Will you help me...my son?"

Francis could not utter a sound. His heart was too full. Instead he hugged his father and wept away the pain of thirty years on Guy's broad shoulder.

Brandon coughed. "What of Kitt?" he asked his mother. "One day he will be the Earl of Thornbury. He should know his heritage."

Alicia resumed her seat and spread her skirts. "Aye, in good time, but not now. He's barely twenty and as wild as an eagle—much like you were, I may add. Let us not clip his wings just yet. Who knows? By the time he is as old as you, the wheel of fortune may turn yet again and the Tudor threat will be a thing of the past, like the faint memory of a nightmare by dawn's clear light. Now away with you three and make merry with your families. Kill a fatted calf, so to speak. Our prodigal son that was lost has come home again."

Brandon lifted up the portrait. "Where shall I put this, Mother?"

She waved it back to the window seat. "Leave it for a while. I have not seen it for many a year and tis a good thing to feast one's eyes upon a father's face. Is that not true, Francis?''

''Amen,'' he murmured.

The three moved toward the door but paused when Alicia asked, ''Did you know that my father's personal badge was a sunburst? The sun in splendor—Jobe hit the nail squarely on the head.''

In silence they closed the door behind them.

''Join us in a cup of malmsey?'' Guy asked at the top of the wide staircase to the great hall.

Francis gave him a sheepish grin. ''First, I have a great deal of fence-mending to do, if my sweet mistress has not gone to ground.''

Jessica's wedding day dawned with a flash of bright sun and a blessed warmth in the air. After the ritual bath, Celeste, Kat and Belle perfumed her, dispensed a great deal of marital advice and dressed her in the most gorgeous gown Jessica had ever owned. The ivory-satin bodice and crimson-velvet skirts had been cut in the Venetian style. An army of seamstresses had labored on her clothes throughout the past two days and nights. Milky pearls twined through the dark curls of her unbound hair crowned by a bridal wreath of cowslips, primroses, daisies and ivy.

Francis's stepsisters adjusted their new gowns of pale green silk and fussed with each other's laces, ribbons and jewelry. They had never performed the delightful office of bridal maids and the Cavendish trio were determined to enjoy their moment to the fullest. Ignoring the girls' excited chatter, Jessica paced back and forth, twisting her fingers.

When Francis had finally found her shivering in the unheated chapel, he had all but slit his wrists with his apologies and testimonies of his undying love. In forgiving him,

Jessica had made him promise one more thing—that his real father would escort her to her wedding. Since that time three short days had elapsed—time enough to read the banns at morning Mass and to prepare the wedding breakfast. The nearest neighbors and all the villagers had been hastily invited. Everyone had promptly accepted. After a long winter of boredom since Twelfth Night had marked the end of the Christmas season, the inhabitants of Wolf Hall and environs looked forward to the coming festivities.

Caught up in the whirlwind of wedding preparations Jessica had barely seen Francis. When she had asked him about his conference in Lady Alicia's solar, he had merely smiled and said that it had been a landmark event. Nor would he elaborate when she pressed him for the details. Francis only wanted to talk of his love and their wedding day. He spent most of their brief times alone together kissing her, stroking her and driving all her questions far from her mind. Just thinking of him waiting for her now at the door of the castle chapel made her weak with desire.

A sudden sharp knock startled Jessica from her reverie. The time had come! Her escort had arrived, but which man would it be? Had Francis chosen Brandon because of their past relationship? Or had he asked Guy to do the honors? Tonia and the twins looked at her with open anticipation.

"You are not going to faint, are you?" Gillian—or was it Alyssa?—asked. Jessica still could not tell the twins apart.

"You can't back out now," Tonia added with a note of warning. "Belle will skin you alive if you disappoint Francis."

Another knocking, more insistent, propelled Jessica into action. With a purposeful stride, she crossed the floor, took hold of the latch with her moist hand and opened the door.

Sir Guy Cavendish, resplendent in a red-and-black velvet doublet and hose, swept off his plumed hat to her.

Just like Francis!

"Is the bride ready?" he asked, offering her his arm. A large silver medallion of a wolf's head hung from a wide silver chain around his neck. The wolf looked almost as if he winked at her.

His three daughters descended upon him in a billow of silk and high spirits. "We are, Papa!" shouted Gillian—or was it Alyssa?

With a laugh, their father arranged them in a line behind him. "You will be brides soon enough, I warrant, but not this day. Jessica, are you really ready to become a member of this family?"

Such an easy question—now! "With all my heart," she replied, placing her hand over Guy's. "Lead on!"

"And then we can eat!" crowed Tonia.

Francis never stopped smiling the rest of that memorable day. Not even when he fumbled and dropped Jessica's wedding ring on the paving stones. Not even when Jessica wept with her joy throughout the Mass. Not even when Tonia and the twins distributed dozens of cow bells to the assembled guests and they rang them incessantly during the feast. Not even when two of the dogs got into a fight under the head table. Nor when Jessica wept anew when the cooks brought in their special confection—a towering cake covered with pastel pink and green sugar frosting that reminded her of the *palazzi* of Venice. Not even when Jobe hoisted the bride over his shoulder and announced he was abducting her. Jessica had squealed with delight during the wild race that followed as Jobe led the groom and the rest of the family on a frenzied chase around the castle.

Jessica had never been so happy in her life. Nor had she

ever seen Francis look so handsome as he did that day, attired in a doublet and hose that exactly matched his father's right down to the winking silver wolf. When she placed her mark on the wedding register, Francis wrote her name and told her that soon she would learn how to sign for herself—Mistress Jessica Bardolph Cavendish.

"A new name, a new wife and a new future together," he whispered to her when at last they were alone in the depths of the castle's best bed.

Jessica rolled toward him and lightly ran her fingertips across his naked shoulders. He groaned with his pleasure.

"Once again, I have you under my hands," she teased, her blood throbbing with passion.

He grasped her wrists and pulled her tight against his hard body. She fitted his contours as if the good Lord had made them a matched pair. He stroked the indentation of her spine. "But for once I have you under mine," he murmured in reply. "You have led me a merry dance, *cara mia*. I swear you nearly drove me mad all the way back to England on board that poxy ship."

Jessica twined her arms around his neck and rubbed herself shamelessly against him, savoring his strength and his obvious desire. "Then take your revenge, my love. It is high time that you drove *me* mad."

His lips hovered a breath above hers. "With the greatest of pleasure," he answered just before he enveloped her in a kiss that banished all doubts and fears forever.

"I love you, Francis Bardolph Cavendish," she sighed as he knelt above her.

"Welcome home," he murmured as their bodies joined. "Home forever."

* * * * *

Author Note

The story of Jessica and Francis is a work of fiction but it is set within a time and place that was very real in the mid-sixteenth century. Venice during the Renaissance was every bit as lush, colorful and decadent as described in these pages. Art, music, international finance and book publishing flourished beside the darker arts of intrigue and midnight assassinations. The Venetian secret police and the Council of Ten were sinister forces to be reckoned with. The secret letter drops called the *bocca di lione* still linger in some of the city's walls; their open mouths forever waiting for another anonymous note. Early forms of cipher codes and messages written with invisible inks had their origin in Venice. There were no recorded escapes from the infamous *prigione* until around 1750 when the famous lover, Casanova, managed to break out through the roof. I hope my readers will allow me a little artistic license in arranging Jessica's earlier escape. Resourceful men like Francis and Jobe could certainly have rescued her!

Of the many holidays that were celebrated in Venice during that time, none surpassed the midwinter festival when the entire city gave itself up to the pleasures of *Carnevale,* meaning literally "farewell to meat" that signified the forty days of fasting and prayers during Lent. Masques, dancing, fireworks, games of chance, street corner theater, acrobats, and other wild delights ruled the days and especially the nights. I have included some of the more interesting carnival traditions in my story.

Finally, a note on the famous courtesans of Venice: their beauty, intelligence and sexual expertise were legendary for several hundred years. During the Renaissance, Venice was known as "the best fleshpot in Italy." Tutoring in the arts of love by a Venetian courtesan was considered a vital part of a young nobleman's education. By the end of the 1500s, there were more than 11,600 "daughters of Venus" plying their trade in Venice—roughly twelve times the number of the chaste patrician wives.

TORI PHILLIPS

After receiving her degree in theater arts from the University of San Diego, Tori Phillips worked at MGM Studios, acted in summer stock and appeared in Paramount Pictures' *The Great Gatsby*. For the past twenty years she has been a docent and actress at the Folger Shakespeare Library in Washington, D.C., where she researches material for her historical novels. Tori has written short stories for *Teen* and *Sassy* magazines, freelance newspaper features, poetry and has published four plays for Dramatic Publishing Company. She has won a number of writing awards, including the prestigious Maggie Award for Excellence in Historical Romance, and her work has been nominated by *Romantic Times Magazine* for a Reviewer's Choice Award. *Publishers Weekly* praises Tori, saying that "she's literate, witty and tells a good story." Tori lives in northern Virginia with her husband, Marty. When she is not working at her computer, she relaxes by reading and ice skating—though not at the same time. Tori loves to hear from her readers. Please write to her at: P.O. Box 10703, Burke, VA 22009-0703.

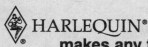

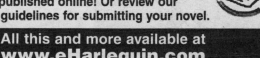

HARLEQUIN®

bestselling authors

Merline Lovelace
Deborah Simmons
Julia Justiss

cordially invite you to enjoy three
brand-new stories of unexpected love

The
Officer's
Bride

Available April 2001

HARLEQUIN®
Makes any time special ®

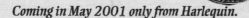
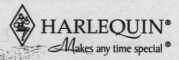

Harlequin truly does make any time special. . . . This year we are celebrating weddings in style!

To help us celebrate, we want you to tell us how wearing the Harlequin wedding gown will make your wedding day special. As the grand prize, Harlequin will offer one lucky bride the chance to **"Walk Down the Aisle" in the Harlequin wedding gown!**

There's more...

For her honeymoon, she and her groom will spend five nights at the **Hyatt Regency Maui.** As part of this five-night honeymoon at the hotel renowned for its romantic attractions, the couple will enjoy a candlelit dinner for two in Swan Court, a sunset sail on the hotel's catamaran, and duet spa treatments.

A HYATT RESORT AND SPA®   Maui • Molokai • Lanai

To enter, please write, in, 250 words or less, how wearing the Harlequin wedding gown will make your wedding day special. The entry will be judged based on its emotionally compelling nature, its originality and creativity, and its sincerity. This contest is open to Canadian and U.S. residents only and to those who are 18 years of age and older. There is no purchase necessary to enter. Void where prohibited. See further contest rules attached. Please send your entry to:

Walk Down the Aisle Contest

In Canada	In U.S.A.
P.O. Box 637	P.O. Box 9076
Fort Erie, Ontario	3010 Walden Ave.
L2A 5X3	Buffalo, NY 14269-9076

You can also enter by visiting www.eHarlequin.com
Win the Harlequin wedding gown and the vacation of a lifetime!
The deadline for entries is October 1, 2001.

Makes any time special®

PHWDACONT1

Got a hankerin' for a down home romance?
Pick yourself up a Western from Harlequin Historical

ON SALE MAY 2001

CIMARRON ROSE
by **Nicole Foster**
(New Mexico, 1875)
An embittered hotel owner falls for the beautiful singer
he hires to revive his business.

THE NANNY
by **Judith Stacy**
Book 2 in the Return to Tyler historical miniseries
(Wisconsin, 1840)
A handsome widower finds true love when he hires a
tomboyish young woman to care for his passel of kids.

ON SALE JUNE 2001

THE MARSHAL
AND MRS. O'MALLEY
by **Julianne MacLean**
(Kansas, 1890s))
A widow wishes to avenge her husband's murder, but
soon loses her nerve—and then loses her heart
to Dodge City's new marshal.

Available at your favorite retail outlet.